THE TIME OF BLUE MOONS

HM NOUR

CONTENTS

PROLOGUE

"Don't walk to the beach house tonight," I said into the telephone at fourteen years old, standing on the unsteady ground of adolescence and a dark family secret. "He's coming to kill us."

Time is a straight line, but the truth is not. Rewinding the hands of time to the beginning, which is much like the ending, I am lost in my thoughts, before the secrets began, before the time of blue moons.

PART 1 – 1957

CHAPTER 1

THE DRIVE

Interspersed red, black, white, blue, and green specks blurred before my eyes, as notable to my perception in that moment as blinking. Our mint green Chevy hummed along steadily with a soothing, gentle motion. The sun, emerging from behind a billowing cloud, warmed my face with its intangible touch. My mind was occupied with nothing, a random conversation or event, and the obscure everything. Remembering some past occurrence, I dissected and analyzed it while wandering in a labyrinth of details, stuck in this subconscious land created by the comforting movement of the car, indiscriminate objects passing by, and tepid rays upon my face. We drove for hours before a word was spoken between us. This was one of the many ways my mother and I were alike. My features—the shape of my eyes, nose, mouth, and body—resembled my father's. However, my pale skin tone, sandy blonde hair, and blue eyes were inherited from her; my personality was as complete a reflection of hers as seeing my own image in a mirror. It was as if God had sketched the outline of my body from my father's silhouette, but the colors, the life, both visible and invisible, were painted solely by her.

My view shifted from the car window to Mama. Her eyes, focused on the road, also gazed at something abstract before her mind, imperceptible to me. Perhaps all parents, in their attempt to shield their children, forget how perceptive children are to subtle changes in their parents' countenance. Empty eyes cannot be concealed by a deceitful smile. The coldness between my mother and father had strengthened its icy grasp long since winter had thawed. A freezing fog settled in our apartment, depositing ice in every room and hindering their communication. I did not blame them for sparing me the turbulence in their relationship, but despite their efforts, I was not ignorant of its occurrence and hated pretending that I was. I imagined her, similar to myself, analyzing conversations with my father, the ones that I had never heard.

"I can't stand the city for another day," said my mother earlier in the morning after we had stuffed our car, mostly full of books, and begun our journey, just the two of us. After a few minutes, she progressed, "We shall both be content at the beach, my little bird, to see new scenes and meet new characters for our imaginations. We shall be *quite content*." She spoke to convince herself, I thought, more than me.

Thus, we began fleeing to the beach for summer after I completed kindergarten, not long after I turned six years old and my parents' shouting had increased in both frequency and ferocity, culminating in countless slammed doors and my mother's resolve to escape to her family's beach house for the entire summer. Beginning as evasion, under the disguise of adventure, our trips eventually transformed into tradition: one that sustained hope of its arrival from the moment we journeyed home until we embarked again on that comforting path, etched deeper into my subconscious each year.

When she finally noticed me observing her instead of our surroundings, her lips curled up into a faint smile, eventually pervading her entire face, particularly her swirling eyes. Her eyes always exposed her true emotions.

"Mama, where will we be staying during our trip?" I inquired, breaking the silence. We had never been on such a long trip before, and she had not explained exactly where we were journeying.

"Well," she responded, clearing her throat, "we'll be staying at your grandparents' beach house. It sits upon a cliff overlooking a beach called Ruby Cove. There are stone steps, sprinkled with sand, that lead from the house down to the beach. When I was young, I would spend part of my summer vacations there with my family ... until ..." Her voice trailed off.

Ruby Cove, I thought to myself. Mistaking a cove for a cave, I imagined a dark cave full of rubies, twinkling red inside the monochromatic rocks.

"Can you grab the map from the back?" she asked while pulling to the side of the road.

We had driven on US Route 1 since our departure but would need to switch highways in Boston. I reached to the back seat, searching for the map. In addition to books, the entire back row and floorboard had been stuffed beyond capacity with cleaning supplies—a broom, a mop, bottles, buckets, rags—and linens—folds of neatly stacked sheets and towels. I finally found it beside some flashlights on the floorboard under some tattered rags.

Unfolding the Esso road map, Mama said, "This is what truly makes this trip an adventure. We must navigate our way to our destination using our wit and bravery," her eyes alive with excitement. She turned to me and questioned my resolve, "Are you up for the task, little bird? I cannot do it without you."

Without hesitation, I replied, "Yes, I'm ready, Captain!"

She smiled at my enthusiasm. Together, we bent over the creased map, trying to find our current location amongst the names and lines filling the page. It was my first time using a map for travel, and I found myself overwhelmed by the vast expanse of land before me.

Mama patiently explained, "We know we are now in the state of Massachusetts so that should be where we begin our search." She traced the yellow outline of Massachusetts, which looked to me like a child had drawn its boundaries with straight, focused strokes in the west and distracted, free-form squiggles along the coast in the east, and waited for my eyes to settle there. Then, she slowly followed along the red line representing US Route 1, paused, and remarked, "This is where we stopped at the diner to eat and fill up with gas," pointing with her index finger at the city's name, printed in blue.

"That's right!" I exclaimed.

Now I knew why she had told me to remember the names of cities and landmarks we drove past. It was not only to make a lasting memory, as I had believed earlier, but to help us find our way to the beach house.

"Remember that peach pie?" she replied as she closed her eyes: the pie before her mind, the taste upon her tongue.

"Focus, Mama!" I yelled at her, eager to continue our navigation.

She opened her eyes wide and turned towards me slowly. We stared intensely at each other for a few seconds until we both exploded into laughter.

"Okay, okay," she forced out through sputtered giggles after a couple of minutes, wiping away cheerful tears, or cheers, as she called them. "Back to the map. But before we continue, I need to do something," she said, snatching the map and a pen from her purse. "Can you find our last location?" she quizzed me, handing me the map.

I scanned the area diligently, determined to succeed, until I found the correct spot once again. "Here!" I shouted proudly. I giggled and shook my head after seeing she had drawn a tiny pie around the name.

"Correct!" she responded. "Now, we will always know where to find that pie. Let's follow Route 1 from this city to Boston."

Once we had tracked the line around an inch up the page, Mama explained how we needed to change highways in Boston since we did not need to travel any farther north. Instead, we needed to find a route to take us south towards the coast. While I held a finger on Boston, she pointed at the area of our destination, and together, we found the two highways to take us to the beach house. Satisfied with our path, we continued on US Route 1 towards Boston.

In my naivety, I believed Mama and I were discovering the path together for the first time and she was relying on me to help find the way or end up lost. I took my duty seriously and read every road sign, mispronouncing most, scanning for the correct highway to scream out loud. In reality, Mama had traveled these roads many times before; even I had unknowingly made this journey previously. For the first time, I felt the excitement of our trip, a mixture of hope and elation swirling around my stomach. There would be no school tomorrow or the following day, and I was on an adventure with my favorite person in the world. After a few false alarms on my part, we came upon the correct interchange and soon began our way south on the last leg of our journey. As it is with any inceptive trip, with the road unknown to me, my eagerness oscillated between peaks and valleys; as each minute passed, the depths and summits became more extreme, fluttering until I could not contain my anticipation anymore and felt I might explode. A mile seemed to drag on for ten, a minute for an hour, prolonging our arrival. Mama noticed my restlessness.

"Roll down your window," Mama instructed as she rolled down her own, her shoulder-length hair suddenly flying around her wildly.

The cool wind felt refreshing.

"Can you smell it?" she inquired.

At that point, I had only felt the breeze upon my face and bare arms, not discovering it yet in any other sense. I breathed the saliferous air in slowly, deeply.

She smiled. "It's the smell of the ocean. We are near."

Mama turned on the radio as the wind blew in puffing gusts through the windows, the lulling sound and touch of the shifting air all around me. The sun had begun its descent, a glowing orange sphere falling slowly, a cerulean sky high above and shades of burning orange and pink scattered below, contrasting the violet hue brooding underneath the hanging clouds. We faintly heard the counting of "Rock Around the Clock" play on the radio. Mama turned the dial, and we sang all the words together with the sound blasting out the windows, ebbing into the evening noises outside until dissipation.

I felt pure happiness, the kind only children experience, unblighted by the hauntings of yesterday or anxieties of tomorrow. I immersed myself in every aspect of that moment—the colors of sunset, the tangy smell in the air, my mother's laugh, the feel of the wind. I hoped I remembered enough for my mind to return and relive this moment once again someday.

We continued our path south, observing the colors transform as the sun dipped towards the horizon, a spectacular show that culminated with brilliant oranges and yellows, just above the boundary of earth and sky, painted by the last glow of the sun after it receded from view. The pinks, oranges, and yellows faded, progressively overtaken by blue once more. The sky eventually darkened to blue velvet as night engulfed twilight. The rest of our journey passed quickly in flowing conversation, opposite to its silent, reflective beginning.

It was night when we finally arrived at the beach house. From the glow of the headlights, I initially observed the outline of a small cottage with a screened porch at the front. Covered in square cedar shingles typical of coastal houses, the natural color of the house ranged from warm tans to light grays. I exited the car and viewed the colors change gradually as I shined a flashlight along the exterior. Its steep roof, covered in darker gray shingles, slanted upwards, a brick chimney protruding from the center.

Leaving the rest of the luggage for the next morning, Mama and I carried clean blankets and sheets as well as a small overnight bag of our pajamas and toiletries inside the house, using the flashlights to guide our way from the gravel driveway along the stone path that led to the house. Upon opening the door, a musty smell wafted to greet us.

"The house needs to be aired out," Mama remarked on the stale air consuming the lonely house, which had been empty for years.

Inside, I saw small separated rooms with wallpaper and hardwood floors. Mama opened all the windows, allowing fresh air to dilute the fetid odor filling the rooms.

"Let's go," Mama commanded as she walked towards the door.

I obeyed and followed her, though a little confused since we had only just arrived. I wanted to explore the rest of the house, to become acquainted with it. It was all unfamiliar to me like a new classroom at the beginning of a school year. We walked down the front steps to the stone pathway, but instead of curving to the car, we stayed straight towards the stone steps at the bottom of the yard, enclosed by a low stone fence with pillars. A sweet fragrance blew past us, scented by flowers along the wind's path. We strolled by a hedgerow of bushes planted at the edge of the yard, forming a verdant border between the house and cliff, to the stone steps Mama had told me about earlier that led down to the beach.

I heard the waves crashing onto the shore from the clifftop as I gazed upon an infinite black mass. We used our flashlights as beacons to guide our steps down to the sand.

"Mama, I'm afraid," I admitted to her as we began descending.

"Follow behind me and stay close to the cliff. We will go slowly, little bird. No need to rush."

We grasped the rocks jutting along the cliff for balance as we climbed down the steps. It felt strange to feel the jagged edges and differing shapes of the rocks without being able to differentiate them by sight. In the darkness, I was only able to detect varying shades of grays and blacks, which objects were deeper or lighter in color. We finally reached the bottom, to my relief, and sat on the last steps to remove our shoes. I advanced with bare feet from the last rough, craggy stone to the cool, smooth sand. Under my weight, the grains spread between my toes, each consumed by the tiny specks of earth. We walked towards the water, the wind blowing with more fervor as we approached, our feet swallowed by softness with each step.

Mama said softly, "'And forget not that the earth delights to feel your bare feet and the winds long to play with your hair.'" (Gibran 42)

The beach was ours alone; the only sights and sounds were the wind, clouds, and water moving rhythmically to the forces of nature, attempting to establish equilibrium. The waves flowed over the sand, reaching their frothy tips onto the shore, until they were dragged back into the sea. The heavy gray clouds, impregnated with water droplets, hovered just above the horizon, ready to bathe the earth. We stood there together at the shoreline, feeling the repeating push and pull of the water rush over our feet, sinking in the paste of sand and water. Mama held out her arms, her polka dot dress and hair whipping about her, and closed her eyes, submerged in complete serenity. In that moment, I saw her cleansed of the anxiety she carried with her, invisible but evident in every aspect. I felt my feet may succumb to the relentless current, washing me away with the tide, but instead, it was a part of her that was swept away, abandoned to the murky depths temporarily.

Fatigue from our journey eventually overpowered us, much to my disappointment, forcing us to relinquish our reveries on the beach for dreams in our beds. We carefully climbed step after sandy step up the cliff just as gravity pulled the condensed beads down as rain upon our heads. As we reached the front yard, the drizzle transformed into a torrential downpour. We ran up the pathway to the front porch, our sandy feet dripping wet and laughter unheard over the roaring deluge.

After quick baths, Mama and I cuddled in her bed while she read aloud to me, our nighttime tradition since I was swaddled in her arms. My recent favorites were *The Little Prince* and *The Lion, the Witch, and the Wardrobe*, the latter which we began reading again that night at my behest. Mama always read each character in a different voice, just as her grandfather had read to her. She insisted a story was never quite as good without proper voices.

Those books, many that we had read before like *The Children of Green Knowe* and *Alice's Adventures in Wonderland*, captured me, transporting me to another world. My love of literature began in these quiet moments with Mama at the end of each day.

Before I fell asleep at the beach house, I snuck from my bed to the closet in my bedroom. I reached to the back and checked for Narnia: a custom begun after reading the book for the first time. I had thoroughly searched all of the closets and wardrobes in our house and my grandparents', with nothing beyond the back as yet. I tiptoed back to bed, reminding myself to check the rest of the closets in the morning.

CHAPTER 2

NEW FRIENDS

I awoke the following morning to sunlight flooding the entire room, shining, at first, as a soft glow upon my eyelids. I opened my eyes slowly, to a rush of unfiltered light, as they adjusted to the overwhelming brightness. I looked around the bedroom at the unfamiliar surroundings, reminding me we were not at home. I jumped out of bed smiling, remembering last night, and heard music when I opened the door. I followed the music to the kitchen, at the back of the house, where Mama knelt scrubbing the linoleum floor, marbled with gray and white, while singing quietly along with the radio. She turned as she heard me approaching and smiled warmly.

"Good morning, Michael."

A gentle breeze and sunlight filtered through the open windows, a fresh lemon scent permeating the room. Motes of dust floated within a beam of sunlight. I peered around the kitchen, studying its aqua steel cabinets and Formica countertops in the same color, edged with steel, perfectly framing the small space.

The kitchen looked modern, similar to the ones I had seen in magazines around our apartment, not quite matching the rest of the quaint house. A white sink sat beneath a double-pane window facing the backyard. I observed tree branches, thick with leaves, waving in the breeze beyond the window, birds hiding within the foliage.

"Now that you're awake, sleepy little bird, we should go buy groceries."

"I am hungry." My stomach rumbled at the thought of breakfast.

"I'm not surprised," she responded with a chuckle. "It's almost eleven."

From the cleanliness of the house and her tired eyes, it appeared as if Mama had been cleaning all morning while I slept peacefully.

"I know a place where we can eat on our way to the market. How do burgers and milkshakes sound to you?"

My stomach answered for me with a discontented growl before I could speak. We drove downtown, a few miles from the beach house, as I eagerly observed our surroundings through the open windows, my right eye squinted in the sun. The sky, completely clear of clouds, stretched azure blue in all directions, a glaring divergence from the previous night's gloomy appearance. We turned onto Main Street, as Mama informed me, a narrow two-lane road that began with buildings of various heights squeezed together—shops, businesses, and restaurants—on the left side and a small park with an open green space surrounded by mature trees on the right side. I watched the trees transform into a comparable row of structures lining the street on both sides as I discerned the similarities and differences in the buildings' cladding, brick and wood painted mostly in shades of white and red. Awnings with scalloped edges covered the entrances and windows, providing additional pops of color. Mama parallel parked the Chevy in front of a pharmacy. The birds darted between trees and lampposts, whistling merry tunes while chasing one another, relishing the tranquility after a boisterous night of storms.

"We are here!" Mama exclaimed before exiting the car. "It's strange to see how much this area has changed over the years," she continued as we walked past the pharmacy. "This diner, however, has been here since I was a little girl."

As we walked through the door, the irresistible aroma of fried food and sizzling meat seized my attention. I inhaled deeply while internally assuaging my hunger by reminding myself that I was mere minutes away from nourishment. The second thing I noticed, after the smell, was the long counter at the back with shiny red and chrome barstools, running almost the entire width of the restaurant. Behind the counter, I could see the cooks through a rectangular opening, dancing around one another to complete the orders amid a chaos of dinging bells and yelling. As a waitress zigzagged past us and the tables and chairs in the middle of the diner, she yelled for us to sit wherever we wanted over her shoulder. We surveyed our options and quickly opted for a seat along the perimeter rather than the exposed center tables, walking over the large black and white checkered tiles to a booth in the corner, nestled beside a picture window overlooking the street.

The booth seats were covered with the same sparkling red material as the barstools and chairs, trimmed with white, an upside-down white triangle in the center. I bounced from the edge of my seat to the middle and rubbed my hands over the slick upholstery. They resembled the back seat of a car. Mama began skimming the menu as I continued my observations of the restaurant. The repeating doo-wop syllables of "Little Darlin'" flowed softly from the neon jukebox nearby.

Mama joined my survey of the diner after ordering our food. "The layout is the same, but everything else looks different from my childhood. I think I like it even more now."

"Yeah, this place is cool." I loved everything about it: the pictures of cars hung on the walls, pops of cherry red everywhere, the flashing jukebox, dings of the bell and chatter of customers, the smell of salt and meat, the white tabletops with gray and red intertwined boomerangs.

Mama pointed out the window. "When I was a child, I always loved to come walk downtown at night with the lampposts softly glowing upon the sidewalk. And every summer there used to be a dance in the little park we passed on our drive here. They set up a gigantic dance floor underneath a white tent with lights strung from end to end. It was as if they had pulled the stars from the sky and hung them on a string. I loved dancing with the stars just above my head. We went every year at the end of summer."

I looked up and imagined stars hovering above me, twinkling as Mama had described. All thoughts of stars and dances disappeared when our waitress finally brought our burgers and shakes. After saying thank you, I grabbed my milkshake for a quick taste. I held it in my mouth for a few moments, allowing it to melt and my tongue to savor the creamy chocolate flavor.

We finished eating and then headed to the market for groceries. Most of the afternoon was spent cleaning, unpacking the car, and putting away the remainder of our clothes and supplies.

Around three o'clock, Mama said, "Why don't you go spend some time down on the beach? I need to finish some cleaning, but I will join you in about an hour, okay?"

"Okay, Mama," I replied, running to my bedroom to change into my red-and-blue plaid swimming trunks.

I was thankful for Mama's suggestion. I had heard the waves calling out all day, and I yearned to return to the beach. As I crossed the hedgerow, I stood at the edge of the cliff, observing the beach from above. It appeared quite different in the daylight, not just by sight but by feeling as well. At night, it was mysterious, almost magical, in the solitary darkness when the sounds of the restless water overpowered everything, but in the day, it was brimming with life. I pondered this duplicitous nature as I watched the groups of people below, rather small from my point of view, gathering under umbrellas, splashing in the water, and walking along the beach. I heard faint conversations and the screams and laughter of children. When I moved from the shade and began my descent, I felt the sun's warmth upon my face and arms. The cloudless sky offered no reprieve from the sun. Thankfully, a steady breeze blew across the water. As I gazed towards the ocean, the clear sky and water merged together in a gradient of blues, spread out into the eternal distance.

I found a nice spot on the beach, spreading my towel on the sand and then immediately plopping down upon it to prevent the wind from blowing it away. I buried my bare toes in the sand, feeling the cool grains underneath the burning surface. Not far from me, a lady lounged under a large striped umbrella; she appeared older than my mother but not quite my grandmother's age. She smiled at me and nodded hello. A group of children nearby, ranging in age, caught my attention. They were chasing each other in a game of tag. I watched as they soon abandoned one amusement for another, kicking water up high into the air and splashing it all around. The littlest ones giggled each time the salty mist sprayed them. After they tired of this game, they waited at the shoreline until the tide returned and attempted to outrun the water's reach upon the sand. I laughed softly to myself at each new endeavor. Soon, a woman who seemed to be their mother called them for a break. I did sometimes find myself wishing for a sibling. It was not easy for me to approach people and initiate a conversation. What seemed like a simple task to others was extremely vexing, taxing, and overwhelming to me. I tended to watch from the periphery, a reticent observer, until another extended their friendship and granted me a chance.

A little girl with chestnut brown pigtails and a red bathing suit sprinted from the dispersed group of children to the lady sitting next to me. She ran and shouted with such alacrity that she was forced to stop halfway to catch her breath. As she approached at full speed once again, she continued screaming, "Aunt, Aunt!" while her braided hair thrashed wildly around her head.

Her aunt responded calmly, "What is it, my dear?"

Through labored gasps, she replied, "Did you see us running from the tide?"

Her aunt laughed. "I did see you! Now, have a little rest and refreshment before you get back to playing."

She kissed her aunt on the cheek and sat down beside her on a towel. The little girl began singing "Bye Bye Love" before her aunt joined in at the end.

I listened to their singing and subsequent laughter as I lay down to rest my head on the sand with my eyes closed. I felt content hearing the dance of the tide back and forth in the background with the warm sun upon my face. My breathing slowed to the rhythm of the tide: back and forth, in and out, back and forth, in and out. I would have happily remained there forever, entranced by the sea.

Time had no meaning in that moment. My mind became caught in a web of thoughts, a shimmering gossamer lifted by the wind, floating within a daydream or perhaps a dream, as the glaring sun shone down unwaveringly upon me. The heat, intensified further by the absence of wind near the ground, recreated a hazy memory of my sixth birthday party, a month prior. There I was on that perfect spring day, the bleakness of winter forsaken, in the park with my grandparents and a few friends from school. The adults stood together near the pavilion and watched us children run in a pack, here and there, attempting to fly a kite. We repeatedly tossed it into the air to catch the wind. I paused, alone, noticing my parents in the distance standing together upon a hill, as the other children left me behind, their screams fading into the background. My father had arrived late, stumbling around the park as if he had been spinning around and around in circles. Mama had delayed the party as long as possible for him, but Dad had missed the singing and cutting of the cake. Mama looked angry, her thin eyebrows slanted downwards in the middle towards her nose, her eyes swimming in tears. She was yelling something at him. It felt as if I were watching a silent film, desperately trying to read their lips or hear their conversation, although I was too far away to hear anything other than the few words lifted above the others. Trying to understand why they were fighting, I attempted to fit the puzzle pieces of random words together, the ones I remembered from that day.

"Hello! Do you want a soda?" I heard suddenly next to me.

Startled, I opened my eyes, a bit confused to be back on the beach and not in the park anymore. I sat up quickly to discover, once my eyes had adjusted to the sun's brightness again, the little girl in the red bathing suit sitting beside me.

"Sorry! I didn't mean to scare you! I just thought you would like a cold drink. You look quite pink right now, and you're getting redder by the minute." She poked my arm with one finger, turning my skin white from the compression and then immediately back to burning red.

My cheeks flushed a deep scarlet. "Oh, thanks," I replied, diffidently accepting the drink.

"No problem. Are you here all by yourself? That seems dangerous. How old are you? I'm six, but my birthday is next month on July 18. I'm here with my great-aunt," she spluttered, pointing at the lady beside us.

I waved at her for a second time. "My mother will join me soon. She's right up there cleaning the beach house," I responded, pointing towards the cliff.

The girl's deep brown eyes, the color of coffee, grew with excitement. "You're staying up there on the cliff? Us too but further back. You're so close to the beach! Did you climb down those steps near the cliff?" she asked in one ebullient breath.

She continued before I could answer, "I've been wanting to climb those steps forever, but my aunt said no," glaring over her shoulder in her aunt's direction. "We are even staying at a house not far from here. We could walk to this beach and take those very steps, but she instead drives to the public parking area. Truthfully, I'm not certain she can make it down those steps. Can you believe that?" She paused to sigh and contemplate her terrible misfortune.

I jumped at this moment of silence to talk. "The very first time I climbed down the cliff was last night, just after we arrived from our road trip. We walked down in the dark using only flashlights. It was cloudy and stormy without any moon to help light the way. We walked down slowly, holding onto the rocks for balance. When we finally made it down, we had the whole beach to ourselves."

With wide eyes, she gazed back at the cliff behind us and then at me. "What an adventure! You walked down in the dark? I can hardly stand the excitement!"

"Yes, we really did walk down in the dark," I said, trying not to giggle at her theatrical reply. "Have you been here before? Is there a cave somewhere on this beach?"

"We've been coming here since I was a baby. My oldest cousin, who sometimes comes to stay with us at the beach, told me about a cave nearby. He said nobody ever goes inside because some sort of creature lives there and scares all of the children away. Once, he heard about a little girl who went inside and was never seen again," she recalled, her face animated by both thrill and fear while retelling the story.

My only reaction was fear. I replied, concealing the complete horror in my voice, "Is that story true? Was your cousin just trying to scare you?"

"Um, that does sound like something David would do. I think there really *is* a cave that way, but I've never seen it before," she responded, turning and pointing to her right.

"I don't think I want to see that cave." My desire to see a cave full of rubies had disappeared in one fearful poof.

The gang of children, released by their mother, ran towards us with celerity, screaming the entire way. They yelled at the girl asynchronously, in a jumbled mess, "Come on, Lucy! Let's go play!"

Lucy replied inattentively, waving them away, "Maybe later. I'm talking with my new friend."

I smiled. That was *me*.

The children, a flock of screeching wild beasts, galloped in the opposite direction to resume their games.

"Oh, my name is Lucy, by the way. I forgot to tell you earlier. My dad is always reminding me to introduce myself before I start chatting away."

I laughed. "It's okay. My name is Michael. It's nice to meet you, Lucy."

We continued talking while drinking our Cokes, or rather, Lucy chatted away, as her father put it, while I listened and interjected with the occasional laconic replies. In truth, I preferred it this way, conversations flowing easily without the constraints of guiding them.

"Michael?" I heard from a familiar voice behind me. I turned and spotted Mama walking towards us in white shorts and a blue-striped shirt. She looked like Grace Kelly in *To Catch a Thief*, except her hair was a darker shade of blonde.

"Mama, I'm here!" I waved my hand in the air.

She smiled as she approached us. Lucy immediately jumped up and extended her hand to my mother, as casually and confidently as she had offered me the Coke.

"Hello," she began, "I am Lucy, Michael's new friend." Lucy turned towards me beaming. "See, I am already better at introducing myself!"

Mama laughed. "Hello, Lucy. I am Michael's mother, Margaret. I am pleased to meet you."

Lucy grinned, displaying a gap of missing front teeth. "Oh, you must come meet my great-aunt."

I had observed her from a distance earlier, alone, and then interacting with Lucy. Something about her fascinated me. Relaxing under her umbrella in a beach chair, a paradox amidst her surroundings, she wore a red dress with red lipstick, red cat-eye sunglasses, and her dark brown hair pulled back with a silk scarf beneath a rather large white hat. She appeared out of place, plucked from a movie scene or ostentatious party, and placed in that chair. She seemed like someone who says the word "marvelous" very slowly and enjoys the luxuries of life, someone with boisterous laughs and tendencies to indulge her every whim.

We followed Lucy to the striped umbrella and properly met her Aunt Louise. Instead of handshakes, we were greeted with hugs and an intimacy that felt natural and sincere. Both Lucy and her great-aunt possessed that rare ability to make strangers feel included and distinguished without effort. Lucy's great-aunt might very well end up being all of those earlier assumptions but thus far seemed to be a mystery of first impressions: one by first appearance, the other by first introduction.

CHAPTER 3

BOARDWALK

For the remainder of the afternoon, Lucy and I focused on the construction of a sandcastle, which Lucy took quite seriously, interrupted occasionally for a run through the water or rest under the striped umbrella as necessitated by the overwhelming heat.

"This heat wave is unbelievable! The weather has never been so hot here, even in late July," I heard Lucy's aunt discussing with Mama.

Afternoon faded into early evening. The heat diminished slightly as the sun sank in the west. After achieving satisfaction, or boredom, with our sandcastle, we walked along the edge of the water, contemplating our next game, when Lucy darted off unexpectedly to the large umbrella where Mama and her aunt were chatting. I followed and heard, as I approached, her suggesting a walk together to the boardwalk.

I said, "Oh, I've never been to a boardwalk. I didn't even know there was one here. Where is it?"

Lucy's aunt replied, "It's about a mile down the beach, just beyond the other side of the cliff."

"Please," I implored, sitting on Mama's lap. "Please, can we go, Mama?"

She smiled. "Well, I would hate to waste this beautiful evening. We can go, little bird."

I jumped out of Mama's lap to rejoin Lucy on the sand. Lucy and I both shouted, "Hooray!"

Together, Lucy and I shook the sand off the towels, sprinkling the gritty specks back onto the beach. When the grains briefly floated and caught the sunlight, in a shimmering, suspended twinkle, it felt as if we were inside a golden snow globe. I rolled up my beach towel and left it beside the stone steps. Mama and Aunt Louise, as she repeatedly insisted on being addressed, packed up the chair, umbrella, and other supplies. We turned and left the private beach, reserved for families that lived nearby, and the cliff's edge behind, carrying the beach supplies to their car, parked at the public parking lot above the beach in the same direction as the boardwalk. Free of the load, Lucy and I removed our shoes for the remainder of our walk. The sand, finally cool enough to allow normal steps instead of hops, collapsed beneath our feet, leaving footprints behind. Indiscriminate blobs in the loose sand transformed into clear impressions in the compressed, wet sand near the shoreline. I wondered who had made the other footprints we passed along the way. Ahead, I spotted a Ferris wheel and the boardwalk. As the boardwalk continued past the Ferris wheel, above the sand, and into the water, it resembled popsicle sticks lined up and glued together in the distance.

We encountered more people, scattered groups gradually growing into a crowd, as we approached our destination. The sun hung to the left of us, slowly savoring each bit of summer day, while we walked towards the clear northern blue before us. The high tide forced us further up the shore; the breeze blew a sweet relief from the open ocean to us that late afternoon. With a closer view, I observed the colorful seats circling around the Ferris wheel. I had never ridden a Ferris wheel before and imagined how it felt to ride one. Lucy chattered beside me about everything she had learned in first grade while my mind cycled between her words and my own thoughts.

Lucy suddenly stopped and stood on the sand seriously, little escaped curls blowing about her face. "'And then my heart with pleasure fills, / And dances with the Daffodils.'" (Wordsworth 329)

Lucy's words had caught Mama's ear, halting her steps. Aunt Louise continued walking and chatting, not yet noticing that she was alone. Mama listened and then clapped softly for Lucy.

"Wonderful, Lucy! That is one of my favorite poems. I also love Emily Dickinson and Khalil Gibran."

"He's Lebanese, like me!" Lucy exclaimed, recognizing the second name. "Well, I'm actually half Lebanese. My dad reads his book to me. But I don't know Emily Dickerson."

Lucy then turned to me and requested we dance like daffodils down the beach. With my lanky limbs and clumsiness, I awkwardly tried to sway my head and wave my arms as leaves while walking simultaneously, which resulted in Lucy collapsing onto the ground in a fit of giggles. It took quite a few minutes, in addition to a stern look from her aunt, for Lucy to compose herself enough to continue our jaunt.

"I'm sorry," she apologized, leaning in close to me, "but once I get the giggles, I can't really stop myself. You must let a fit of giggles finish themselves. That's what my Daddy tells me."

I leaned in closer to her face and touched her shoulder. I whispered, "Tag," and ran from her as she smiled. Lucy began chasing me, no forgiveness nor remorse needed between us.

Finally, we arrived at the boardwalk. The trip, to me, seemed to take longer than the walk on the yellow brick road in *The Wonderful Wizard of Oz*. We climbed up the wooden steps from the sand, pausing in amazement at the blinking lights and large crowd as music played overhead. The storefronts faced the beach, displaying signs large and small that advertised jewelry, hot dogs, cotton candy, popcorn, Coca-Cola, clothes, beach supplies, and radios, all attempting to lure shoppers to their door. I absorbed, in wonder, this new place and all of the people, most of them seeking shade or refreshment from the beach, sunburnt and dusted with sand. They walked among the shops or loitered outside, drinking Cokes and eating popcorn or hot dogs while waving off the daring seagulls. The smell of butter and roasted meat overwhelmed the sweat and sun lotion.

Lucy grabbed my hand, as I was still mesmerized by the signs and crowd, and dragged me behind her. Mama and Aunt Louise followed closely behind us as we quickly swerved into the open spaces between people. Lucy pushed open a door to the ding of a bell, and I saw "Mae's Arcade" written in white letters just above the handle when we entered. In front of us, pinball machines were lined up in perfect rows against the walls. In the back corner, I spotted a picture booth with a floral curtain covering the entrance. Lucy looked at me, smiling, trying to see if I approved of her surprise. I did.

After a quick hello to an employee behind the counter, we walked slowly along the rows of games, stopping at each one to inspect and comment on the minuscule world inside. Two older boys were bent over one of the pinball machines. We watched as one boy pulled back the plunger and launched the ball up the side and into the playing field. When the ball hit the circular red bumpers, they lit up and emitted a ping. Once the ball rolled to the bottom center, he pressed the red buttons on the sides and flipped the ball up again. The ball quickly shot up to the top and bounced from bumper to bumper, a melody of pings, until it succumbed to gravity and fell down again. Our eyes chased the ball up, down, and side to side. Another flip hit the metal ball straight into the middle of the target, lighting all the bowling pins. A loud bell and flashing lights signaled a strike.

"Wow," I whispered to myself.

Lucy looked at me with an exuberant smile and gleaming eyes. "Come on! Let's check the rest of the games."

I glanced over at Mama. Aunt Louise, an animated look upon her face, was talking to her, but Mama was looking at me instead, beaming, always content when I was happy.

As we finished inspecting the rest of the machines, Aunt Louise walked over to us, bent down, and asked, "Would you like to play?"

"Yes!" we shouted in unison.

"Here you go." She placed a nickel in each of our open hands.

"Thank you, thank you," I said, falling into her for a hug.

After considering our options thoroughly, we decided that we both wanted a turn on Spot Bowler, so we waited patiently for the other boys to finish with the machine. Never playing before, I was quite terrible and secretly happy the older boys did not stay to watch us. I did, however, hit the ball a few times, which was enough for me. Lucy cheered loudly each time I hit the ball with the flipper. From her reaction, one might assume I had made a lot of strikes. My favorite part was pulling the plunger back as far as I could and watching the ball fly to the top when I released it. Lucy was surprisingly good, and unlike me, she actually did hit one strike while playing.

Once we both had finished our turn, Lucy ran to her aunt, pulled her down, and whispered into her ear. Aunt Louise fumbled through her purse before handing something to Lucy. Lucy kissed her cheek and then ran back to me.

"How about a picture?" she asked, gesturing towards the photo booth.

"Cool," I responded with a grin.

The man who had greeted us upon our arrival showed us how to operate the booth. Lucy inserted three coins, each landing on a hidden pile of money with a clang, and we stepped inside, closed the floral curtain, and posed for our pictures. We had previously decided on two silly and two serious poses in alternating order, directed by Lucy before each camera flash. A few minutes later, our pictures dropped into the metal slot on the front of the booth. Lucy ripped the strip in half, with two pictures on each side, and handed me one piece. We left the arcade, rejoining the crowd on the boardwalk, after showing our pictures to Mama and Aunt Louise.

While considering our next adventure, Aunt Louise declared, "I'm hungry. Let's eat hotdogs!"

No one objected to her idea, so we bought four hotdogs and Cokes from a vendor, plus an ice cream cone for Aunt Louise. We crossed onto the pier for a picnic above the waves, sitting beside a fisherman who waited for a tug of his line. The setting sun shone gently upon our faces as we looked towards the Ferris wheel.

Aunt Louise began eating her ice cream before her hot dog. "I always eat dessert first," she explained to us between licks of her vanilla cone. "In my wisdom, I have found that it's the proper way to begin a meal."

It must be fun to be an adult and do whatever you want, I thought to myself. I took the first bite of my hotdog; the succulent roasted meat tasted even better mixed with the peppery fizzle of soda, bubbling inside my nose. Between bites, I peered over the edge of the pier, watching the waves crash against the round legs, the water sloshing up the sides. I spotted the fisherman's line submerged beneath the surface.

Our hunger satisfied, we walked back towards the Ferris wheel, towering above the shops. Suddenly, the center of the Ferris wheel lit up, displaying a star in the middle. The six tips of the star pointed at every other seat. We watched as couples boarded, the wheel turning slowly with a creak until the next seat was ready for loading. When the last seat was occupied, it began to turn faster, round and round, the shining star spinning before us.

As we stood watching the ride, Mama approached me and Lucy from behind and kissed the top of my head. She smelled faintly of flowers and laundry detergent, a distinctive, familiar scent that would always be hers, one of those nostalgic scents of childhood that transports you back with one whiff. She grabbed my hand, gently placed a quarter inside, and squeezed it before letting go. I knew its purpose without words.

I linked arms with Lucy at the elbow and asked if she would ride the Ferris wheel with me. Lucy vehemently squealed, which I interpreted as a yes, and dragged me along running to the ticket booth. Exchanging our quarter for a ticket, we waited in line for our turn. That flitting winged creature appeared in my stomach as we stood in line, gaining intensity as we boarded our red seat, slowly rose into the air, and turned faster and faster. I waved at Mama when we reached the bottom and secretly held my breath as we climbed backwards, that fulgurant spark zipping about my stomach. Lucy merrily shrieked and waved throughout the entire ride. She had no fear. My favorite part was that fleeting moment at the very top, bathed in the last bits of sunlight, when it felt as if we were flying. I tilted my head back, a bird surrounded by boundless blue, before falling back to earth.

The radiance of the setting sun lingered that evening, as all seems to in summer, in a never-ending twilight, which was fine with me since I did not want the day to end. We walked back home after riding the Ferris wheel, finding and retracing our remaining footprints, those not erased by the reaching waves, as the boardwalk slowly faded behind us. We reluctantly said our goodbyes, waving at Lucy and Aunt Louise as they trudged up the weathered stairs to the parking lot, sand tumbling with each step, until they were out of sight. Mama and I continued our walk along the beach and around the cliff, chatting about our boardwalk adventure. The sun's last visible glow was shining like a nightlight from below the horizon. We sat upon the cool sand together, once we were just below the beach house, enjoying the quiet after a busy day, each dissecting the conversations and occurrences to the sound of waves collapsing onto the shore. All of a sudden, darkness surrounded us as the protracted twilight ended, tricking us earlier into believing night shall never appear.

CHAPTER 4

BLUE GLASS

Without even realizing it, Mama and I settled into a routine the week after we arrived. We went shopping for groceries or other supplies on Mondays. Tuesdays and Thursdays were cleaning and laundry days, working around the house most of the day and then venturing to the beach once the chores were completed. Those days began with breakfast on the back patio, when the weather obliged, listening to the world awaken, the slight scatter of waves in the background. Following breakfast, we switched on the radio for a quick dance party and then began cleaning. I helped as much as I could until Mama, drained of patience, kicked me to the backyard to play. I usually spent my time hunting for spiders in the grass. Fridays and weekends were left open for adventure. Occasionally, my grandparents visited us. Nana and Pops, my mother's parents, typically took us on day trips to neighboring cities or local landmarks. Though I was surprised to discover that they rarely visited anymore, the beach house belonged to them, so they knew the area better than anyone.

On Sunday evenings, my dad called, mostly to talk to me and hear of our latest adventures. Mama typically said hello, asked about work, quickly transitioned the conversation to me and how much I missed him, and handed me the phone soon after she picked up the receiver. He asked me lots of questions, and I loved recalling all of the things we had done each week, perhaps embellishing some of the details. At the end of every call, before we said goodbye, Dad promised to come visit us soon. He always talked about taking me deep-sea fishing on a boat and joked that we might accidentally catch a sea monster, which would drag us all the way to Greenland. Mama's mood always seemed to change after his calls. Sometimes, I even caught her wiping her face, as if she had been crying.

On Wednesday mornings, Mama and I walked downtown, sometimes buying ice cream to eat along the way, resting on the walk back home at the little park just on the edge of downtown, the one I had noticed on our first drive to the diner. On one such outing, we were eating our ice cream cones, returning to Main Street on a perpendicular road, when Mama suddenly stopped. After finally realizing she was not behind me, I returned to join her observation. She stared at a small building, its height larger than its width, constructed entirely of old cream-colored stones. Inspired by Gothic architecture, its façade contained three recessed windows with pointed arches at the top: a large one in the center flanked by two smaller ones on each side. The internal tracery of the large window began at the bottom with three straight lines that branched into an intersecting pattern, creating six diamonds towards the top. The glass of the three largest diamonds was stained sapphire blue. A similar branching tracery intersected the two smaller windows on the sides with one blue diamond in the center of each. At the bottom of the building, three pointed archways led to a covered portico around the front entrance, the doors hidden within.

We licked our vanilla ice cream as we admired the small but ornate structure, discovering new details with each glance.

"It reminds me of churches I have seen in pictures from Europe," Mama remarked. She then turned towards me, her eyes glistening in the sunlight. A slight smile asked, "Shall we go inside, little bird?"

I nodded enthusiastically.

We walked towards the entrance, halting just before the archways. I looked up along the edge, chewing the last bit of my cone. In an almost straight line, I saw the archway, stones, and windows above. We passed through the middle archway, which felt like entering a secret passage, to the double doors. The wooden doors, tall and rectangular, formed an arch with the curved window above them. The window, the same width as the double doors, was divided into branched segments like the recessed windows on the front of the building. Thinking it must be a church, I began recalling the sins I had committed during the school year—telling small lies, the ones kids begin experimenting with at my age, and stealing a seashell from school that I had returned the following day; the latter was kept a secret from Mama, for I did not want her to be ashamed of me. I prepared my guilt and act of contrition mentally as we neared the entrance. Part of growing up with Catholicism in my school and home was accepting the never-ending shame in my life and then regularly asking for forgiveness through confession. Just to the right of the doors, a square bronze plaque read "W. M. DuPont Public Library." Mama and I looked at each other in surprise. She must have thought it was a church too as she also looked a little relieved. I curiously wondered what sins waited in her mind to confess.

We entered the library to see a rather large front desk greeting us, out of proportion to the size of the library. To the right and left, there were rows and rows of shelves filled with books—tall, short, thick, thin, old, and new—in an array of colored bindings. Similar to people, each book had a distinct appearance and personality. Simultaneously, I wanted to read every book within view but became overwhelmed by the prospect of doing so. I looked up to see the high vaulted ceiling above us, stone ribs arching to the top.

After a deep inhalation, Mama whispered, "I have always loved the smell of books, especially the older ones. They smell a bit old but familiar somehow."

I closed my eyes and took a deep breath. I smiled. The library smelled stale, much the same as the beach house when we first arrived. *How curious for a building full of new ideas to smell old*, I thought to myself.

After walking to a shelf and pulling out a book, Mama continued, "Oh, and the feel of a new book in your hands. Touching the binding, etching the letters of the title with your finger, imagining what's inside, and the excitement when you turn to the first page. Ever since I was a little girl, books have been my friends."

Unbeknownst to us, someone had approached quietly from behind while Mama was talking. After Mama had replaced the book and we turned around towards the front desk again, we were startled by an elderly lady, quite a bit shorter than Mama, who smiled at us. She wore thick-rimmed black eyeglasses and a tidy outfit of white blouse, plaid skirt, and brown cardigan. A poof of short brown curls encircled her head, pulled back neatly with gray streaks on the sides. Despite the apparent effort, little curly wisps escaped on the top, the only unkempt part of her appearance.

"Welcome to the library," she said softly.

I tried to figure out how she had sneaked up behind us without a sound. She did not seem particularly lithe to me as I examined her thoroughly.

She looked directly at me. "Follow me, young man. We have a children's area I think you will enjoy."

Mama and I followed her to the back of the library after a quick glance and chuckle between us. We came upon a border of low bookshelves and walked to the small rectangular tables in the center. The bookshelves were packed with books neatly squeezed together until they stood up straight. Larger chairs for parents, I assumed, were scattered around the perimeter. A large globe sat in one corner next to a window with a built-in seat. A selection of books was displayed on top of a long row of bookshelves, and on top of another row against the wall, I spotted pottery pieces, small baked clay, that resembled animals shaped by inexperienced fingers.

The librarian caught me staring at them. "Ah, yes, those were made by the children at our local school. You will definitely want to get a closer look." She then walked over to the book display and continued, "Here are some of our most popular children's books. Of course, I can help you find any book if you have a particular one in mind. You just come and find me at the front desk if you need anything. My name is Ms. Prince."

"Thank you, Ms. Prince," I replied before she turned and left us.

First, I examined the pottery, piece by piece, leaning in closely to see the tiny faces and bodies. I attempted to guess each animal I came upon. Some were easily distinguishable by their prominent features: the neck of a giraffe, the ears of a rabbit, and the trunk of an elephant. Others were more challenging; I could not determine whether one figure was a pig or dog, a second was a zebra or horse, and a third was a tiger or cheetah. After visiting the clay zoo, I ambled over to the other row of bookshelves to check the display of books on top. I walked slowly as I looked at each book's cover, judging based on its appearance whether I might like it or not, against the advice of that famous idiom. I grabbed a book about animals, which seemed interesting, probably because my mind was still occupied with the artwork.

I carried my book to the window seat and climbed on, peering around the library from this new perspective. I saw Mama cozily ensconced in an armchair behind a book. I smiled, knowing Mama was never happier than when she was surrounded by her friends. I looked towards the front of the library, which was blocked by the rows of bookshelves. My view wandered up to the three arched windows we had seen from outside. The late morning sun shone through the windows. From the translucent light, I realized that the other segments of glass had been stained white in addition to the blue diamonds that had captured my attention outside. The white fragments reminded me of frosted glass during cold winter days, the sunlight trapped behind foggy panes. Once again, my eyes shifted to the blue, seized by the sapphire diamonds that pulled my gaze like a current, incessant yet calming. I liked watching their brilliance change with the waxing and waning sunlight from bright blue to deep indigo. Sometimes the colors transformed quickly, in a capricious kaleidoscope, when clouds zipped by in a hurry. I had hardly opened my book when Mama told me it was time to go.

We said our thanks and goodbyes to Ms. Prince although I knew she would see us sooner than she realized. Before it left our view, I turned back for another glimpse of the library, settled inconspicuously on the edge of downtown. I wondered how many would never discover its arches or stained glass but, at the same time, felt grateful that we had wandered to its doors. As we were talking, the midday sun shining from above all around us, I looked up from the broken sidewalk to Mama's face, basked in sunlight. At that moment, I realized the blue glass from the library windows resembled Mama's eyes, in intricacy as well as transparency, shining or fading according to the light within her. Our time at the beach house had already restored their brilliance. On that day, her eyes scattered the sunlight like malleable, shifting diamonds perched upon the morning grass.

We soon arrived at the park and headed straight for a bench surrounded by flowering bushes. I ran to the green space in the middle of the park, sprinting back and forth until I collapsed onto the ground with my arms outstretched, heart pounding, inhaling and exhaling rapidly. I closed my eyes for a few minutes; a slight breeze blew a gentle caress across my arms and legs, compared to the sea breeze blown from the ocean. I could smell the earth below me. It smelled of dirt and minerals.

After resting, I joined Mama on the bench. She was writing in her red journal, the one she always carried with her. She had once told me, "You never know what might inspire you. It helps to write your ideas down when they strike you, even if you save them for another day." I peeked at the page and read:

Between the bush
And blushing tree
A butterfly glides blithely.

Black tiger stripes,
A swallowtail
Using yellow wings to sail

I watch the feast
Beyond the glass
As billowy clouds stroll past.

A whipping gale
Out of the north
Blows the branches back and forth.

Pink snow flurries,
Do not despair
As they scatter through the air.

For you, I'll grow
Fields of flowers
To behold your fleeting hours.

I looked around at the bushes surrounding the bench on all
sides. Indeed, I spotted two large yellow butterflies with black
stripes resting on a bush with cone-shaped blooms, tiny purple
flowers covering every inch. They were the largest butterflies I had
ever seen, their wingspan wider than the distance from my thumb
to my little finger. I examined my hand, stretching my fingers to
see how far apart they could spread. Mesmerized by them, I
watched as the butterflies floated delicately, one at a time, to a
nearby tree, sipped nectar from the pink flowers, and then flew
back again to the bush.

"Are those swall tails?" I asked Mama in a whisper, afraid I
may disturb their feast.

"Yes," she replied. "They are tiger swa-llow-tails. The first
time I ever saw them, when I was a little older than you, I became
enchanted by them, watching them for hours from a window that
summer in Tennessee at my grandparents' house. I did not know
their name, so I drew a picture of them, ensuring the colors and
placement of the stripes were perfect. Then, the next time I went
to the library, I used my picture to discover their name by
comparing it to the images and descriptions in a book of insects.

I just could not stop searching until I knew the name of this butterfly. Seeing them here is like bumping into an old friend unexpectedly."

"Aren't they wonderful?" she asked me, her eyes of blue glass twinkling.

"Wonderful."

We sat there together on the bench, watching the butterflies glide between the bushes and the trees, over and over, for the remainder of our time at the park until we walked back to the beach house for a late lunch.

CHAPTER 5

NOBSKA

I did not see Lucy nor her great-aunt the week after we walked to the boardwalk or the week after that. I looked for her red bathing suit and listened for her laughter, both loud and distinctive, every time we went to the beach. I thought perhaps they had left the beach and gone back home, wherever that was, wondering if she would remember me and our perfect day together. Mama and I kept busy with our schedule, relishing the relaxing days as much as the active ones. Nana and Pops came for their first visit during the third week of our stay at the beach house. Mama laughed when Nana showed us the itinerary she had planned for all of us: a trip to Nobska Light and a cranberry bog tour, among other things. None of us, including Pops, had a choice in the matter, but I loved the adventures that she had organized for us.

A few days after my grandparents arrived, I awoke one morning to Mama and Nana busily packing a picnic basket full of wrapped sandwiches, the last bit of banana bread, baked before their journey to utilize the last of their bananas, and vegetables grown in Pops' garden. Pops figured if Nana got to bring her banana bread, then he could bring his proudly grown bounty along as well. I overheard their conversation before I joined them.

Nana said, "Really, Margaret, I don't know why you asked us to update this kitchen."

"I thought you might like to cook for Michael in a new kitchen and maybe, I don't know, you and Dad would come here to stay more often. You never come anymore."

Nana changed the topic. "Where is your husband? Why is *he* not here?"

Mama admitted, her voice sinking, "Mom, you know we've been fighting a lot lately. I think some space between us will help."

"Just work it out. Jimmy is your husband, so it's your only choice," Nana replied in a harsh, admonishing tone.

Their conversation stopped when Nana spotted me walking into the kitchen. She squealed, wrapped me in her arms, and squeezed as she rocked me back and forth.

"Good morning!" she sang merrily, continuing to embrace me firmly. "We are going to have a picnic at the beach near the lighthouse today. Now, go change your clothes, my darling."

"And bring something warm!" Nana shouted down the hallway after I had already disappeared.

We drove to Nobska Point, located on the southwestern tip of Cape Cod. When we arrived after the short trip, Pops parked rather precariously beside a narrow road without a shoulder, running parallel to Nobska Beach, where we would have our picnic. As it was only ten o'clock in the morning, we walked to the lighthouse first. I carefully exited the car, sitting partially on the road, anticipation swelling inside me. I could see the lighthouse before us in the distance, stoically standing on a hill overlooking the Vineyard Sound, an inlet of seawater between the mainland of Cape Cod and nearby islands. It appeared in my vision as a picture from a storybook, becoming more real the closer we got to it.

Nana utilized the walk to scold Pops about his choice of parking spot, smacking him gently but repeatedly with her purse and questioning whether he was trying to kill us all. Mama and I walked behind them, quietly laughing so Nana did not hear us. Nana was intense in every way: her joy brimming with loud laughs and singsong words and her anger exploding with roaring screams and flailing limbs. I had once heard Mama telling a friend what it was like growing up around her. She explained how difficult it was to gauge her mother's mood and how it would change rapidly without warning. If she were happy, the whole house would be happy. The atmosphere would be yellow, cheerful, and bright. If she were sad or angry, storm clouds would instantly appear overhead, coloring everything gray. During those times, everyone would be required to be miserable, just like her.

Even as a child, I noticed the cautious way Mama approached Nana, always trying to anticipate and placate her capricious tendencies. Mama had adapted into the peacekeeper of her family. Apart from her faults, Nana was funny, kind, and loyal to her family. Curiously, she never acted this way towards me, which confused me when my immaturity and innocence painted people as good or bad, superhero or villain, and nothing in-between. She perhaps attempted in her own way to rectify her misdeeds by spoiling me excessively—a solution which required no admission of guilt on her part nor apology to my mother.

We finally made it to the lighthouse grounds safely after a short but treacherous jaunt. The winding road, with no shoulder nor sidewalk, curved sharply around Nobska Point, making it impossible to watch for oncoming cars. In reality, I never thought we were in any real danger of being hit by a car. In the time it took us to complete our walk, we only encountered three cars, which were all driven cautiously as they passed us.

"Look," Nana remarked, pointing while glaring at Pops. "There's a parking lot right here. Why in the world didn't you park here instead of making us walk?"

She whacked him with her purse again.

Pops countered firmly, "Well, for one, I didn't even know there was a parking lot right here. Secondly, we would have had to walk down to the beach anyway with all of our picnic gear. I still think it's best that we parked down by the beach."

Because of his defiance, Nana struck him one last time on the rear end. Pops yelped and then screamed, "That's it!" as he chased her up to the lighthouse, both of them giggling like schoolchildren. Pops never took anything too seriously, including Nana.

I paused alone at the bottom to observe the scene in its entirety. Lush grass covered the area, contrasting brightly with the low white picket fence surrounding the perimeter. I gazed up at the black-and-white lighthouse, sitting magically on the knoll above me. The tower was painted white. Thin arched windows, covered with peaked casing and divided into four panes, climbed up and around the tower at various heights and locations. Tiny round portholes encircled the top of the white tower. Above, a black iron balcony with railing enclosed a small black room, encased in large windows all the way around. *That must be where the light shines out*, I thought to myself. This compartment was covered by a black pointed roof with a sphere upon the summit. The rod protruding from the sphere reminded me of a saber drawn and aimed towards the heavens. Behind the lighthouse, I saw a house with a distinctive red roof, the color of red clay.

Satisfied with my survey, I passed through a gate and walked up the steps, wooden squares with loose pebbles in the center, to the lighthouse. I looked out at the water, surrounding all before me, my eyes swimming in blue. The elevated position made the ocean feel even more prodigious, more overwhelming than it did when we were at the beach. I was glad that Nana had advised me to bring a sweater. Usually a welcome respite from the sun, the wind whipped wildly above the water, incessantly battering me from all directions at once. I thought I spotted land ahead, which seemed impossible to me. I knew there were islands beyond the sound, but my eyes must have been playing tricks on me to see them so close to the mainland.

Pops, now standing beside me, remarked, "That's Martha's Vineyard," as he pointed in the same direction that I stared. He then pointed to the right and said, "Over there are the Elizabeth Islands. And way over to the left out of view is Nantucket, separated from the mainland by the Nantucket Sound."

Pops turned around when he heard a man's voice behind us. He smiled and walked over to shake hands with him. Pops waved me over excitedly to join them, along with Nana and Mama.

"This is Mr. Osborne Hallett," Pops said. "He is the keeper of this lighthouse. Mr. Hallett is my friend, and he agreed to give us a quick tour."

The introduction sparked a curiosity in me about keeping a lighthouse, what it meant and how to do it. We all exchanged pleasantries and then followed Mr. Hallett to the entrance, which looked like a small house with an oversized door. As we entered the stairwell, I looked up and observed the clay brick wall, each brick unique in varying shades of red and dark gray, curving around until it completed a circle. A black staircase spiraled all the way up along the wall. We climbed up the tower's twisting staircase, pausing briefly, one after another, at the little curved windows to peer out from each vantage point. The sun streamed through the windows, lighting up the dark stairwell. These were the same windows I had seen from outside. At each stop, I rubbed my hand gently, to avoid scraping my skin, along the coarse, cold bricks.

It did not take long for us to climb up the thirty-three steps. At the top of the stairs, we entered through a door to an odd little room painted completely white with a twisted black ladder in the corner. Before ascending to the lantern, the glass enclosure that contained the lens, I walked back out to the stairwell and peeked over the banister for one last look. I loved the way the staircase coiled along the wall, the spiral growing smaller on the way down, resembling a snail's shell. As soon as I climbed up the eight steps of the ladder, the lens caught my eye immediately. It was elevated upon a black stand directly in my line of sight. I stood, frozen, gaping at that strange clear glass object, rising taller than me in the center of the small room. It looked like a bulging barrel in the middle with spikes protruding from the top and bottom. Through a narrow opening, I saw a tall, thin light bulb.

The lens, with its bizarre angles and protrusions, captured the sunlight as well as images of the sky, water, and nearby occupants simultaneously, bending and blending everything into distorted refractions of random sights. Bits of sunlight were scattered as gold flecks around the lantern room. It was a captivating madness, like looking through glasses of water all lined up but held at different angles. I thought I could easily get lost staring into it.

Mr. Hallett was recounting the history of the lighthouse in a rehearsed manner, as if he had given this verbatim speech on countless occasions. "The light was originally built on top of the keeper's house in 1828 but was later rebuilt in 1876 as a 40-foot cast-iron tower. The very one we are standing in now! It was built in Massachusetts and transported here in four different sections."

His attention shifted to the lens. He extended his hand to invite me closer and continued, "This is called a Fresnel lens, named after the French physicist who developed it. Originally, a fifth-order, or smaller, Fresnel lens was installed but was later replaced with this fourth-order lens in 1888 (Friends of Nobska Light). It is a bigger multifaceted lens than the fifth-order, and its light can reach further out to sea. It is confusing but with these lenses, the bigger the number, the smaller the lens."

Mr. Hallett asked me, "Do you see this light in the middle of the lens?"

I nodded.

"Well, it is much easier to be a lighthouse keeper these days than it was forty or so years ago because this light uses electricity. But before then, oil lamps were used as a light source. The keeper and his crew had to ensure that the light never extinguished, for souls might be lost to the sea if this occurred. It is a great responsibility to guard the light."

"But, sir, how does the light shine way out there?" I inquired, pointing towards the water. "How does it reach the ships?"

"Great question, young man!" Mr. Hallett walked closer to the lens and pointed at the bottom spikes. "These ridges on the lens bend the light in varying degrees until they converge, or meet, into one bright beam that shines farther away. It is a wonderful invention that has saved many lives."

He looked directly at me again, noticing my interest in the lens. "Did you know that each lighthouse has its own signal pattern?"

"No," I responded.

"The different patterns help ships distinguish between the lighthouses. Our signal is one white flash every six seconds. So, a captain could see our signal and know his approximate location. We also have a red sector on one side that is used to warn sailors in dangerous shoals. If a ship is too close to the shoal, they will see a red light, telling them to change course or risk running aground."

Mr. Hallett then walked over to the windows and said, "We also have a foghorn, which is turned on when visibility is less than five miles."

I stepped over to one of the windows, enjoying the view of water stretching far into the distance. My view was dissected partially by the railing of the gallery outside. Upon further inspection of the railing's spikes, I realized that they were not spikes at all but tiny lighthouses instead. It was a clear day with only little puffs of clouds spread throughout the sky, allowing me to see to the end of the earth. The sunlight reflected on the water, shimmering like glitter on the surface. At this height, I could see the islands more clearly. I moved around the perimeter, excusing myself past the others, to look out every window. In the left corner, beside the red pane used to warn of dangerous shoals, I saw the peak of the red gabled roof atop the keeper's house. Moving past the red sector, I eyed the curving road below and cars wheeling around its bend and out of sight. Little ripples of water moved continuously over the rocks towards the land. On the other side, I spied the parking lot and a portion of the mainland. I completed my tour of the windows and turned back to the lens, blocked by bodies. The lantern appeared quite small with all of us inside. Mama walked over to join me after I had returned to the windows and stared at the water once more. I pointed out the tiny lighthouses on top of the railing to her.

I wished we could have stayed in the lantern for hours, but Mr. Hallett needed to continue his duties. We descended the lighthouse, declared our gratitude, and bid farewell to Mr. Hallett. As we walked down to the car and carried our supplies to the beach for our picnic, I found myself repeatedly looking back at the lighthouse. The beach, hardly a beach at all, was just a small strip of sand beside the water. I thought the incoming tide might swallow it completely. It was enough, however, for a picnic, and despite its size, the beach provided a perfect view of the lighthouse.

The wind blew continuously at the beach but with less strength than it did around the lighthouse. Mixed with the high sun beaming down, the breeze produced clement conditions for our picnic. We spent the rest of the afternoon lazily, relishing our lunch and intermittent conversations, coming and going as the waves waltzed upon the shore. The lighthouse stole my gaze, in quick glances between words and lingering stares during pools of silence, throughout the remainder of our visit. Rising above the rocks along the edge of the water and overgrown bushes of wild green growing on the knoll, it appeared mysterious, almost lonely.

Pops returned from the car, after snoozing a bit on the blanket following lunch, with a childlike grin and an object hidden behind his back. The sun illuminated the flecks of gold in his hazel eyes, amber starbursts the color of honey around his pupil. He asked me to close my eyes and then promptly revealed the red kite, as if he could not wait another minute to reveal the surprise. For a brief moment, the kite reminded me of my sixth birthday party and the daydream I had wandered into on the day I met Lucy. I laughed, grabbed the thick spool of string, and ran while Pops held the kite and tossed it up into the air, the tail waving about, hoping the wings would catch the wind and rise. After a few attempts and lots of laughter, mostly due to Pops' goofy hops during each throw, the kite climbed higher and higher as I released the string with Pops' assistance. Mama and Nana cheered from the picnic blanket.

"We've never flown a kite this high before," Pops remarked, amazed at the height it had reached once all the thread had been unraveled.

"I know!" I tilted my head back and watched the kite with one eye squinted.

Pops and I had been flying kites together since I had learned to walk, according to Mama. Pops, a pilot who fought in World War II, was fascinated by them and their similarities to airplanes. He always explained the principles of lift and drag, eventually transitioning from the kite into the science behind an airplane's ability to fly. He often repeated the same stories of learning to fly over and over again, as older people tend to do. I did not mention this to him, for I loved hearing his stories, under any condition. Pops never discussed specifics of the war, although I thought he would have lots of exciting stories to tell about his flights and the people he met. Whenever the Second World War was brought up in conversation, Pops quickly fled the topic through a change in subject or dash from the room. Once, when he and I were in town together, an old friend of Pops approached us, shook his hand, and offered his condolences for George Junior. The encounter lasted a mere minute, but still, I saw Pops' eyes fill with tears, on the verge of overflowing and with them, his control. I had never seen Pops cry before then, or any other man, and I believed perhaps men did not need to cry. Nana and Mama seemed to cry all the time. As we continued down the sidewalk that day, in slow steps with heavy thoughts, Pops reeled in his sadness, bottling his emotions once more.

After he had composed himself, he said in a soft, thoughtful voice, "My father and grandfathers told me that real men don't cry. So, I've spent my whole life trying not to show my sadness or fear or any weaknesses."

He then bent down after a long pause to look into my eyes, a tear slowly rolling down his face, and admitted, "After all these years, I'm not sure that was good advice."

It was advice, at my young age, I only understood on the surface. It seemed silly to hold back emotions. As a child, I was allowed to cry or scream whenever I wanted or needed to do so. It was not until I grew, wading further into the waters of time, when these allowances were no longer granted, and I gained the experience of being a male with emotions that I comprehended the depth of his words. I would only see Pops cry once more in my lifetime.

I knew very little about George Junior, Mama's older brother. I knew he had died during World War II at a very young age. I saw pictures of him, the same heart-shaped face and eyes as Mama, scattered around Nana and Pops' house. His face seemed familiar to me although I had never met him, perhaps because he and Mama looked so much alike. Junior was only mentioned in passing, when a memory surfaced, carried by some little reminder of him, a topic no one seemed able to linger on for very long.

The bright red kite danced, back and forth, across the blue sky with its long tail swinging after every move. I could feel the power of the wind push against the kite, rippling with a whish, as the string was pulled within my hands. The kite, at the mercy of the fickle wind, swayed gently for a stretch of time and then unexpectedly swooped wildly, slicing through the air with a whoosh. Pops chuckled each time this happened, but I worried that I might release the handle and lose the kite.

Mama walked over and asked for a turn. "I can't resist the fun any longer," she said as she took control.

She laughed, in her quiet way, as the kite dipped and then climbed up again. I stood back and watched Mama fly the kite with the lighthouse in the background. It was a beautiful scene of white, black, and red. Not wanting to be the only one without a turn, Nana joined our group and demanded a go. Mama handed the kite to Nana, who squealed loudly in delight when it jerked her arms. I looked away for a moment when suddenly I heard Nana squawk as the kite plunged to the ground.

"Of course the wind hates me," Nana sulked puerilely, holding the drooping string.

Mama, Pops, and I looked at Nana and then at each other, trying our best to look empathetic until Pops exploded into laughter like a firework whose fuse had abruptly ended. After this outburst, Mama and I could not hold it in any longer, even to spare Nana's feelings. We joined Pops' guffaw, which only made him cackle louder, and before we knew it, all three of us were on the sand in a fit of never-ending giggles and tears. Nana stood there, despondent, staring at us.

"Well, I'm so glad my misfortunes can amuse you," Nana said shakily, her sadness quickly turning into rage. A Southern drawl, remnants of her childhood, stretched out the end of the sentence.

It snuck into her speech when her guard had been lowered, during particularly emotional moments or under the influence of alcohol.

"Oh, Betty," Pops spluttered but could not quite finish after the laughter overtook him again.

Determined to make amends before Nana lost her temper, Pops tried his best to end the cycle of giggles. "Oh, Betty, it's just a kite," he stammered, immediately rejoining us with a few barks.

Nana glanced at me, happy upon the sand. Her anger vanished before she allowed it to progress into a fight as she dropped the string and began laughing. Soon, she was on the ground with us, unable to stop.

Mama leaned in close to me, her eyes glistening, and whispered, "Cheers, little bird."

CHAPTER 6

LIGHTHOUSES

As we left the lighthouse behind and drove back to the beach house that evening, our day weighed heavily, exhaustion from the excitement tugging on my eyelids. I tried to resist, at first, immediately opening my eyes each time they closed, stubbornly refusing to surrender. Fatigue eventually won, however, after a hazy battle. I heard faint snippets of conversation as I swayed between consciousness and sleep.

Nana said, "Margaret, he returned from the war a different man. You should show him more patience."

I never heard Mama's reply or if Pops had a thought to add, but next I remember hearing Mama ask, "Why don't you come visit the beach house more often?"

I dozed off but forced myself awake again and heard Nana crying. Through her sobs, she spluttered, "I just miss him so much. All of the memories … he haunts me there. Sometimes I see him in Michael … all those emotions come rushing back when …"

The heaviness combined with the car's movement overtook my willpower. The voices became muffled and distorted until, eventually, I heard no more. I awoke to Mama gently shaking my arm, the car parked in the gravel driveway of the beach house.

The lighthouse remained in my thoughts long after we had left the beach that afternoon. The following Wednesday, when Mama and I returned to the library and our normal routine after Nana and Pops left, I asked Ms. Prince, the librarian, for help finding a book about lighthouses. She smiled and asked if I had ever visited a lighthouse as she walked over to a wooden cabinet full of small square drawers. She opened one of the drawers and flipped through the cards, searching for a book that matched my request.

While she searched, I said, "Yes, we went to visit one last week."

She replied, "Lovely, dear," in her quiet voice, laced with honey, as she continued flipping through more cards until she paused on one, jotting down the information in her tiny notepad.

"Follow me, dear," she requested, leading the way, row after row of books, her square heels tapping lightly with a click-clack on the tiled floor until we reached the correct shelf.

Ms. Prince pulled out a hardback book and handed it to me. "Here you are. I believe you will enjoy this one with lots of pictures," she said, her thin lips, lined with dark mauve lipstick, curling into a slight smile.

"Thank you, Ms. Prince," I responded, returning the smile.

She added, "The author of this book is Edward Rowe Snow. They call him Flying Santa because he flies to lighthouses during

Christmas and drops presents from the airplane for the keeper's children."

She patted my back gently and walked back to her desk, the click of her shoes becoming fainter and fainter. I carried the book to the children's area, where Mama was writing in her red journal. I found a seat at one of the lower children's tables and placed the book in front of me. I inspected the front cover, wrapped in a dull black cloth with gilt letters on the top half, shimmering gold in the light, spelling the title *Famous Lighthouses of New England*. Underneath the title, separated by a small golden circle, the author's name Edward Rowe Snow was written in a smaller font, just as Ms. Prince had said. I picked the book up and rubbed my fingers over the cover, uneven from the cloth's pattern, difficult to discern by eyesight. Then, I traced each golden letter with my index finger as I recalled Ms. Prince's remark.

Flying Santa, I thought to myself, imagining packages, wrapped in brown paper and tied with little parachutes, falling slowly to the reaching hands of children, a lighthouse looming behind them. I opened the book and saw, behind the cover, an illustration of a lighthouse and two ships, one in the foreground and one further away, being battered by reaching waves and fierce wind, spraying water above the tall, thin lighthouse. Even from a single black-and-white drawing, I felt the power of the waves and heard the howling wind.

I turned the page to see the first photograph, a black-and-white picture of Boston Lighthouse from 1945. I turned the book sideways to view the white tower, constructed of bricks with a double black gallery, in the correct orientation. It stood in the center above scattered rocks. A helicopter hovered next to the lantern. I inspected the picture, amazed at how closely the helicopter's blades spun next to the lighthouse, and wondered how it did not crash into it. On the back, the next page revealed another photograph of Boston Lighthouse. This one, printed in color, looked quite different from the first with a farther perspective and upright orientation. The lighthouse, hiding behind two overlapping boulders, rose high into the blue sky, blanketed almost completely with thin clouds. For some reason, the muted colors in this picture conjured a feeling of tranquility. The other showed movement, overwhelmed by the sound of the helicopter's blades. Looking at the second, I imagined the sound of distant waves lapping onto the shore, the squawk of seagulls. The caption below it read "Boston Light On A Summer's Day, Oldest Lighthouse in America."

I flipped through the book, searching for more pictures, when I discovered a folded paper tucked between two pages. At first, I thought perhaps someone had left it as a sort of bookmark until I noticed a small white sailboat through the thin paper. Curious, I removed the paper carefully, as it seemed quite delicate, and unfolded it. Upon first glance, it looked like a map of green-speckled land, as if mottled by a paintbrush, and deep blue water with white sailboats and ships scattered throughout. I placed the map onto the table and bent down to observe the fine details. The jagged coast, dotted with tiny white lighthouses and their names, stretched from the bottom left of the map all the way to the top right. An enlarged compass and lighthouse appeared on the right side. Underneath these on the bottom right, enclosed in a rectangle, I saw an inset of buoys, perhaps amongst the lighthouses on the map. It was difficult to differentiate them, however, without a magnifying glass. After a quick overview of the entire map, I began in the bottom left corner, examining the names and illustrations slowly. First, I saw Watch Hill Light and, above an inlet, a building that looked like a church. I followed along the shoreline, reading the names Block Island, Point Judith, Beavertail Light, Gay Head, and West Chop, until I noticed the peculiar bend of Cape Cod, curving at the tip like the shoe of an elf.

"Cape Cod!" I whispered to myself, wondering if I could find the lighthouse we had visited.

I followed down the western part of the Cape, similar to the route Pops had shown me on his map that morning before we drove to Nobska Point. Before long, my finger indeed landed on Nobska Point, written in white letters on the mainland. Below the name, a white lighthouse was sketched at the edge of the land, covered partially by a nearby lighthouse on Martha's Vineyard. Nobska Light appeared inconspicuously, the area surrounded by many islands, lighthouses, and names. Countless eyes had probably overlooked it completely, but I could not take my eyes off of it. I stared at the tiny white tower for a while, then closed my eyes, and instantly appeared before it.

"Mama!" I whispered and motioned for her to come over to my table.

She smiled as she approached, her eyes drawn to the map spread out on the table before me.

"What is this, little bird?" she asked in a hushed but eager voice.

"This is a book about lighthouses that Ms. Prince picked for me. I found this map inside, and look at what else I found!"

She bent down next to me and looked where my finger pointed. She read the name and gasped. "You found the lighthouse! Amazing! I can't believe you found it."

"I know. It's so cool! Look at all of the islands and lighthouses around it. Pops told me about the nearby islands, but I never imagined there were this many."

Together, we scanned the map, laughed at a few names that inspired vivid pictures in our minds, and pondered who had decided upon those particular names such as Beavertail, Sandy Neck, Marblehead, Great Duck, and Goat Island. With the latter, I imagined an island solely inhabited by wild goats that had chased the keeper off the island, overtaken the lighthouse, and declared it to be Goat Island.

My gaze inched back down the Northeastern coast, satisfied with our list of silly names, when I spotted a particular one that caused me to stop.

"Oh, Mama look! This is Boston Light, the oldest lighthouse in America."

"I had no idea it was the oldest lighthouse. How did you know that?" Mama asked, impressed by my knowledge.

"I learned it from this book." I flipped back to the front pages to show her the two photographs of Boston Light.

After she had sufficiently absorbed the details of both, she kissed my head and returned to her red journal. I continued my study of the map, moving from lighthouse to lighthouse, until I finally reached the top right corner of Maine. There must have been over a hundred lighthouses drawn on the map although I did not count them. At that moment, sitting back in my chair and taking them all in, I secretly wished to visit every single one. I desired to know them like I knew Nobska Light so when I read their names, they held meaning for me and immediately elicited a memory, like the name of a friend.

It was time for us to leave the library before I was able to peruse the remaining pages of the book. I returned it to Ms. Prince on our way out.

She asked, "Well, how did you like the book, Michael?"

"I loved it! It was perfect. I would like to look at it again next week if it's available."

Ms. Prince beamed as she accepted the book, pleased that I approved of her choice, and promised to hold it for me until our return next Wednesday, complete with a wink. I conveyed my thanks as I leaned in to give her a hug. She smelled of books and peppermint candy, the ones she kept in her cardigan pocket and offered me occasionally.

We said our goodbyes and continued our walk to the park. That night before bed, Mama asked if she could read me a story about a pirate and a lighthouse. In an instant, I agreed since the map and lighthouses still occupied my thoughts.

She grabbed her red journal from the nightstand. "The pirate, known to many as Red Beard, stepped onto the rocky shore of an island with his black buckled boots. He took a moment to steady himself on land, for he had been swaying back and forth on the sea for two months straight. The last month was particularly turbulent, as storms created waves towering so high, Red Beard thought they might split his ship asunder, the ocean swallowing its fragments down to the murky depths forever.

"All that gazed upon his looming figure feared him, and rightly so. He wore an eye patch on his left eye, a story better left for another time, sitting above a permanent scowl wrapped within his infamous red beard, tangled and billowing from his face, perhaps concealing small bits of his lunch. He always wore black pants, tied at the knee, with a white shirt underneath a red waistcoat and unbuttoned jacket, complete with a gold earring and a large tricorn hat on top. He was quite fond of this hat, and the unknown lurking beneath his eye patch might have something to do with the theft of his hat, ridicule of his hat, or, if you believe rumors, that one time he forgot his mother's birthday. He had no wooden leg nor hook instead of hand but bore a large jagged scar across his chest. There were no chatting parrots anywhere to be seen. Red Beard had no idea why pirates were always depicted with parrots upon their shoulders, one of the more common stereotypes pirates faced.

"Finally steady upon dry land, Red Beard climbed up the beach, slipping on the loose pebbles and sand, to observe his surroundings. He saw a mixture of sand and rocks spread out before him. Over to the right, a lighthouse, the one he had spotted from his ship, sat high above the beach, watching the water. He turned around and saw his own ship, *The Scurvy*, anchored beyond the shallow water, bobbing gently. Red Beard always left his crew behind on the ship while he explored a new island alone. According to his mother, Red Beard had problems sharing, even as a young lad. It's quite unfortunate not to share. So, why didn't his crew just abandon him on the island and steal his ship? Good question. Because of his fearsome reputation, of course. Red Beard ensured he was unpredictably evil in front of his crew. He once pushed a man off the ship just for touching his beloved hat. I told you he loves his hat. It's rather unhealthy, if you ask me.

"Now, Red Beard had no map to follow nor riddle to solve. That's another matter to discuss. In stories, pirates always have a map with a giant X covering the exact location of the treasure. Wouldn't that be nice? Unfortunately, it is never quite so easy in real life. So, how did Red Beard know to come to this island in search of treasure? Your guess is as good as mine. Maybe just luck or a fever dream or that one time he fell overboard during a storm and almost drowned. Perhaps while sinking below the waves, he met a fair mermaid with purple hair and sequined tail, who saved his life and whispered of an island with a lighthouse and hidden treasures.

"Despite the reason you choose to believe, Red Beard was on this island searching for treasure. He headed towards the red-and-white lighthouse, as there was nothing else in sight. The harsh winds blew incessantly across the small island, battering one about from every direction, making it an impossible environment for plants and other living things to thrive. After a short walk, he arrived at the striped tower, rising high above him. The unkempt lighthouse appeared to have been deserted, the exterior paint chipped, dirty, and in desperate need of another coat, just like Red Beard. The waves crashed against the jutting rocks along the coastline, spraying the salty water onto the island.

"Red Beard walked around to the back of the lighthouse, searching for the entrance. He found a door with a bronze plaque positioned beside it that read 'Treasure awaits at spiral's end.' Below these rather odd words, the inscription continued 'Golden Spiral Lighthouse, Gale Point 1712.'

"Befuddled, he read the plaque again. 'Treasure awaits at spiral's end.' A riddle! Treasure! At last! He opened the door and entered the stairwell to see a black staircase spiraling along the interior wall, all the way up.

"Spiral! Treasure! At last! This was not the first island Red Beard had visited in his most recent quest for gold. He had been unsuccessful at the last two islands. He had found more sand in his underpants than treasure. Murmurs on board his ship had reached his ear, questioning his leadership. He needed some good fortune, or else his crew might throw *him* into the sea next. Pirates really are an untrustworthy lot. Red Beard chuckled to himself, satisfied with his cleverness and assured the treasure waited for him at the top of the lighthouse, as promised by the plaque. He climbed the stairs as quickly as he could until he realized he was not even halfway up yet after looking out one of the windows. Determined to scoop up the gold coins in his hands, and warm his frozen toes, he kept climbing with tenacious speed until he, at last, reached the top.

"Finally, he entered the lantern, snorting and gasping for air, only moments from holding his treasure. He looked everywhere, but all he saw was the translucent lens in the middle, lonely and aimless, without any light to shine into the distance. He circled the lens twice and peeked outside to the gallery through the large glass windows, desperately searching for a chest or purse or bag or any container fit for holding treasure, really. He found nothing. Perplexed, he stepped out to the stairwell landing and removed his hat, pacing the few steps allowed, back and forth, while swinging his hat and considering his next move. He knew he could not return to the ship empty-handed again. Back and forth he paced for several minutes. He had always found that swinging his hat gave his mind the clarity to solve problems. Again with the hat!

"He continued waving his hat, ideas churning in his mind, contemplating whether he should surrender to defeat, go home to his mother and a nice cup of tea, and open that hat shop he secretly dreamt about.

"'What about the ship full of pirates waiting for me!' he said to himself, his fear echoing in the tower.

"Unexpectedly, he released his hat, swinging right out of his hand and over the banister. He dramatically screamed and flew to witness his hat floating down the center of the stairwell. In his despair, a revelation was revealed to him. Red Beard saw a spiral twisting down. Spiral! Ah, the treasure must be hidden at the entrance! From this perspective, another spiral ended at the bottom. He raced down the stairs to retrieve his beloved hat (and treasure). It's all for the treasure, of course. Descending stairs is a much easier task than climbing up them. Reaching the bottom quicker than the top, he replaced his hat upon his head and searched in every corner for the gold. He found nothing except a sprinkling of sand on the floor, carried in on his black buckled boots.

"'Treasure awaits at spiral's end,' he muttered to himself.

"He looked up. 'I must have missed it hiding in the lantern.'

"At once, he ascended the stairs, determined not to be tricked out of the treasure. Nothing. He descended again. Nothing. Up and down. Up and down. Up and down. He slipped on the last trip down, near the bottom, and rolled down the last ten steps. Sweat dripped from under his hat and down his brow. His face was now redder than his beard. Shall we change his name to Red Face? Perhaps now was the time for resignation, to finally accept defeat."

Mama paused here for an intermission of giggles. In my mind, I clearly saw Red Beard climbing up and down the lighthouse.

"More!" I said, bouncing on the bed closer to her.

She smiled. "Do you think Red Beard will accept defeat?"

"Never!"

Mama chuckled at my reply and then continued. "Nope! Stubbornly, Red Beard stood upon shaking legs and began climbing, step after step. Up and down. Up and down. Up and down. Up and down. Eventually crawling on his hands and knees up and scooting on his booty down, he, at last, collapsed onto the ground, surrounded by sand. He lay there for some time, unaware that *The Scurvy* had long since reeled in anchor and sailed away from the island. You see, the brother of the pirate that Red Beard had pushed into the sea for touching his hat had been waiting for the crew to lose confidence in their fearless captain. It did not take much persuasion for them to abandon Red Beard. To begin with, one really should not put much faith in pirates.

"This is where we leave Red Beard: inside the lighthouse, upon the ground, without his ship or treasure. As time passed, his story turned into rumors and then eventually transformed into legend. Some say he went mad on that island and spent the rest of his life climbing up and down the lighthouse, looking for a treasure that was nowhere to be found. Some say he boarded the dinghy, christened it *The Scurvy II*, and attempted to chase down his ship. No one really knows the truth. But, if you ever pass by a small island known as Gale Point, you will surely hear the wailing lifted upon the breeze. Whether the stormy wind or Red Beard's cries, no one shall ever know."

Mama closed her journal and looked at me. "Did you like it?"

"Yes! I loved it! Did you write it, Mama?"

"I did. I'm so happy you like it. I was inspired by our visit to the lighthouse and you."

"Me?"

She laughed. "Yes, you. I watched you stare at the spiral staircase at the lighthouse. I saw how mesmerized you were by it. I even saw you peeking over the top to look at it spiraling down. And your last glance up before we left the stairwell. I wrote it for you to remember your first visit to a lighthouse. And to make you laugh."

"I think it's wonderful, Mama." I leaned in and hugged her. "Thank you," I said, muffled into her nightgown.

I hopped into my own bed and pulled the covers over me. "Tomorrow I'm going to draw Red Beard."

She kissed my head. "I would love that, little bird. Good night."

CHAPTER 7

MEETINGS AND PLANS

I fell asleep that night with images of Red Beard climbing up and down the lighthouse. The next morning was Thursday, a cleaning day. After breakfast, I stayed outside on the patio to begin my portrait of Red Beard while Mama began cleaning. I worked on my drawing all morning until lunchtime, satisfied with my initial sketches. I intended to ask Mama to reread the story that night so I could ensure all of my details were correct. It had to match the story's description perfectly. After we finished lunch, Mama and I walked down to the beach together, eager to wade in the cool water and wash away July's humidity. I paused briefly on the stone steps to stare at the giant clouds, puffs of cotton filling the sky, hanging so low I felt I could reach up and touch them.

We found a nice spot on the sand, spread out our towels, and dashed to the water. Suddenly, just when we made it to the shoreline and felt the rush of water over our feet, I heard a raucous scream as I was tackled to the ground from behind. The refreshing tide washed over my body. I heard Mama laughing while I tried to compose myself out of disorientation. As I lifted myself up from the wet sand, the paste sticking to my arms and legs, I spotted a red bathing suit and bouncing brown curls.

"Lucy! You scared me to death! Where have you been? I thought you had gone home." Elation made words spout from my mouth like running water.

"I'm so happy to see you! I was afraid you would be gone before we returned. We went to see my cousins." Lucy rolled her eyes.

Mama said hello to Lucy and went in search of Aunt Louise, which was not difficult since she had howled and waved from her striped umbrella as she watched our reunion. I chased after Mama to say hello to Aunt Louise.

"Hello, darling," Aunt Louise said, fabulously drawn out at the end. She nearly squeezed the breath out of me.

As soon as I could escape her embrace, I sprinted back to Lucy. We spent the next hour catching up on all the adventures that had occurred over the last few weeks. I told her about visiting Nobska Light and our picnic on the beach. She listened with eager eyes and ears, as if I were the only person on the beach, or in the whole world, reciting the most exciting story she had ever heard. Lucy accomplished this in a way, with her wild laughs and carefree confidence, that made me feel special without blinding me with the spotlight. She insisted I tell her everything we did while she was away, for her trip was really quite boring and not worth discussing. I recalled every day for her, but the only events worth mentioning were the ones when my grandparents visited us.

"We also toured a cranberry bog with my Nana and Pops."

"That sounds exciting! Tell me everything!"

"Well, with the way my Nana talked on the drive there about seeing the floating red cranberries, I was expecting much more."

"What did you see then?" A perplexed look enveloped Lucy's face.

"Not much. Turns out cranberry bogs are only exciting during harvest in the fall. I did learn that cranberries float on water because of the air pockets inside them. And they use bees to pollinate the flowers. And I saw the goats and sheep they have on the farm."

"Cranberry flowers! What do they look like?"

"Pink flowers that look like tiny claws." I bent my fingers into a claw to demonstrate their appearance.

She giggled. "Oh, I love flowers!"

"We also went to the Fourth of July parade downtown! It was really fun. The floats and fire engines threw tons of candy. And we saw fireworks later that night at the boardwalk. I wish you were here for it! Okay, now it's your turn. You must have done something exciting since I saw you."

"Hmmm, nothing as exciting as what you did." Lucy paused to think, and when a worthy event finally popped into her mind, her eyes and subsequently her entire face brightened. "I did go to the movies with my cousins! I finally saw *The Wizard of Oz*, which I've been dying to see," she said dramatically, her hand on her heart to demonstrate her sincerity.

"Cool! I read *The Wonderful Wizard of Oz* with Mama, but I've never seen the movie."

Shocked at this news, she stared at me with her mouth open and then gushed. "It's amazing! You have to see it sometime!"

Lucy forced me to promise I would see it at some point in my life, which made me laugh since she had only just seen it herself. She struggled with not being able to discuss the film with me, and we were forced to change topics quickly before she blurted the whole story and sang all the songs for me.

I looked at her, the wind blowing her chestnut curls, strands of shimmering gold in the sunlight, around her face. "I really missed you, Lucy."

Lucy brushed the hair off her face, beaming with happiness. "I missed you too. Let's promise to meet every week for the rest of summer." She extended her hand to shake on the deal.

I grabbed her hand. "Deal!"

Lucy squealed, as if she had been pinched by a crab, but only because she remembered some bit of news she wanted to report. "I forgot to tell you. I also celebrated my birthday with my cousins! I can't believe I'm seven!"

"Happy birthday, Lucy!"

Lucy spent several minutes describing every detail of her party, from her outfit to the decorations and cake.

"It sounds like a fun party. Can you believe I don't have *any* cousins? I really wish I did."

"It was a fun party, but I wish you were there. I have seven cousins, but I only see them maybe once a year since we live so far apart. They're okay, I guess."

I wondered if she was trying to spare my feelings with her lukewarm response or if I only thought cousins were better than they truly were because I did not have any. Our conversation sparked an idea in my head. I reminded myself to discuss it later with Mama.

After ensuring we were up to date on everything, as if we were never apart, we spent the remainder of the day lying upon the sand searching for objects in the fluffy clouds. I was quite good at the game, often playing on my own. Lucy succumbed to many of her giggling fits after I described the creatures I imagined, always with a silly twist to make her laugh, such as a camel doing the limbo.

As we were saying our goodbyes for the day, I whispered something in Mama's ear.

Mama listened thoughtfully, looked into my eyes, and whispered, "I love it." She then turned towards Aunt Louise and Lucy and said, "Michael and I would like to invite you to our house on Saturday, around six o'clock."

Before Aunt Louise could say a word, Lucy answered while jumping up and down. "Yes!"

Aunt Louise looked at Lucy seriously, then at us, and burst into belly laughs. "Of course we would love to come!"

Later that night, Mama and I began planning for Saturday. Lucy was unaware that it was actually a surprise birthday party for her. We needed to buy ingredients for a cake and some snacks as well as a birthday present. We decided to go shopping the following day, Friday, and then spend Saturday morning getting everything ready.

As we snuggled in bed chatting about the party, I said, "I think I will make a birthday banner for Lucy."

"What a wonderful idea! I will also need some help with the cake. Show me your muscles."

I obliged, flexing the arm closest to Mama.

She squeezed my arm and gasped. "That's exactly the kind of muscle I need for stirring the cake batter!"

I giggled. "Oh, Mama, I'm so happy!"

"Me too, little bird."

We hugged in silence, reveling in the moment, until guilt crept inside my thoughts.

"Mama, do you miss Daddy?"

Surprised by my question, apparent from her changing expression, Mama said, "Yes, I do." She paused. "But he had to stay behind for work."

"I know he has to work, but what about the weekends or vacation? Does he even miss us? Every Sunday when we talk, Dad keeps saying how much he misses me and how he will try to come visit, but he never does."

Mama sat up and turned to face me directly. "Of course he misses you and loves you so much! I think he's just tired from work and doesn't feel like driving all this way. Try to enjoy the last few weeks we have at the beach. Soon, we will return home to Daddy and school, and you will miss these carefree days."

"I do miss him, but is it okay to feel happy without him?" I asked, conflicted by the polarity of my feelings.

"Yes, you can miss him *and* be happy at the same time. We, as humans, are capable of many emotions, even different ones at the same time. Be happy without guilt, little bird. Trust me, Daddy would be so happy to know you are happy."

I nodded, hugging her tightly. I felt better after our conversation, but Mama's face crumpled afterwards, not in a fleeting manner. I noticed it when she kissed me good night. Something else worried her. I lay awake that night, thinking about Lucy's surprise party and Daddy, wondering what he had been doing all summer while we were away and if he would ever come visit us.

I awoke to the sun, bright and warm, entering my bedroom window. I smiled, looking forward to the day ahead and the next, and then remembered my dream from that night. Mama and I were standing on a small island with a lighthouse, the same scene depicted on the inside cover of the book from the library. A wild storm blew with blustering wind and rain. We screamed at Daddy, who sailed a boat on the churning waves, trying desperately to reach us on the island. Our strained voices could not be heard over the violent whistles of the wind. The sea swells carried the sailboat in the opposite direction of the island. I had woken up in the middle of the night, safely anchored in my bed, before discovering if Daddy ever made it to the island. *How weird*, I thought to myself before jumping out of bed and running towards the kitchen. Mama and I had a busy day ahead of us, making certain everything was perfect for the party. There definitely was no time for analyzing dreams, even one as strange as that one.

After breakfast, Mama and I created a list of all the supplies we needed and set off for downtown with the windows open. I hung my arm out the window. Instantly, my hand became an airplane, slicing through the wind and clouds. Mama parked along the sidewalk near the diner where we had eaten on our first day at the beach. First, we walked to the little bookshop a few stores down to look for Lucy's present. We had spotted the storefront with its enticing display of new books during our usual Wednesday walks downtown although we had never entered, opting instead to visit Ms. Prince and the library.

Upon entering, a dull ding announced our arrival as my eyes beheld the bright, happy colors everywhere. Comfortable armchairs with buttons and velvet upholstery were placed in hidden nooks, surrounded by bookshelves stretching from floor to ceiling. To the right, along a wide bookcase spanning the entire wall, I eyed a rolling ladder. I secretly wanted to climb the ladder and glide across the entire width, but instead, I began searching for the children's section. Mama walked off to the right, hunting for a book of poetry, while I went to the left, down a corridor stuffed with books, a mosaic of different colors, heights, widths, and textures. I stopped in the middle, spinning around as I looked at all the books. It was a wondrous feeling to be enclosed by all of those bound words, new worlds hidden within, perhaps even better than paintings hung in museums. I continued along the narrow hallway, the hardwood floors creaking beneath my feet, towards a room at the back, flooded with light, sunken at the bottom of a few steps. Bunting, made of colorful triangles, hung from the ceiling. Some sort of painting on the back wall captured my curiosity, reeling me in to it involuntarily, as if I were caught on a line.

When I arrived at the top of the steps, I stood there, absorbing the delightful sights. Two rectangular skylights in the ceiling allowed sunlight to cascade into the room, creating an effulgent glow all around. The multicolored bunting that I had spotted from the corridor was strung from wall to wall, each section overlapping the other like rolling waves. Unlike the rest of the bookshop, the bookcases only covered the bottom half of the walls. Above them, a mural, depicting an enchanted world, had been painted. I descended the steps, in awe, for a closer view of the faraway mountains, blue and green, some capped with snow; glimmering castles; hot air balloons with polka dots; pastel clouds floating like giant puffs of cotton candy; a rainbow hovering above a rushing waterfall that filled a pool of water below; and a forest covered in bluebells with giant toadstools, bewitched trees, stone steps covered in moss, and a tiny cottage. Magical creatures were hidden throughout the painting. I spotted a red dragon sitting atop one of the mountains; a lion with a flowing mane of orange, reminding me of Aslan, hiding partially behind a tree; fairies twinkling like fireflies throughout the forest; a pirate ship floating beside the waterfall; and mermaids swimming below the pool's surface.

"Hello there," I heard behind me, followed by the groaning descent of steps.

I turned briefly to see who approached. I saw a tall man dressed in slacks and a short-sleeved button-down shirt. He wore round glasses, encircling his deep brown eyes. His face appeared kind and joyful, in a way one recognizes easily but fails to explain with words.

"Hello," I said, immediately turning back around to search for more hidden creatures.

The man walked over and stood next to me. "Do you need any help finding a particular book? My name is Henry."

"Well, I haven't even had time to look at the books yet."

Henry pointed at the wall before us. "Do you like this painting?"

"Yes!" I replied before even taking the time to consider his question.

He laughed quietly. "I just finished painting it recently, and I really needed to hear an expert's opinion. So, I thank you for your help."

My eyes shifted from the mural to him. "*You* painted this?"

"Yes. I had been thinking about it for a long time. You see, it was an idea that was planted like a seed in my head. And every day I tried to ignore it, but the seed kept getting watered by my imagination. And each day it grew and grew until I could no longer ignore it anymore."

I glanced at the top of his head. His brown hair was sticking up a bit in the middle, as if he were overdue for a haircut or had just gotten out of bed.

He noticed and said, "Oh, this is embarrassing. Is the plant sticking out of my head?" He touched the top of his head, feeling for vegetation within his hair.

I giggled. "No, but I thought I might check. I love your painting. I'm glad you listened to the idea."

He smiled. We both turned to look as we heard Mama's soft voice behind us in the hallway, calling my name.

"I'm here, Mama," I said in her direction. Then, I said in a softer voice to Henry, "My name is Michael, by the way."

Henry extended his hand and said, "It's very nice to meet you, Michael."

Mama joined us as we were shaking hands. She smiled, holding a hardcover book in one hand. "Hello, sir. I am Margaret, Michael's mother."

"Hello. Please call me Henry instead of sir. I am Prince Henry, I mean Henry Prince, the owner of this bookshop."

Mama repeated, "Prince," in a low voice to herself and then stared vacantly, distracted by a thought, as if something had startled her or she had remembered something suddenly.

She soon composed herself again. "Okay, Henry it is. It's very nice to meet you and finally visit your shop. We have walked past it many Wednesdays but have never stopped."

"Wednesdays, huh? I suppose Wednesdays are not very good days to read books, are they?" he replied.

Mama laughed. "That does sound rather silly, doesn't it? Michael and I always walk downtown on Wednesdays, usually to get ice cream. We then walk to the library and park on the way back home."

Henry scoffed. "The *library*? Do you know that scoundrel of a librarian? She's always taking my customers! Whoever heard of free books? How can a capitalist survive in such a world?"

"Yes, of course! We love Ms. Prince. I really don't think she would intentionally steal anyone's business. Anyway, libraries are important for people who—" Mama abruptly stopped.

"Are *you* related to Ms. Prince?" Mama asked with a wide smile, her eyes sparkling.

"That scoundrel is my aunt. I suppose you could say books run in my family."

Mama and I began laughing. She said, "Okay, you got me. I thought your name sounded familiar."

"I'm just kidding. Sometimes I can't stop myself from a good laugh. These books don't talk back to me anymore," Henry said with a chuckle. "No, in all seriousness, I'm really glad you don't have an aversion to books, even if you prefer to visit the library instead of me."

At the idea of Mama disliking books, I said, "Mama would live in the library if she could."

Henry burst out laughing and after calming himself, remarked, "Oh, I don't think my Aunt Irene would allow that."

"Very funny," Mama said playfully. "Michael, I do expect better of *you* than to tease your own mother!"

I had hardly ever seen Mama talk to a stranger, or anyone, that easily before. Henry had a way about him that made others comfortable, much like Lucy. Lucy! I suddenly remembered why we had come to the bookshop—a present for Lucy's birthday.

"Mama, did you find a book for Lucy?" I asked, referring to the book she held in her hand.

"Yes, little bird, I found a book of poetry for Lucy." Mama handed the book to me for inspection. "It may be a little advanced for her, but I believe she will cherish it forever."

"Emily Dickinson," Henry said after glancing at the teal cover with gold letters within my hands.

"Yes," Mama replied. "Michael, do you remember I talked to Lucy about her poetry when we walked to the boardwalk?"

"Oh, yeah, I do remember that," I answered. "She will love it!"

"It's a great choice," Henry said. "Before you leave, would you like to have some tea and cookies with me?"

I answered before Mama had a chance to say anything. "Thank you, sir, but we have a very busy day. We are getting ready for a birthday party tomorrow."

Mama grinned as she listened to my explanation, and when I had finished, she said, "Michael is quite right. We have lots to do for the party, but we appreciate the kind offer. Since we have visited your beautiful bookshop and intend to return, may we join you for tea another day?"

"Of course! I understand you two walk this way on Wednesdays. Would you, by chance, walk here next Wednesday for a tea party?"

"That sounds lovely. We would love to, wouldn't we, Michael?" Mama asked.

"Yes!" I replied swiftly.

With the tea party settled, we all walked to the front of the store. Mama paid for Lucy's book, which Henry wrapped in brown paper.

As Henry handed me the book, he said, "I hope your friend likes the present and the party goes well! I look forward to hearing all about it next Wednesday."

"Thank you, Henry. I can't wait till next week," I responded.

He accompanied us to the door to say goodbye.

Mama said, "Until Wednesday," with a smile before we walked to our car.

Henry stood outside waving at us until we drove past his bookshop and out of sight.

CHAPTER 8

BIRTHDAY PARTY

We finished shopping for the remaining supplies on our list and then drove back to the beach house. I spent the evening working on Lucy's birthday banner. Mama drew the letters for me because I wanted it to be perfect. I lay on my belly upon the floor, concentrating on staying inside the lines as I colored the letters with crayons, their waxy smell reminding me of school.

After breakfast the following morning, we baked the cake together. Mama let me add the measured ingredients and stir them together. When the batter was mixed well, I lowered my face into the bowl, just above the mixture, and inhaled deeply. That irresistible scent would be nothing to the one emanating from the oven as the cake baked. The chocolate aroma slowly filled the entire house. Mama opened the windows as the oven warmed the kitchen, but I did not want the smell to escape outside, only to fill my nostrils. Mama allowed me to lick the remaining batter from the bowl and spatula before we made the vanilla frosting. I hung

91

around the kitchen, unable to leave the cake, while Mama prepared sausage balls, a cheese tray with sliced ham and crackers, and fruit cocktail for the party.

Soon, the cake was baked and taken out of the oven to cool. I bent over the warm cake, now solid instead of batter, and heard a faint crackling sound. I inhaled deeply once again. The smell unlocked memories stored deep inside my brain, only happy ones of birthdays, holidays, parties, and picnics, joyful times we were together with family and friends. Once the cake had cooled enough, I helped Mama frost it, ensuring every chocolate inch had been covered with white icing.

"It looks perfect, Mama, and smells even better!"

She simply smiled while she continued cleaning the mess we had made in the kitchen. The next few hours dragged on despite my attempts to distract myself from the clock. Time eventually passed, as it always does. I sat on the front porch waiting for our guests to arrive while Mama finished getting dressed. It was a calm evening: the light blue sky covered in thin, wispy clouds. The heat from midday lingered in the air but became more tolerable with each passing minute. After more anguished waiting and fidgeting, I spotted Lucy and her great-aunt walking around the corner to the stone fence and up the path. Lucy led the way, wearing a white dress and her hair pulled back off her face, a few short curls hanging in the front. She carried a colorful bouquet of flowers in her hands.

"Hello!" I screamed and ran to greet them.

Aunt Louise trailed behind, carrying a casserole dish in her hands, a large bag on one arm, and her leather purse on the other.

A wide grin spread across her mouth, lined with bright red lipstick.

Lucy said, "We walked here! Our house isn't too far at all!"

Aunt Louise waddled into the house.

"I want to show you something," I said as I grabbed Lucy's hand and led her towards the edge of the cliff.

Lucy looked down at the beach and squealed with delight. "The stone steps! I must walk down a few before going inside!"

She handed me the flowers, descended five steps, and paused to relish the view from above with her arms outstretched.

"It's amazing! Everything looks so different from up here!" she shouted at the beach.

I laughed at her excitement, remembering the day we met, when she could not believe I had walked down those steps. After Lucy rejoined me, I walked over and climbed onto the cobblestone fence that enclosed the yard. Lucy skipped after me, and together, we stepped from stone to stone, gray and weathered with green, yellow, and white patches of lichen, balancing on the fence with our arms spread out on each side, even though the fence was not very high. Once we reached the end, we took turns stepping up and jumping from the pillar that framed the pathway. Lucy held the flowers firmly with both hands each time she jumped. We then followed the path inside the house, heading straight for the kitchen, where I knew Mama would be. Mama was placing Aunt Louise's casserole into the oven when we arrived.

Mama turned, accepted the flowers from Lucy, and gave her a welcoming hug. "Thank you for the beautiful flowers, Lucy.

Well, it looks like we shall have a feast tonight! Louise brought Chicken Divan."

"That's not all I brought!" said Aunt Louise, reaching into the large bag she had carried on her shoulder.

I noticed her outfit for the first time, as it was blocked earlier by everything she carried upon their arrival. She wore a black cocktail dress, red high heels in the same color as her lipstick, and a gigantic diamond necklace with matching earrings. Fabulous, as always, Aunt Louise once again looked misplaced, this time in our kitchen. I pondered whether Mama felt underdressed in her old yellow sundress, the one she had worn a hundred times. I looked at Mama, a drastic contrast to Aunt Louise. She did not appear embarrassed or uneasy but radiated pure joy and beauty.

We all looked intensely at Aunt Louise as she fumbled through her bag. I wondered if she might pull a rabbit out of it like a magician.

She finally began pulling out bottle after bottle as she announced each one. "Gin! Lemon juice! Syrup! Club soda! Cherries!" She placed them all on the countertop in a neat row and then bellowed, "Tom Collins has arrived!"

We all exploded into laughter. Lucy collapsed onto the ground while Mama and I bent over, holding our aching bellies.

"You even brought cherries for the drinks?" Mama asked.

"Why, yes, of course! They must be authentic, darling!" Aunt Louise answered.

After another fit of giggles, Mama replied, "You are the most wonderful person I have ever met!"

Once the laughter had finally subsided, we relocated to the back patio to eat the appetizers while the chicken casserole warmed in the oven. Aunt Louise stayed behind in the kitchen to prepare the mixed drinks. When she finally emerged, she walked backwards through the screen door, groaning as she opened it in her elegant dress, more fit for a wedding than our little party. She turned around and walked towards us, holding two large drinks garnished with cherries on top. She handed one to Mama.

Mama admitted, "I've never met Tom Collins before."

"Well, I'm happy to introduce you to him. Cheers to wonderful friends!" Aunt Louise raised her glass up in the air.

"To wonderful friends and my newest one, Tom Collins," Mama said as she raised her own glass and clinked it with Aunt Louise's.

We indeed ate a feast that night on our little patio. The evening danced towards twilight, floating along like our conversations and laughter. Lucy and I dashed off to play with my Matchbox cars, returning to the table for quick bites until Mama brought out the Chicken Divan.

"Aunt Louise, I thought you always started a meal with dessert," I asked as we began eating the casserole.

"Ha! You are correct, Michael! Above all, I am never a rude guest and don't presume that we'll have dessert. I'm quite content to begin tonight with a drink!"

I giggled to myself when I remembered the surprise that awaited an unsuspecting Lucy. Aunt Louise would eat her dessert at the end, after all.

"Michael, please help me carry the dirty plates inside," Mama said with a wink after we had finished eating.

"Okay, Mama." I jumped from my seat and began stacking plates.

We toted all the plates inside and prepared for the surprise. Mama placed seven pink candles on the cake and lit each one while I grabbed the birthday banner. I opened the screen door, screeching to announce our return, and led the way towards Lucy. I watched her eyes, moving along the banner as she read each word and finally understood their meaning. Her mouth agape in surprise, the shock had rendered her utterly speechless for the first time. Aunt Louise squealed in delight as Mama set the cake down on the table in front of Lucy. All three of us began singing "Happy Birthday to You." Lucy's mouth broadened into the biggest smile as she looked at each of us in turn, her eyes glimmering in the glow of candles. Lucy shut her eyes so tightly to make her birthday wish that her nose scrunched at the top. I wondered what wish she would make. She opened her eyes, glanced at me briefly, beaming, inhaled deeply, and blew all of the candles out in one breath.

Lucy placed her hands on her cheeks as the smoke lifted from the wicks, dancing in swirls, and disappeared. "Thank you, thank you, thank you!"

"You are welcome, sweetheart!" Mama replied. "It was all Michael's idea."

While Mama sliced the cake and served it, I ran back inside to retrieve Lucy's birthday present.

"More surprises?" Lucy asked upon my return, still flabbergasted by the cake. She unexpectedly pounced and grabbed me in an embrace. She squeezed me tighter and whispered, "Thank you, Michael."

"No problem. Now, open your present!"

Lucy giggled as she accepted the gift. Ripping the brown paper, she held the teal book in her hands, inspecting the cover and title written at the top.

"Poems by Emily Dick-in-son." Lucy looked at Mama and said, "You told me about her on the day we walked to the boardwalk! Oh, thank you, Ms. Margaret!"

Lucy ran over to give Mama a hug and then sprinted back to me for another squeeze. "This is the best birthday ever."

It was finally the time for cake, a moment I had been waiting for all day, ever since its irresistible aroma filled the kitchen. Lucy and I savored each bit of chocolate cake, chatting between bites about how we baked it in the morning. Beside us, Mama and Aunt Louise ate their cake while giggling like children. Her inhibition shattered by the alcohol, Mama became more like Aunt Louise— loose-lipped and unrestrained, sober or otherwise. I was happy to see her guard down, able to enjoy the party she had worked hard to make possible.

"Another Tom Collins?" Aunt Louise asked as she rose from her chair.

"Oh, no, I shouldn't," Mama replied. "I don't drink often, and I'm afraid this one has gone straight to my head."

Aunt Louise laughed as she walked inside, presumably to make herself a second one. She burst through the door a few minutes later, screaming, "Well, I drink all the time, my dear, so I made myself another! Ha!"

As she veered from the stepping stones to the yard, one of her heels sank into the ground on her wobbly walk back to her chair. She yelped. "Margaret, I'm stuck! Call the fire department!"

Mama darted over to her and bent down to inspect the situation as Aunt Louise repeatedly attempted to pull her shoe from the ground without spilling her drink. Mama then fell to the ground, laughing uncontrollably.

"I don't believe we'll need the fire department, Louise!" Mama yelled at us from the ground, "Children, we need your assistance over here!"

We ran over and pulled Mama up. Then, Lucy and I held onto Aunt Louise's arms to steady her while Mama wriggled and yanked her heel from the ground. Aunt Louise very practically focused on not wasting a drop of her Tom Collins, balancing her body weight on one foot like a fancy flamingo.

Finally free, Aunt Louise walked on tiptoes to her chair. She sighed dramatically upon sitting. "Thank you, my darlings. Without you, I'd still be right there in the morning! Stuck like a scarecrow!"

I imagined her flailing wildly at crows while she held her drink. Lucy and I dashed to her side for a hug and then back to our seats. Mama walked over and cut us another slice of cake before we even had a chance to ask for more.

She said, "Enjoy the cake, little ones," her face gleaming in the golden glow of sunlight.

The wind rushed around us in a gust, lifting our hair and clothes briefly, and then disappeared. A softer but steadier breeze followed, blowing gently through the tree limbs, shaking the branches from side to side. The full leaves rustled against one another. I closed my eyes as I felt the wind against my face. The thin clouds had been painted underneath with purple and pink strokes by the waning sunlight. July's heat had departed with the passing breeze. Her yellow dress stained with green in the back from her tumble to the ground, Mama sat down beside Aunt Louise once more.

Aunt Louise sipped her drink and asked, "So, it's none of my business, but I see you wear a wedding band. Where is your husband, my pretty little thing? You may punch me in the nose, if you wish, for such a nosy question."

Mama replied, initially in a restrained manner, "He is back home. He couldn't come because of work."

Aunt Louise remarked, "That's too bad. I bet you and Michael miss him. Tell me how you met and fell in love. I need to hear a good story."

Mama's tongue had been loosened by the drink and a friendly ear. Words flowed from her mouth like a rushing river. "Well, I met him when I was a little girl. James, my husband, was best friends with my older brother, George Junior. James was a little older than my brother, but they went to school and grew up playing baseball together. James was always at our house. I'm quite a bit younger and used to chase after them, begging to play. Junior always said no immediately, but James was kind to me."

I listened intently to the story, as did Lucy.

"One time, when I was eight or nine years old, I fell down outside and scraped my knee. It was bleeding and covered in dirt. James found me crying by myself and carried me inside to my mother. He stayed with me while she cleaned my wound, making sure I was okay. I grew up feeling like an annoyance to Junior, but James acted like a sweet older brother to me."

Mama paused briefly and began twisting the wedding band on her finger. "After that, I developed a secret crush on him, but of course, he only saw me as a little girl and Junior's sister. James joined the Marines right after Pearl Harbor, and my brother followed him, as he always did in everything. My father went to fight too. It was just me and Mama left behind—the loneliest years of my life. We even came here to this beach house, which belonged to my grandparents, but the memories and worry accompanied us. We thought we could escape the war. My father came back; my brother never did. He's still officially missing in action. We never received his body, only false hope and a telegram with neatly typed regret."

Mama paused again, this time for a longer period, and wiped a few tears from her face. She cleared her throat before proceeding. "I never knew what happened to James until he showed up at our house in January 1946, shortly after he had returned. He had heard about Junior. I was quite changed by then, about to turn seventeen years old, no longer the little girl he remembered. He became close to my family again and visited every week, usually multiple times. My father liked to sit outside and chat with him, perhaps about the war or Junior. His presence comforted us all as if Junior were still around. Not long after he returned, I discovered my former crush on him had survived all those years. I never said anything to him until I had graduated high school and begun college nearby. One night, we went for a walk after he ate dinner with us, and I plucked up the courage to tell him that I had loved him since that scraped knee. We started dating after that and eventually got married, much to the happiness of my parents. He asked me to leave school and focus on being a wife and mother. In those days, I would have done anything he asked of me. I just wanted to be his wife. My mother also encouraged me to quit, saying my place should be at home. I did quit, eventually gave birth to Michael, and here we are."

Aunt Louise rested the stem of her glass against her chest and sighed. "What a love story!"

"Is it?" Mama asked, her face blank of expression, carried away with her drifting thoughts.

I turned around to focus on my cake once again, trying to appear less interested in the story.

Lucy leaned in closely with her hands clasped and whispered, "How romantic!"

I said, "Yeah, it is." In truth, I had never heard that story, and my parents did not seem like the same people in it anymore.

The sky had noticeably darkened, and the wind began to feel cold instead of refreshing. I heard the waves more clearly in the distance as the other sounds quieted around us. People had abandoned the beach for their houses, leaving behind the waves and sand. Mama escaped from her daydream, brought on by her introspective time travel, and walked over to Lucy. She asked to borrow her book of poems. She turned to the index, found a particular poem, and then flipped to the corresponding page.

Mama said, "'Tell all the truth but tell it slant' by Emily Dickinson." She recited the poem for us:

Tell all the truth but tell it slant
Success in circuit lies
Too bright (bold) for our infirm delight
The truth's superb surprise

As lightning to the children eased
With explanation kind
The truth must dazzle gradually (moderately)
Or every man be blind.

CHAPTER 9

TEA PARTY

The following Wednesday morning, as arranged, Mama and I walked downtown to have tea with Mr. Prince. I had much to tell him about Lucy's birthday party. The birds filled our walk with merry warbling, a welcome cheeriness, as the sky looked sullen with gray clouds, hanging low and heavy. I thought the rain might pour from them at any moment onto our heads. Mama had dressed more formally than she usually did during the summer, perhaps because she did not know Henry very well or how one typically dresses for a tea party. She wore a black-and-white gingham skirt with a black sleeveless button-down shirt, tucked in at the waist, with a black belt. It was an outfit she usually wore to church, a safe bet for an atypical occasion. She appeared to regret it, however, since it had turned out to be quite windy on our walk. Mama laughed as the wind repeatedly lifted up her skirt and she tried desperately to hold it down. I attempted to assist her when I felt a gust of wind. I imagined we looked rather ridiculous, suddenly afraid of the wind and a silly skirt, as we walked down the sidewalk, but Mama had a gift of finding the laughter in most annoyances. We arrived at the bookshop and waited until Henry had finished helping a customer. He wore navy blue slacks with a brown belt and a white button-down shirt with vertical blue stripes, tucked into his pants. His brown hair still stuck up a bit in the middle.

He welcomed us and led the way to a back room used for storage. We followed him through a door, up a narrow stairway, and into an apartment above the bookshop. It was quite small, as if everything had been squeezed together. Henry walked to the tiny kitchen with light yellow cabinets and walls painted to match, poured water into a kettle, and placed it on the white range to warm. I had never seen a room with so much yellow before, but somehow it suited Henry's cheery disposition.

Henry said, "Please make yourselves comfortable," as he sat at an oval table with a white top, positioned in a breakfast nook adjacent to the kitchen. The nook's large window overlooked an alley. We walked over to join him.

Mama said, "Thank you, Henry. It's kind of you to invite us."

"Oh, it's nothing," he replied. "It's nice to make new friends."

I asked, noticing them through the doorway upon our arrival, "May I look at your paintings?"

"Of course! Explore wherever you'd like, except my bedroom." Henry leaned in closer to me and whispered, "It's quite messy. Don't tell."

I walked to the living room. Almost every inch of wall space had been covered in artwork, large and small. I studied paintings of nature: flowers, mountains, and oceans; paintings of people: full figures, faces, and silhouettes; and abstract paintings, open to interpretation, that did not look like anything but brush strokes and splatters on canvas.

Henry walked to the kitchen and arranged the teapot, cups, saucers, and plates onto a tray. They were bright turquoise with roses painted on them.

"What can I do to help?" Mama asked, standing up from her chair.

"Absolutely nothing," Henry said with a wide grin. He scooped two spoonfuls of tea leaves from a tin and dumped them into the teapot. "Well, you can do something for me, Margaret. Talk to me. About *anything*. Most of my day is spent in silence between customers. Tell me about your favorite book."

"Well, if you had asked me that a few weeks ago, I would have had an entirely different answer. It has not changed in a few years, but a single book can come along and change everything."

"Curious. Hmm, I quite agree. Go on."

"I love English literature, particularly the classics. My favorite used to be *The Woman in White* by Wilkie Collins, which is still a close second."

The kettle whistled from the stovetop.

Henry broke out into a song to the tune of "Following the Leader" as he tended to the kettle. "The kettle is a-whistling, a-whistling, a-whistling. The kettle is a-whistling. That means the tea is done." He sang the last note in a lower pitch, drawn out for theatrics.

Henry poured the boiling water into the teapot and covered it with the lid. I returned to the table after first hearing the kettle and then Henry's funny song.

Henry said, as if nothing had happened in the interim, "I read that book in school. I agree; it *is* wonderful. A marvelous mystery! I'm quite intrigued now. What is your new favorite book?"

"Can you guess it?" Mama asked.

Henry inhaled deeply as he pondered the matter. He crossed his arms and looked at Mama inquisitively.

Mama laughed at him. "Are you trying to read my mind, Mr. Prince?"

He chuckled. "No, but I wish I could. I'm just trying to make an educated guess based on what I know about you, which is limited at present. Shall it be another mystery? Or something else entirely?"

Henry carried the tray to the table, walked back to the kitchen, and grabbed a covered plate.

He turned around and took a guess. "Based on my knowledge of women and classic English literature, I believe your favorite book is *Pride and Prejudice*."

Mama looked at him seriously. "And is your knowledge of women vast?" A smirk crept onto one side of her mouth, though she tried to suppress it.

"Honestly, no," Henry replied frankly. Then, he turned to look at me and said, "Too nerdy," before winking behind his round glasses.

Henry set the large plate down and uncovered it. "I present to you: my mother's authentic scones with clotted cream and strawberry jam, freshly prepared this morning. By her, not me. My mother is English, so I asked her to bake them for our tea party. And if there's one thing the English take seriously, it's tea."

Mama and I each took one scone and added it to a plate. The scones looked like biscuits to me.

Mama remarked, "Tea *is* quite serious and can even divide an empire. These scones look scrumptious! And I'm quite impressed with your tea set."

"Ah, that would also be a gift from my mother. For the opening of my bookshop. It's the first time I have used it for guests, actually."

Henry placed a small tea strainer onto a cup and poured the teapot over it. I bent down and watched curiously as the strainer caught the tea leaves and allowed the golden brown liquid to pass through the holes. He repeated this two more times and then positioned the teacups before us. The tea's vapor rose and danced like a charmed snake from my cup.

"I have sugar cubes and milk, if you would like."

Mama politely refused but allowed me to take one sugar cube. I wanted to watch it melt in the hot tea. Henry added only a splash of milk to his teacup. I wondered if that was how the English typically drink their tea.

While waiting for her tea to cool, Mama said, "It was not a terrible guess, I suppose, as I do find *Pride and Prejudice* quite clever and amusing. I'm afraid it is not even my favorite Jane Austen book, and I'm quite annoyed that you lump all women together in a single category."

Henry sipped his tea and replied, "All right then, I apologize for my terrible guess. Will you tell me now or must I guess again and offend you even more?"

"My favorite book, at present, is *Jane Eyre*."

"*Jane Eyre*. The Brontë sisters. I'm embarrassed to admit I have never read it although I've read her sister's *Wuthering Heights*." Henry noticed my perplexed look. "Michael, these books were written by the Brontë sisters. They were three talented sisters that all wrote poetry and novels. They are very famous now but at the time published their books under pseudonyms, or fake pen names, because they lived in a time when being female had its disadvantages."

Mama scoffed. Henry and I looked at her. Surprised we had heard her, her cheeks flushed red.

Mama smiled like a child who had been caught in a lie. "Pardon me. The disadvantages of being female is a subject better left for another day, preferably at night when stronger drinks are served."

Henry laughed. "I agree. Now, back to *Jane Eyre*. May I ask why this is your favorite?"

I nibbled the edge of my scone, the first one I had ever eaten. I was surprised by its dense, crumbly texture. It did not taste like Nana's biscuits as I had expected, but I liked it and returned for a bigger bite. I glanced into my teacup and noticed the sugar cube had dissolved without a trace. I sipped the warm tea. It tasted of oranges.

"Perhaps the story itself is not all that remarkable, compared to the intricacies of Dickens or Collins, but the words themselves

...” Mama stopped to gather her thoughts. “It’s not prose but poetry. Her words are magical. I can’t really explain it well, but promise me you will read it one day, Henry.”

“I will add it to my list of books to read, which is rather long.”

Mama switched the attention to me. “Michael also loves reading. You should ask him about his favorite.”

“Young gentleman, you have a smear of jam and cream on your nose. Would you like to leave it for later?” Henry jokingly asked.

“No, no,” I replied with a laugh, wiping it from my nose. I anticipated his question. “My favorite book is *The Lion, the Witch, and the Wardrobe*. I wanted to ask you when we met if you had painted Aslan in your bookshop. I thought I saw him hiding in the forest.”

“Ah, very perceptive of you, Michael,” Henry said. “Children do see what most adults cannot. It is indeed Aslan. Like you, I also love *The Lion, the Witch, and the Wardrobe*. If you look closely at the painting, there are other hidden characters from books and some from my own imagination.”

Mama looked confused by our conversation. I explained, “Mr. Prince painted the mural in his bookshop, in the children’s area. There are hidden creatures in the painting.”

“Oh, I did see the painting last week but didn’t examine it closely. I would like another look sometime.”

“You shall look today, as you leave our tea party,” Henry said.

We spent the rest of our time together becoming more acquainted with one another through the usual questions that precede intimacy. Mama told him where we lived and how we came to visit this beach for the summer as well as how she spent her summers growing up here. Henry discussed growing up in the area, spending his summers and attending university in England, and how he had always wanted to own his own bookshop. Once every drop of tea had been drunk and the morning had hurried into noon, we left the bookshop after Mama and I looked at Henry's mural, as promised. As we opened the door to leave, we knew the cloud's promise of rain had been fulfilled when the wind blew the raindrops into the bookshop.

Henry looked outside. "I must drive you home. You cannot walk home in this wind and rain."

Henry and Mama argued back and forth on this matter for some time. Mama insisted he must not close his bookshop for us. They eventually reached a compromise of borrowing Henry's umbrella and a promise of stopping at the library if the rain became heavier.

"My aunt can call me on the telephone from the library. I will drive immediately to pick you up if you need me. I don't want Michael to get wet and sick."

"I promise we will call if we need you, but I rather like a walk in the rain," Mama said with a smile.

Henry and I shook hands goodbye. He leaned into Mama for a quick hug. She offered more thanks for the invitation.

Before we left, Mama asked, "How do I return your umbrella?"

"I will be at the dance in the downtown park next week. Will you bring it to me then?"

"Until then," she said as we walked away, huddled together under the large umbrella.

CHAPTER 10

FAREWELL, FOR NOW

July ended as quickly as it began. So many wonderful things had happened over the past month, more than had occurred in the past two years, it seemed. Memories of them would be enough to fill my head with happy thoughts after we returned home. The heat of summer hung around as August appeared with bitter truths. Our time at the beach would end soon, as I knew it would when we first arrived, but I had never dwelt on this thought for long. Now, the end was upon us and inescapable. Along with our days at the beach being over was the feeling of being different people with different lives, not necessarily different people but different versions of ourselves. I wondered which version would stay at the beach and which would return home.

Lucy and I met on the beach almost every afternoon after her surprise birthday party. We were determined to spend as much time together as possible in the remaining days. Mama and Aunt Louise became even closer, chatting earnestly about life and laughing at its joys as well as disappointments. Mama seemed drawn to her for some reason, a kindred spirit of sorts. I had observed Mama with strangers. She, like me, had a hard time talking to them, as if she shielded her heart or hid her true self like a turtle retreating into its shell. It took time and trust for her to open up. But with some people, she immediately felt a connection and dropped her armor and superficial pretense. With these people, like Aunt Louise, Mama would reveal everything to them, emptying her heart of its burdens.

We said goodbye to Lucy and Aunt Louise the following Friday, after a long week together, and walked up the sandy steps to the beach house that evening. The next night, Saturday, would be the dance, the one held every year to celebrate the end of summer. Excitement for the dance lasted all week, always sneaking into our thoughts and conversations. We arranged to meet at our beach house so we could all walk to the dance together.

Lucy and Aunt Louise arrived early Saturday evening, both wearing formal dresses. Lucy wore a shiny pink dress with a collar and a large bow in the back. Aunt Louise wore her signature black, adorned with sequins that shimmered in the light, and high black gloves. I wore the only formal thing Mama had packed for me, meant for church instead of dances: light blue shorts with a belt and a white shirt, tucked in, with alternating stripes of red and light blue on the placket and collar. Aunt Louise walked into the house, carrying a garment bag on a hanger, and began searching for Mama. Lucy and I played inside while we waited for them since Lucy did not want to ruin her dress before the dance. I grabbed our transistor radio from the kitchen and tuned it until Lucy approved of a song. While practicing our dance moves in the living room, we were interrupted by Aunt Louise and Mama. Aunt Louise walked in first with Mama hidden behind her.

"Presenting Margaret!" Aunt Louise announced in a booming voice.

She stepped to the side, allowing us a view of Mama. She wore an off-the-shoulder red dress. The top was tight-fitting with a high waist. From the waist, it flowed away from her body down past her knees. Her lips and cheeks were stained red, the same color as her dress; her hair had been curled and pinned up off her face. She looked like a movie star.

"What do you think?" asked Aunt Louise, a question Mama would never ask.

Lucy screamed, "Wow! Ms. Margaret, you look great!"

I agreed. "Mama, you really do!"

"I'm not so sure. Louise bought me the dress. I never really wear red. I-I … it will attract attention." Mama stammered as she attempted to explain her reservations.

"Well, let them look! You look marvelous and simply must wear this dress. For me!" Aunt Louise commanded. "Now, we really must be going if we are to walk there in these high heels! The dance might be over by the time we make it."

Mama agreed, reluctantly, so we began our merry trek towards the park, the same park that Mama and I had visited every Wednesday throughout the summer. The sky was completely cloudless with a faint breeze—the perfect weather for an outdoor dance. I felt deliriously happy as we walked on that familiar sidewalk, bits of green growing through its cracks. I thought back to that first morning, right after we arrived at the beach house, when the park appeared within my view on our drive to the diner. Mama had mentioned a summer dance that day, but I never thought it still occurred or we would be attending with such good friends. As we approached the park, the view looked quite different than the one to which we were accustomed. A large white tent had been erected in the middle of the green space where I always ran. The tent had two peaks on the top, resembling mountain summits, and was secured with white straps around the perimeter. People in dresses and suits stood underneath the tent. On the far side, I spotted what looked like a small stage, raised from the ground, with musicians and instruments on top. There were also lots of people standing outside the tent, mingling in small groups. Children ran around them and screamed. We continued walking along the sidewalk towards the park's entrance, taking in all the sights, until we finally made it inside, near the border of trees.

We were approached, just as we arrived, by Henry and his aunt, both with big smiles. Henry greeted us warmly, and then Mama introduced Henry and Ms. Prince to Lucy and Aunt Louise. Dressed more formally than usual, Henry donned a gray suit with a subtle plaid pattern and a tie, reminiscent of Cary Grant.

After all the introductions and salutations, Ms. Prince said, "I hear you've abandoned us at the library for the new bookshop in town."

"Not quite," Mama answered. "Their prices are outrageous and the owner even more so."

Henry heard this, scoffed, and then continued his chat with Aunt Louise, who looked quite enamored with him.

"We will always love your library and promise to visit before we leave," Mama said. "Could Henry's parents not join us tonight? I was hoping to meet them."

Ms. Prince replied, "No, unfortunately. They recently traveled to London. Henry's younger brother, Charles, lives there."

"Oh, I'm sorry to miss them," Mama remarked.

As a big group, we all walked towards the tent. We stopped along the way, every few steps, to say hello to people. Henry seemed to know everyone there, as if he were the mayor or campaigning to be one. We finally made it to the tent, my anticipation soaring and my cheeks sore from smiling at everyone. It was a marvelous sight to behold. The peaks I had noticed from the outside rose high into the air. I tilted my head back all the way, almost tipping backwards, to see their full height. They were supported by large poles which dissected the interior of the tent, similar to a tree trunk. Strings, full of lights, had been hung from the center poles to the outside ones, dipping from the middle to the lower periphery. It was exactly as Mama had described it in the diner—stars pulled down from the sky and hung on a string. Underneath the stars, the gigantic dance floor was spread from pole to pole. The musicians had begun warming up, each playing different tunes over one another.

Lucy and I spotted some children running through the tent and then out the other side. We asked Mama and Aunt Louise if we could go play with them outside the tent. They both agreed, so we headed in the same direction with a plan to follow the trail of screams and laughter. Once we had exited the tent, we came upon a copse, the one that bordered the green space on one side. We looked left and right for any sign of them, just at the edge of the trees, and decided to go right, deeper into the dense woodland at the back of the park. Not long after we had begun walking, we heard the noises of children coming from within the thicket of trees. I had never ventured into the forest when I visited the park with Mama. It looked eerie in the evening, the trees creating a world of shadows. Before we entered, I glanced behind me at the tent, the lights glowing above the dance floor. Outside, the haze of twilight endured. Lucy grabbed my hand as we stepped beyond the light. We walked on a little dirt path between the trees and soon found the other children in a little clearing. As we moved closer, a child jumped from a tree swing, tied with long ropes to a thick branch high above us.

We joined the other children, who barely noticed our arrival, and waited for a turn. Lucy climbed onto the swing first, immediately forgetting her earlier worry of keeping her dress clean. She giggled with each pass, the little curls around her face bouncing in the wind. When it was my turn, I grasped the twisted ropes, frayed and bristly, with both hands and pushed myself backwards on my tiptoes. As the wooden seat sloped downwards and I could reach no further ground, I kicked out my legs ahead. I felt that zip in my stomach, the same one from the Ferris wheel, as I swung forward into a rush of wind. The weatherworn ropes were so long that one oscillation seemed to last forever, the branch bending and the tree moaning with each swing. The breeze lifted my hair and then pushed it down again. I closed my eyes and gently rocked back and forth, free and happy, until the swing slowed and my turn ended.

I looked up at the canopy of leaves, green and full, blocking the summer sky from view. Trees curved to the right or left, bending towards the sunlight, fighting for survival. Eventually, the faint light in the woods dimmed around us as time passed. I stood with my back against a large trunk, touching the rough bark with my hands. A portion of the roots was exposed above the surface, gnarled and stretching outwards. Suddenly, something flashed momentarily in front of me. I stared ahead, still and silent. Again, I saw a flicker of yellow light, tiny and fleeting.

I walked over to Lucy and whispered, "Fireflies."

She smiled and followed me into the thick of the trees, towering above us like giants. We waited until we spotted a glimmer of light within the gloam of the forest and chased after it. By nightfall, more and more fireflies appeared, bursts of fluorescence winking one after another in the darkness surrounding the trees. I finally caught one inside my cupped hands. I opened them, just a crack, to show Lucy. I gazed at the firefly, still blinking, as I held its magic for a brief moment before I released it back to the land. Lucy and I joined in the quiet dance of the fireflies. We stepped towards the floating light, away when it went dark, and then towards another, around and around the neon flickers in the night air. To me, it felt as if we were standing in an enchanted forest. I could see Aslan hiding behind a tree, fairies hovering among the fireflies, bluebells and gigantic mushrooms covering the ground, just like Henry had painted in his bookshop.

Lucy and I eventually tired of chasing fireflies and wished to return to the dance. We walked through the woods, holding hands again, as sticks snapped below our feet and branches reached above our heads, resembling crooked fingers in the dark. I sighed in relief when we finally exited the woods and saw the white tent rising before us again. The music, which had been muffled within the woods, played loudly as we entered the tent and walked to the other side, where we had left Mama and Aunt Louise. Lucy and I scanned the area for them, first discovering Mama, who conspicuously sat in her red dress with a drink in her hand. She seemed distracted by something, staring and smiling at the dance floor with the occasional laughter. After we joined her, we learned what, or rather whom, she had been watching. Aunt Louise and Henry were dancing together, but they appeared to be putting on a performance instead. The band played a song with a fast drum kick, an irresistible beat that tempted feet to hit the dance floor. They were swing dancing with lots of kicks and turns, complete with Aunt Louise's squeals of delight. Henry attempted to lift her above his head in a sort of grand finale, which was a challenging feat since Aunt Louise was nearly as tall and as heavy as him. Aunt Louise could not contain herself anymore after the failed lift and broke down cackling on the dance floor. Mama rushed to help her before she exposed herself in front of everyone, seemingly forgetting that she wore a dress. Together, Mama and Henry lifted her from the floor and assisted her to a chair.

Aunt Louise groaned, "Oh, I was having so much fun. Why must it end?"

"You exhausted me," huffed Henry, sweat glistening on his forehead. "I need a break."

The band started again with another fast song.

"Come on, Michael!" shouted Lucy as she grabbed my hand and jerked my body to the dance floor.

We kicked, spun around, jumped, and threw our hands into the air as the music demanded. Mama smiled at me as I danced without constraint or concern, as a child should. With Lucy beside me, I felt brave and carefree. We sat down to rest once the song was over, my heartbeat thumping beneath my ribs like a drum. Henry, rested and dry, stood and turned to Mama.

"May I have the next dance?" Henry asked, offering his hand to her.

"Of course."

Mama placed her left hand in his, a gold wedding band encircling her ring finger. Her cheeks flushed red, a bit deeper than the blush upon them, only discernible to familiar eyes, as they walked to the dance floor holding hands. The music resumed with a slower melody, calming the ambience. Henry and Mama stepped closer together with their right and left hands clasped, respectively, and as their bodies met, each wrapped their opposite arm around the other. They swayed from side to side in harmony with the notes lifted from the instruments. Henry said something with a mischievous smirk that made Mama tilt her head back slightly, laughing towards the stars strung above their heads. I watched them as they danced, moving among the other dancers.

In her flaming red dress and his gray suit, they resembled a couple from a film. Henry twirled Mama under his arm and then dipped her. She arose giggling.

Mama lifted herself onto her tiptoes and raised her head towards Henry's ear. She whispered something to him. I watched his face as they revolved around slowly, first hearing her words with squinted, focused eyes and then comprehending, or attempting to, with wider eyes. Henry's expression seemed to change with each revolution as they turned round and round. I wondered what she had whispered to him when they turned once more and I saw Henry's eyes shifted to the side below a furrowed brow and a faint glint in Mama's eyes. Whether from welled tears, my imagination, or the reflecting lights, I could not tell. Soon after, the song ended, and they returned from the dance floor. Mama sat down with us while Henry walked over to a row of tables, lined up and draped with tablecloths, and paused at the table with skinny glasses of champagne on top. He stood there a few minutes, as if choosing among the identical flutes, finally snatched three, and returned to us. He offered one to Aunt Louise, who happily accepted, and one to Mama.

"A toast!" Henry bellowed as he lifted his glass into the air.

Surprised, Aunt Louise spit some champagne back into her flute, which was almost half empty by then. She and Mama raised their glasses, waiting for his toast.

"To the past, which you can't change but want to, and to the future, which you can change but won't."

Mama and Aunt Louise sipped their bubbling champagne. Henry gulped the entire contents of his glass and then turned to me and Lucy as the music blared in the background.

"I want to dance with you two!" Henry shouted, pointing at each of us.

Lucy and I jumped from our seats, grabbed his hands, and ran to the floor. Henry picked up Lucy from behind and spun her around with her legs stretched out. He then did the same to me. The spinning pulled my legs outwards and tickled my stomach. We strutted around in circles with the silliest dance moves imaginable, laughing hysterically. Aunt Louise cackled and encouraged us with intermittent whoops from her seat, next to Mama, who laughed quietly to herself. Mama danced with another man, one we did not know, who had approached and asked her while Henry danced with Aunt Louise again. Lucy and I danced between them, holding hands with outstretched arms. Henry's gaze seemed to return to Mama, in surreptitious glances, until the music stopped and we all abandoned the floor for a rest.

Many hours had passed since our arrival, and my feet and legs ached from all the dancing. The midday heat had dissipated, and it would not be long before the invisible humidity would form dew drops on blades of grass. I hid my exhaustion from Mama, however, since I did not want the night, or the summer, to end. For some reason, it felt like as soon as the dance ended, the summer and our vacation would too. I never wanted to say goodbye to Lucy, Aunt Louise, Henry, or our favorite places. I did not know if I would ever see them again. The dance eventually did end as the band quit their instruments. By that time, most people had already scattered from the tent towards their houses. Mama had removed her high heels for the walk back to the beach house. Henry, long since sobered up from the champagne, insisted on driving us all home in his car after noticing how tired Lucy and I were. I was relieved when Mama agreed, for I did not know how my legs would carry my body all the way. Lucy and I fell asleep in the back seat, leaning against Mama, who sat in the middle between us. Henry dropped Aunt Louise and Lucy off first and then drove us home afterwards. I awoke slightly as Henry scooped me from the back seat and carried me to my bed. I slept sweetly with new memories in my head, drifting off quickly as voices murmured about an umbrella outside the beach house.

PART 2 – 1961

CHAPTER 11

NIGHTMARES AND DAYDREAMS

Each summer, a perennial carousel, ended in the same way: stifled tears, extended goodbyes, promises of letters, silent car rides, the beginning of new school years, and letters that eventually tapered off and stopped as the year progressed. Our last goodbye that first summer of 1957—after we bid farewell to the library, Ms. Prince, the park, Henry, Aunt Louise, and Lucy—went to the beach. We stood there in the morning sun, not long after it rose for the new day, staring at the water, just as we did the very first night of our journey. Coincidentally, Mama wore the same polka dot dress she had worn that night, when the wind blew it wildly against her frame. With many miles to drive back home to our old lives, we turned from the sand and waves, treading up those stone steps one last time. Mama's invisible burdens, anchored just beyond the shallow water, caught her with an abstract line before we left the sand. She pulled them behind her, up each step, clunking like a prisoner's shackle.

Neither Mama nor I spoke as we drove away. For the sake of the other, we dared not shed a tear. We were afraid that if we did begin crying, together, our tears would fill the car and drown us both. I rolled down my window and stuck my head outside for one last glimpse of the beach house, mentally saying farewell to the stone fence and steps, the porch, my room, the kitchen, and the backyard. We remained silent for the next hour and then gradually spoke in short snippets, becoming longer and longer as we drove further from the beach. We spent the ride trying to remember who we were before that summer, as if we needed to rediscover them before we returned home. I removed a strip of paper from my pocket and stared at it. Lucy had written her address on it, making me promise I would write to her all year and keep her informed of everything that occurred while we were apart, until we hopefully met again next summer.

"That way," Lucy had said as she handed it to me, "it will be like we never left each other."

I folded the paper and crammed it back into my pocket. The drive home seemed to pass more quickly, perhaps because the roads were familiar or the excitement was absent on the return trip. When we arrived home, I was happy to see Dad, who waited for us outside on the stoop, smoking a cigarette in front of our brown brick building. I could no longer hear the beach, only car horns and sirens in the distance, nor look to the edge of the earth, now blocked by towering buildings, the sounds and sights of the city. Dad greeted each of us with a kiss and promised to take me to the park the next day for a game of baseball. The fighting between my parents halted after we returned home. The distance and time apart appeared to heal their wounds, as space, physical or temporal, does with most grievances in life. While unloading my suitcase from the car, I watched my parents. Dad, his tall frame bending down to Mama, vowed to quit drinking and spend more time with me as he held her face within his large hands and stared directly into her eyes. Mama stared back at him as if she wanted to believe his words could carry their own weight.

I fell into my old bed that night and stared up at the ceiling and then around my small room, trying to become reacquainted with it. Suddenly remembering something, I rolled out of bed, crouched onto my knees, and reached with my hands into the darkness under my bed. I found my old tin lunchbox, missing its handle, where I hid my treasured possessions. I unlatched and opened the lid, discovering a stack of baseball cards, a few spare coins, a small red ball, and four metal jacks loose at the bottom. I ran to my shorts, lying dirty upon the floor, and fumbled through the pockets until I found the scrap of paper with Lucy's address. Then, I opened my small suitcase to a mass of tangled clothes, and underneath a shirt, I saw familiar faces looking up at me from inside two tiny black-and-white rectangles. I grabbed the picture, ripped at the bottom, from the photo booth at the arcade. I carried the paper and photos over to the lunchbox, knelt down, and placed them on top of the baseball cards. After I replaced the lunchbox and climbed back into my bed, I began planning what I would write to Lucy in the first letter the following morning, even though nothing had really happened to warrant a letter yet.

Over the years, we each discovered our own ways to pass the time until we returned to the beach for summer. For me, an idle mind only wandered within, creating mirages from the memories and a yearning for certain people and places that were beyond my reach at present. To prevent my own mind from venturing too deep into my thoughts and getting lost in the past, I kept myself as busy as possible with schoolwork, baseball, hanging out with my best friend, Joe, and trips to the library to research space, my latest obsession, particularly the moon.

Just before my tenth birthday in the spring of 1961, I pulled out the lunchbox from under my bed. Dad and I had just returned from my first baseball game at Yankee Stadium. I still felt the intoxication from the roar of the crowd, the smell of hotdogs, and the sound of a bat cracking against a ball on that lazy Sunday, which had utterly mesmerized me. I opened the lunchbox, stuffed over the years with a stack of letters from Lucy—full of the missing pieces of her life, ranging from school to her favorite hobbies of reading, writing, and painting as well as tales of her traveling adventures with Aunt Louise—and memories from the beach— scallop shells, periwinkle shells, one perfect moon shell with a spiral in the center, leftover tickets from the boardwalk, and four sets of photo booth pictures. I picked the pictures up from the top of the thick pile and marveled at the passage of time revealed through mine and Lucy's changing images. Beneath the pictures lay an advertisement for a telescope that I had torn from a magazine. It showed a young boy with his father, both in suits, standing next to the telescope and gazing at something beyond the page. I smiled as I remembered the wad of money that I had been saving for that particular telescope, stashed secretly at the very bottom of the lunchbox. On top of the magazine page, I placed my ticket stub from the Yankees game.

"You must have brought good luck to the Yankees," Dad had said on our way back home, beaming since the Yankees had finally beaten the Tigers after losing the last two games to them. Although we only watched one game that day, the Yankees had played a doubleheader against the Detroit Tigers and won both games.

I removed the Yankees cap Dad had bought me at the game and placed it on my dresser, observing the white intertwined letters stitched on the front. We did not witness a Roger Maris nor a Mickey Mantle home run that day, but it did not matter to me. Baseball provided a connection, a bridge, between me and Dad. There had been a distance separating us when I was younger, leaving Mama to raise me essentially by herself, as if a father were unnecessary in the early years of childhood. Apart from an occasional pat on the back or brief words over dinner, I felt invisible to him as a child. Baseball had changed that. Dad helped me practice on the weekends and attended all of my baseball games. These moments together over the past year had shown me a glimmer of the man Dad could have been, the what-ifs of a life detoured by war.

A few weeks later, when Mama and I began our annual drive to the beach on a rainy June day in 1961, I felt conflicted in my emotions. My life seemed to be split into two distinct parts: one at home, passing quickly in its bustle, and one at the beach, simmering slowly in the summer. Life at home had been good over the past year, better than I could ever remember. I began to wish, for the first time, we could stay home for the summer. It seemed the older I got, the more my life at home and my life at the beach diverged.

As we drove along, rain pattering softly against my window, I glanced down at the book within my hands and stared at it for a while. It recalled a memory, one I had not thought of since it had occurred, of a package Mama had received in the mail, not long after we returned home the previous summer of 1960. Unlike Lucy and me, who were preoccupied with school, Henry faithfully wrote letters to us throughout the year, sometimes including his drawings or an occasional painting. His letters often recommended the titles of new books that he had come across. Owning a bookshop allowed him access to the latest publications, which he then shared with us.

The package was wrapped in brown paper, just like Lucy's book of poetry had been, and addressed to Mama. Dad had discovered it after returning home late from work one evening. He picked up the small package, after loosening the tie around his neck, and inspected it thoroughly, turning it over in his hands. He paused on the return address in the top left corner. The smell of alcohol wafted around him in a cloud, following him wherever he went. Dad had recently landed a new job on Wall Street with the help of his uncle, the only person on his side of the family with whom he had a relationship. His new job came with longer nights and more stress. Dad's lapses in sobriety, though far between, threatened to dismantle the peace in our home. Even with one drink, Dad easily slipped back into the bottle, always waiting for his next stumble. At the time, I had wondered how long he would stay down from this particular one, "just a celebratory drink with work colleagues," according to him.

"Who sent you this, Margaret?" Dad demanded. His volatile temper ignited the alcohol upon his breath.

Mama smiled and cheerfully replied, "Who, darling?" as if she had not noticed the package within his grasp.

Dad held it up higher with one hand and repeated, "This! Who sent you *this*?"

Mama glanced at the parcel. She walked over to him, twisting her head to read the words upon the front.

"Oh," she explained, "it's just a book I ordered from a bookshop."

"All the way from there?" he asked, looking at the address once more. "What's wrong with the libraries and bookshops here?"

"Nothing, of course," she replied. "It's a new book, only available at certain ones."

"Well, next time wait until it's available here, if you can. We can't afford to spend all our money on silly books!" Dad barked at her, tossing the package onto the ground with a thump.

Mama said softly, her head bent down, eyes upon the ground, "You're right, dear. I'm sorry."

Sitting there listening, I did not understand why Mama had apologized to him or failed to mention that Henry was our friend, not just a random bookshop owner. She did not even attempt to explain anything to him. Dad left the house without saying a word, instead allowing the slam of the front door to do so on his behalf. Henry had indeed sent a book to us, confirmed after we unwrapped the package together. Mama had waited to open it with me.

Henry included a short note with the book that read "Cheers! Here's a book that will broaden your perspective. Sent you my personal copy as it's not available widely yet. Let me know what you both think! Don't forget to return it next summer, unlike my umbrella! Yours, H."

I inspected the book cover, a little worn from use, with the same level of enthusiasm as presents on Christmas morning. Mama seemed just as excited as me but better at tempering her enthusiasm. I first noticed the illustration covering most of the front: a tree with a close-up view of its branches and leaves. Above the tree, in large printed letters, I read the title *To Kill a Mockingbird*. The edges of the cover were creased slightly.

Curious name, I thought to myself. *A tree and a mockingbird.* I wondered what the story would be, as I always did before beginning a new book.

"Shall we begin reading it now?" Mama asked, unable to wait any longer, slipping Henry's note into her back pocket.

"Sure," I responded.

We went to my room and sat upon my bed, leaning back on pillows propped up against the headboard. At nine years old, I preferred to read books independently, long past the days of needing help, but occasionally, Mama would read to me, like old times. There was something comforting, at any age, about hearing her soft voice string together a book's prose. The book also seemed to distract her from the argument with Dad. Mama held the book with both hands, ensuring I could see the words to follow along.

We snuggled close together as she opened to the first page and read the opening paragraph.

Her sweater sleeves, the ones she typically pulled down over her freezing hands, slid down her forearm as she held the book before us. On her exposed skin, I spotted a portion of a bruise on her left arm, partially covered by her sweater. I pulled her sleeve down and saw four bruises, blue ovals lined up in a row, blurred and fading.

"Mama, what happened?"

"It's nothing. Your father had another nightmare and grabbed my arm in his sleep."

I stared at her with incredulous yet concerned eyes and waited for a further explanation. It seemed more than "nothing" to me.

"I suppose I was a soldier the other night. A lot of soldiers have nightmares after returning from war."

"I know. I hear him screaming out at night sometimes. They seem to be getting worse."

We read a few chapters that night without any further discussion of her arm. Later on, I lay in bed and pondered the mystery of Jem's broken arm, important enough to be mentioned in the first sentence. Thus far, the book seemed quite different from what I had expected, which made it even more intriguing. I turned over a few times and eventually fell asleep, my mind adrift in a familiar scene. I dreamt Dad and I were on a boat being pulled by a sea monster, a dream to which I returned often, each time a little bit different. That particular night, Dad was asleep on the deck of the boat. As we were being carried away, Dad began to scream in his sleep. I squatted down beside him, shaking his arm, attempting to wake him. I called out for him to wake up. Suddenly, he pounced like a tiger and slammed me onto my back. His shaking body on top of mine, he wrapped his large hands around my neck, squeezing tightly. I tried to talk, but no sound escaped my blue lips. I awakened, still within his grasp as I left the dream, and sat up in bed, rubbing my neck as if I had been strangled in real life. The terrors of my nightmares formed so vividly before my mind sometimes, distorting reality. For Dad, the visions in his dreams had actually occurred. I wondered if he struggled to distinguish fact from the warped illusions turning in his head.

My thoughts were interrupted in the present as we parked in front of a small white building. Inside, through the large front window, I saw booths lined up on one side. Two gasoline pumps idly sat behind our car.

While eating our lunch of sandwiches, I asked Mama, "Why don't Dad or Pops ever talk about the war?"

"Good question." Mama paused to consider her answer thoughtfully as she chewed.

I remembered, during her silence, what Pops had told me on the street all those years ago about real men not crying. I wondered if Dad had heard similar advice, recycled from his father and grandfathers, nonsense wrapped in gilded armor. Mama had encouraged Dad to talk about the war with anyone—his doctor, her, his friends, or even Pops. Dad's reluctance to speak about the war, however, evaded all of her efforts for many years. One night after dinner at Nana and Pops' house, Mama brought a beer to Dad and Pops, sitting outside, and suggested they talk about their war experiences together. They nodded in agreement and completely ignored her suggestion after she walked back inside the house. It was easier for them to talk about baseball and work.

"I can't really answer for them," Mama said, "as I don't have firsthand experience of the war, and I expect they each have their own reasons for not wanting to discuss it. Your father once said to me, 'I prefer to ignore the war since ghosts of friends and enemies already visit me in my sleep, or else my whole life will revolve around something that happened on the other side of the world.' I suppose some memories are too painful to remember."

My thoughts shifted back to the memory of unwrapping *To Kill a Mockingbird*. The following morning, after we had begun reading it together, Mama confessed to me, "I stayed awake all night and finished the book. I'm sorry I read it without you. I just couldn't stop."

I grinned. "It's okay, Mama. There is nothing to forgive. Just don't tell me what happens."

In truth, though I had kept it to myself, I preferred to read this book on my own, take my time, and sit with my thoughts.

After taking a sip of her Earl Grey tea, Mama said, "I was awake reading when your dad returned home late last night. We talked about everything. He apologized for the overreaction. His job has been really stressful, and he started drinking again to deal with it."

She paused, holding the mug between both of her hands. "I also showed him my arm, which I wasn't planning to do. The bruises completely shocked him. He had no memory of it. After a hundred more apologies, he agreed to see a doctor about the nightmares."

I felt relieved, able to exhale the breath I had held since she showed me her arm.

Since that incident, Dad had faithfully taken the medication prescribed by his doctor, which seemed to be helping his nightmares, proven by the absence of screaming overnight. He had also stopped drinking again, at his doctor's suggestion, because alcohol interacted with the sedatives. Dad seemed motivated to improve himself and his relationship with Mama. I would never know the daily battles he fought, hidden inside his head, to maintain control.

I remarked, after returning from the daydream back to the diner, "I'm really proud of Dad for getting help."

She smiled, tears forming in her glistening eyes. "Me too, little bird. He's really trying. For *us*."

We finished our lunch, and I pumped our gas before we were on our way again. The sky had begun to clear. Sunlight streamed in beams through the dissipating clouds. The golden rays appeared as if they were poured from heaven, scattered into spotlights shining upon the ground.

Mama asked as the car accelerated, "Are you going to miss your friends this summer?"

"Yes," I answered immediately. "Joe begged me to stay home this summer. He said we could go swimming and play baseball every day."

"Do you wish we stayed home?"

I was unsure how to answer. Mama loved spending summers at the beach house. It felt selfish to take it away from her.

"Sort of," I reluctantly replied. "At least, I wish Dad could have joined us this summer."

"I do too. You know he has a hard time taking that long off from work, though."

"I know. Dad did tell me he would try really hard to come visit at the end of summer before we return. I know he's said that before, but this time it felt like he meant it." I tried to convince her and myself.

Mama looked at me, smiled, and returned her gaze to the road. "I'm sure Dad will try his best." Her words attempted to reassure me while her eyes shifted undecidedly.

After a long day of traveling, we finally turned onto the road to the beach house. Lined with trees on both sides, the road began with a thick crown of leaves. The trees, hunting the sparse sunlight, bowed over the road, forming a tunnel above. I loved driving through the tunnel of trees, a magical entrance to another world. The closer we drove to the cliff, the more the trees thinned out until the tunnel opened up to allow the sunlight admittance. Our car pulled into the driveway, the gravel popping like popcorn in hot oil under the tires. I looked at the little beach house, unchanged, waiting the whole year for our return. Immediately upon opening the car door, I heard the water and smelled the air, clean and fragrant, a scent forever redolent of my childhood. I suddenly forgot about my friends and the city, realizing this was exactly where I wanted, and needed, to be.

CHAPTER 12

LOOKING UP

"Can you tell me all you know about the moon?" I asked Mama one night when I was six years old as she wrapped my quilt snugly around my frigid body.

We had just returned from a trip outside in the chilly autumn air. Mama had suddenly remembered, as I climbed into bed the first time, that there would be a full moon that night. Earlier that week, we had been discussing the names of full moons and how this particular one, in November, was called the Beaver Moon, which caused me to giggle. When she said the name, I imagined the beavers from *The Lion, the Witch, and the Wardrobe* staring up at the round moon, named after them.

"That's our moon, dear," Mr. Beaver would say to Mrs. Beaver as she smiled at the sky.

I jumped out of bed in a flash after Mama suggested a quick adventure. We grabbed our shoes and coats, mine buttoned over my pajamas, and ventured into the darkness. We ran between the buildings, holding hands and laughing while we searched for a glimpse of the full moon. That night, we only saw the yellow glow of the Beaver Moon behind thick clouds. I marveled at the moon's brightness beyond the silver covering. I did not feel much disappointment, however. As I climbed back into bed, my heart still pounding wildly from our spontaneous hunt, the moon held my attention.

Mama considered my question and answered, "I know people, including Native Americans, named the full moons after crops or other observations of nature as we've already discussed. I also know the moon reflects the sun's light, affects the tides, and February can never have a blue moon."

"What's a blue moon?" I asked of the intriguing name.

"A blue moon is a second full moon within the same month as the first. February is not long enough, even during a leap year, so it will never have a blue moon. When I realized this as a child, it broke my heart. I loved looking at the full moon, and as you know, my birthday is in February. So, the thought of *never* possibly seeing a second full moon in my birth month made me cry."

I cracked a half smile, unsure whether it would hurt her feelings.

She noticed and assuaged my guilt. "It is pretty silly, isn't it? To cry over a full moon?"

Silliness aside, I understood her fascination with the moon. I found myself looking up at the sky constantly, always searching for the moon first. Ever since the launch of Sputnik, the first artificial satellite, in October 1957, I had become obsessed with space, along with millions of others around the world. Instead of

Christmas or birthday presents, I asked for money, even though Mama deemed this a rude request, in order to save for a telescope. I longed to see the surface of the moon in detail, the craters and dark spots my eyes could not discern. I even went to Nana and Pops' house on the weekends to cut the grass or complete other odd jobs for them. Mama insisted I help them for free, as they were my beloved grandparents. Nana ignored her, as usual, and sneakily handed me a folded wad of money, with a less discrete wink, as we said goodbye to each other. At the end of each weekend or celebration, I pulled the tin lunchbox from under my bed and placed the money at the very bottom. Before I closed the lunchbox and hid it in the shadows below my bed again, I stared at the photographs on the very top, the subtle transformations in mine and Lucy's faces as we aged beyond childhood, our features growing more defined over the years.

I had finally saved enough money following the most recent addition from my tenth birthday. I had witnessed rare double blue moons earlier that year, in January and April 1961, each one encouraging me towards my goal. Pops had driven me to buy it after my birthday party. I darted to my room once the candles were blown out, pulled out the lunchbox, and quickly counted my stash of money.

I announced to everyone—Mama, Dad, Nana, and Pops— as the cake was being sliced, "I finally have enough money!"

Pops agreed to take me shopping but only after we ate cake with the rest of the family. The taste of cake had never been less appealing to me. I forced a few bites although my mind was distracted. I had waited years, an impossibly long time for a kid, to save enough money, but all of a sudden, it was as if all my patience had vanished and been replaced with zealousness. As Pops and I walked into the shop, I immediately knew which telescope I wanted to purchase, the same one pictured on the ripped magazine page inside my lunchbox. It stood there in the corner, propped upon its tripod stand, a black cylinder with gold metal bands holding the finderscope, a smaller scope used to aim the main scope. The finderscope reminded me of something a sailor would use to spot land ahead or other vessels, perhaps pirates. I had first seen the telescope advertised in a magazine, ripped the page out, and written a letter to the company for more information. When the brochure finally arrived in the mail, I read it over and over, keeping it under my bed next to the lunchbox.

"I'm ready to buy this one," I informed Pops not long after we entered the shop.

"It doesn't work like that, Michael. You can't just buy the first one you see. Here, let's check out every telescope they have and heckle the salesman a little," Pops said with a smirk.

"Okay, Pops," I replied as we began our investigation.

We inspected every telescope within my price range. Pops asked so many questions that I began to pity the salesman who answered them all as well as he could. Some of his questions did not even have answers. Pops also attempted to negotiate the price on one of the more expensive telescopes.

Pops, satisfied with his answered questions and amusement, asked me, "Well, which one will it be? We've sufficiently looked at all of them."

He began chuckling as I pointed to the corner and answered, "The Deluxe Skyscope."

"You already made up your mind long before today, didn't you?" he asked, not expecting an answer. Pops then looked at me seriously. "There's nothing wrong with decisiveness, but always research all your other options first."

I listened patiently to his advice and nodded.

On the drive back home, I kept glancing at the back seat for another look at the telescope, belonging to me at last.

Pops remarked, "I'm really proud of you for saving your money for something worthwhile. Most adults struggle with this concept."

"Thanks, Pops. I can't believe it's mine." I beamed, glancing one more time to the back seat.

That evening, we returned home to a glaring Nana, who demanded to know what took us so long. Once we had recalled our trip to everyone, Pops came to my room and helped me set up the telescope beside my small window—overlooking the street below, a row of buildings ahead. Pops scorned my insistence on reading the instruction manual, declaring he did not need it since he already saw it assembled in the store. After multiple cycles of profanity upon his realization that the tripod center was upside down and then the cylinder was twisted the wrong way, Pops ultimately agreed to a peek at the manual. I suppressed my laughter as I watched him struggle with the assembly, which was deceptively complicated.

After we arrived at the beach house in 1961, my apprehension of spending summer away from home and friends mollified, I unloaded my telescope carefully from the back seat. Thankfully, for our trip to the beach house, I only had to remove the scope from the tripod stand and disassemble the three fixed legs. The beach house faced south, providing a perfect eastern view from the side of the yard near the cliff's edge. Finally having free time away from school, I was eager to learn how to use the telescope and study the phases of the moon. After I helped Mama unload the car, I walked to the kitchen and picked up the handset of the yellow telephone hanging on the wall. The dial tone hummed in my ear. I turned the rotary dial clockwise with my index finger and waited for the dial to return for each number. The line trilled a few times until I heard a rather loud hello.

"We're here!" I said, immediately replacing the handset and returning outside to my telescope.

By the time I had reconnected the metal tripod legs, the sunlight had completely disappeared behind the trees to the west, transitioning into the soft glow of eventide. I moved the tripod stand to the edge of the cliff and attached the telescope on top. Over the hedgerow of bushes, I peered through the finderscope into the distance, moving the entire cylinder slowly across the twilight sky. Not yet accustomed to my telescope after only owning it for a month, I practiced looking through the scopes and adjusting it, even when there was nothing particular to look at in the sky.

The summer sky, still bright from the long days stretching towards summer solstice, prevented me from viewing any stars through my telescope. The moon, even a sliver, was nowhere to be found yet. I returned to the finderscope and lowered it to the water, where I found a sailboat with a red-and-white striped sail, riding atop the waves up and down. It felt intrusive to spy on the inhabitants, so I inspected the sails, tautly capturing the wind, and discovered a fish printed upon them, near the top, when I suddenly heard a loud screech behind me, just before someone grabbed me from behind. I screamed out and darted to the side before falling to the ground, away from the stranger's grasp. I jumped to my feet again, ready to dash to the house until I heard laughter from the shadows. Once my apprehension had subsided, I immediately recognized the laugh, a sound I had longed to hear all year. From behind the shaking hedgerow of bushes, Lucy walked towards me, holding an unlit flashlight in one hand and a book in the other.

She stood joyfully before me. "I scared you!"

I amended her assertion. "All right, all right, but only because I was distracted."

I saw the faint outline of her body. She appeared much taller this summer. Her hair had been cut short, above her chin, into a bob. Her thick, curly hair stuck out far on both sides of her head as if she were wearing a helmet. I ran to give her a hug although I had reason to be mad at her.

As we embraced, I said, "You've grown taller, and your hair has grown wider."

She pushed me away. "Here's a little advice: don't comment on a lady's appearance."

Teasing her in return for scaring me, I replied, "Lady?"

Lucy pounced on me, and together, we fell to the ground, softened by the thick, cold grass.

She pinned me down with her elbow jabbed into my abdomen and said, "I'm a lady when I choose to be one. But I can still beat you up anytime I want. Don't forget that!"

"Okay, you're a lady," I responded, desperate for her to remove her weight from me.

Lucy rolled off of me and onto her back. The long blades of grass enveloped our limbs as we lay there beside one another. We reposed upon the ground in stillness, the earth, wind, and waves in motion around our fixed bodies. I glanced from the sky to Lucy, relishing how easy it was to be with her, in silence or dialogue, sadness or delight. After all these summers together, we were family.

"I'm sorry if I hurt your feelings, Lucy. I just wanted revenge because you scared me to death."

She turned her gaze to mine and replied, "No problem," in a forlorn, cracking voice.

The evergreen luster in her eyes dimmed, drowned by puddles of tears that slowly trickled out a drop at a time.

"Oh, Lucy, your hair looks nice! Please don't cry." It suddenly felt as if the sun had stopped shining.

My plea failed to stop her tears. The leaking faucet had instead been opened completely, and a steady stream of tears rolled down her cheeks. Realizing my words had little consequence, I moved my body right next to hers, now jerking with profound sobs. I grabbed her hand and held it within mine. I stared at the sky, clear and dark, ignorant of the reason for Lucy's grief. We held hands without words for a long time. She eventually stopped crying; her tears concluded with a heavy sigh.

While looking up, she said, "You are right. My hair does look awful."

Unsure how to respond, I did not speak on the matter this time, instead opting for my silent support.

Lucy turned her head to look at me and began to giggle, her face still damp. "The hairdresser really should have warned me that I can't cut my hair this short and expect it to look like it does in the movies."

She sounded like her old self when she laughed, a contagious giggle impossible to ignore. I joined in the laughter, both of us rolling back and forth on the grass.

Lucy reached over and rubbed my head. "Speaking of hair, you've had the same exact haircut since I met you. How about letting it grow out on top like Elvis?"

My face contorted with both surprise and disgust at her suggestion. "Elvis? No way! Besides, if I grow my hair out, I can't wear my Yankees baseball cap!"

She laughed at my reservation.

I changed the topic from hair to something more sincere. "If I'm upset about something, my mama always tells me to look up at the sky instead of down on my problems. Your problems always seem smaller when you're reminded how big the sky is."

Lucy pondered my words for a few minutes as she looked up at the night sky, completely dark now. "Look up. I like that advice." She then sat up and asked, "So, you finally saved enough for the telescope, huh?"

"Yes, I bought it on my birthday!"

"Well, are you going to show me your telescope or not?" she inquired in jest.

Lucy knew how long I had been saving to buy my own telescope. Last summer, she had even remarked, "If you don't stop talking about that telescope, I'm going to buy the dang thing myself."

I hopped to my feet and pulled Lucy from the ground and over to the telescope, still askew from earlier. I first identified every part of the telescope to ensure Lucy understood the terminology, despite her sneers, and then explained how to use the finderscope to angle the main scope correctly.

She stepped beside the telescope and placed her right eye on the eyepiece, looking through it briefly. "I don't see anything. Where is the moon?" She lifted her head to look at the sky with her naked eyes.

"I'm trying to find it, Lucy! You know, its location changes depending on what phase it's in."

Lucy switched on her flashlight and opened the book she carried with her. When she had flipped to the correct page, she began reading aloud:

The moon was but a chin of gold

A night or two ago,

And now she turns her perfect face

Upon the world below. (Dickinson 125)

Before Lucy finished reading, Mama opened the screen door leading from the front porch and yelled my name.

I walked towards the house. "Everything okay, Mama?"

"Have you seen Lucy?" Mama asked, worry lines wrinkling her forehead.

Lucy jumped from the edge of the yard and said, "Here I am, Ms. Margaret!"

"Oh, Lucy, thank goodness! Louise just called and said you disappeared without telling her where you were going.

"Oops! Guess I have to go!" Lucy ran over and jumped into Mama's arms.

Mama rocked her back and forth. "Oh, I missed you, Lucy! Let me have a look at you. You and Michael seem to change every summer."

Lucy pulled her body away from Mama's embrace and stood before her. Mama thoughtfully inspected her for signs of maturity.

"You've definitely gotten taller and cut your hair." Mama touched her short curls. "Your hair looks beautiful! What a great haircut for summer. I can't wait to see it pulled up off of your face with a few pieces dangling in the front."

Lucy smiled, this time only a small gap between her front teeth.

"Now run home before your great-aunt calls again! Come see us tomorrow."

I watched under the glow of porch light as Lucy turned and disappeared, her short curls bouncing down the road.

CHAPTER 13

ALL MANNERS OF HOLES

The following morning, Mama and I walked downtown to visit Henry at his bookshop, which had not changed much over the years, apart from the window display of recent releases. I found comfort in its constancy. I carried with me Henry's copy of *To Kill a Mockingbird*. We had promised to return it to him although both Mama and I were hesitant to part with it. I had finished reading it in the quiet hours past my bedtime, always wanting to read more and more.

With each step on the gray sidewalk, cracked and discolored, my mind swept over the book's injustices until my thoughts shifted to Ruby Bridges, as I placed myself inside her small shoes, shiny and black, with a bow at the top. Last November, I had seen images on our television of Ruby Bridges, six years old, simply walking to school, which revealed itself not to be so simple for her. Surrounded by four towering marshals with yellow badges wrapped around their arms, she looked tiny in her dress and cardigan as furious White people yelled, holding signs, afraid of a little girl who wanted to go to school. I wondered what else I took for granted every day, for my steps had never been questioned nor judged to be wrong. I became entranced by my white Converse high-tops, worn imperfect like the sidewalk, marching one after the other with measured steps.

Suddenly, something from the corner of my eye stole my attention. I stopped and stared at the little park, unaltered from my very first glimpse of it four years earlier. The barrage of green from the trees and grass, a welcome sight, quieted my mind. The tallest trees swayed to the rhythm of the wind, slowly and heavily, colliding with a deep sound remarkably similar to rolling waves. Switching between this contemplation and Ruby consumed the remaining mile of our trip. Mama, looking like Audrey Hepburn in her black cropped capris and white knit shirt with black gingham collar, walked quietly behind me the entire jaunt until we stepped into the bookshop. We glanced around, searching for Henry, who was not immediately seen.

"I'm going to the back, Mama."

"Okay," she answered as she walked towards the counter and I diverged down the corridor to the children's area.

I smiled as the mural came into view. I stood at the top for a moment before I descended the creaking steps and walked over to the bookshelves. I ran my finger along the spines, paused at a title that captured my interest, and pulled out the book for a closer look. I heard a man's voice, presumably Henry's, drifting from the front of the bookshop. I quickly replaced the book and ran towards the conversation, arriving when Mama and Henry appeared stuck in a long embrace. Henry's face, visible to me, radiated undiluted bliss. He opened his eyes to see me walking into the room. His smile widened as his eyes met mine although he seemed reluctant to release Mama.

Henry eventually detached himself and approached me, remarking in astonishment, "*Who* is this tall man?" as he extended his right hand to me.

I laughed and shook his hand.

"Gosh! You've gotten tall! How can you grow so much in a year?" Henry squeezed my hand and yanked me into his body for a hug. He smelled of peppermint, like his aunt.

I teased him in reply, "Don't worry, old man, I'll soon be taller than you, like my dad."

Henry chuckled. "All right, all right, that's quite enough of calling me old man!" He turned around and gushed, "Oh, I'm so happy to see you both, especially today! My parents are upstairs, and I would love to introduce you to them. That is, if you have the time."

Mama smiled. "Our time is our own. We would love to meet them."

We followed Henry behind the counter to the storage room and up the narrow staircase to his apartment. As we entered to a flood of yellow, made brighter by the morning sun, I saw a man and woman, about the same age as Nana and Pops, sitting at the oval table in the breakfast nook beside the large window. They set down their teacups, one filled with tea, the other with coffee, and stood as we walked into the kitchen.

Henry said, after we had approached the table, "Mom and Dad, I want you to meet my dear friends. This is Michael, who grows an inch every night, and his mother, Margaret, who shrinks an inch every morning."

Henry's father and I laughed while Mama and Henry's mother gasped in unison, their eyes darting in his direction.

"Just kidding!" Henry chuckled nervously as his mother glared at him with disapproval. "Margaret and Michael, these are my parents, Elizabeth and John. No comment about their heights."

We shook hands with them and exchanged warm greetings. Henry looked remarkably like his father, even down to his outfit choice and round eyeglasses, but a more polished version, probably due to his mother's influence. The main differences between the two, on my initial inspection, being their height and the gray goatee covering John's weathered face. In John but not Henry, I recognized some sort of resemblance to Ms. Prince, the librarian, who I realized at that moment was his sister. I immediately understood from whom Henry had inherited his mannerisms and learned his manners. His father, John, cracked jokes and laughed in almost every situation, similar to Henry.

His mother, Elizabeth, wore a tweed jacket and skirt, reminiscent of a petite Jackie Kennedy. She stood before us with straight posture and poise, embodying quintessential British refinement. Her light brown hair was parted on the side with large curls framing her face. Henry shared her symmetrical nose but with a wider tip. Elizabeth was remarkably beautiful, her age only revealed through the creases on the corners of her green eyes and mouth when she smiled and laughed. With further inspection and observation, I discovered the nuanced traits Henry had inherited from his mother. Henry was a perfect mixture of the two.

Elizabeth, who asked to be called Lizzie with a posh yet unpretentious accent, took Mama by the hand and led her to a seat beside her own at the table. She quickly grabbed an empty cup and poured tea for Mama. Mama and Lizzie began chatting avidly, as if they were waiting years for that very conversation.

Meanwhile, I walked around the apartment, attempting to find any alteration in the furniture or décor, and finally asked, "Henry, do you ever change anything?"

"Hmm, not really, except my underpants. Although, I did add something to the mural. Did you notice it?"

"No!" I replied, quickly trying to remember any new characters or scenes in the mural but unable to produce an acceptable guess. "I'll go look again before we leave. I barely glanced at it earlier."

"By the way," I digressed, "we brought *To Kill a Mockingbird* to return to you," lifting the book up to show him.

Henry motioned for us to sit, so we settled on his lumpy couch with perfectly placed pillows. I doubted Henry ever sat on the couch since the pillows never seemed to move an inch. Henry's father sat in a nearby armchair, reading a newspaper. Every now and then, he chuckled to himself, causing the newspaper to shake a bit in between his hands.

"So, what do you think of it? I've been dying to hear your reaction," Henry asked, pushing his fallen brown glasses back in place on his nose.

"I loved it. To be honest, I was hoping to read it again before we returned it, but I ran out of time."

"Well, then it's a good thing my shop now has multiple copies, and I planned to give you this one. Tell me more, though. What feelings or thoughts did the book evoke in you?"

"So many. I felt excitement to learn of the events surrounding Jem's broken arm and sadness mixed with outrage over the injustices of Tom. Just this morning on our walk here, I began thinking about Ruby Bridges and her walk to school. On the news, I've seen stories about the Freedom Riders and Martin Luther King, Jr. Is it *really* like this in the South? How can it be the same country, Henry?" My reaction spilled from my mouth as if it were locked up since I began reading the book, desperate to escape.

"I felt the same way. I *feel* the same way as you, Michael. I'm afraid it is still this way in the South. Separate schools, separate restaurants and bathrooms, separate beaches and swimming pools. Some are trying so hard to keep White people above the rest."

"It makes me so angry. We learned about the Civil War and end of slavery in school, so why is it still like this a hundred years later?" I said through gritted teeth.

"This, your reaction, is why I am hopeful, Michael. You are ten years old and feel outraged at the events happening." Henry stood up and paced in front of the couch. "I do believe things will change for the better. Being angry about it is valid, but the best way forward is acknowledging that it's happening and trying to encourage change in those around you."

"Well said," John's voice boomed from behind the newspaper, "by both of you!" He pulled the newspaper down to reveal his face, wrinkled but handsome. He looked at me and winked.

We heard laughter streaming from the kitchen. Mama and Lizzie cackled at some unknown joke, Mama with her head tilted back and Lizzie bent over, holding her stomach.

"What's so funny over there?" asked John, his glasses peering over the top of the newspaper.

Lizzie replied, "Oh, I was just telling Margaret the story of when Henry acted in Peter Pan as a child."

Her last few words were barely audible over the eruption of laughter. Henry rose from the couch and swiveled around to face them, aghast. Their laughter only became invigorated by his expression. John, unable to resist, walked over to join them at the table.

Henry, when he was finally able to speak through the shock, questioned, "Why, may I ask, are you discussing this particular play? The one that ruined theater for me forever?"

I walked to the kitchen as the three of them began laughing, even more excited to hear the story after witnessing Henry's reaction. Everyone, including Henry, had now gathered around the table.

"Mrs. Elizabeth, will you tell me the story?" I politely asked, hoping my manners might encourage her to oblige.

"Of course, Michael! John, will you tell the story this time? You really are a better storyteller than me."

"Certainly, my love." Henry's father cleared his throat. "Henry was cast as Peter Pan in his elementary school play. He practiced every day after school, giving all of us a part to help him run his lines. Elizabeth played Wendy and her mother; I played Wendy's father, the dog, and Captain Hook; and Charlie played Wendy's brothers as well as the lost boys during our family rehearsals. When the big night of the play finally arrived, Henry was absolutely prepared for it. The curtain was finally drawn, and we eagerly awaited his appearance on stage."

John paused for a drink, perhaps to also add more suspense to the story. I wondered if Charlie was Henry's brother and where he lived, for I had never met him. Henry covered his face with both hands.

"The first scene we saw Henry on stage was in the children's bedroom. Everything was going well until he tried to teach the children how to fly. Henry wore a harness with a rope attached, and when he tried to take flight, the stagehand jerked him up unexpectedly, causing Henry to squeal loudly and then tip upside down while hanging in the air." John waved his hands around and used them for demonstration. "So, he was upside down, fairly high off the ground, swinging around the bedroom screaming. Then, Henry attempted to pull himself back upright and somehow stretched his legs out and ripped his green tights. But he slowly tipped back over and swung around upside down with a big hole in his tights for what seemed like an eternity before they could safely bring him down. They finally lowered him to the ground, headfirst, and poor Henry just lay there on the stage until they closed the curtain. The crowd wasn't sure how to react, so everyone just sat in eerie silence. We rushed backstage, afraid he had been injured. Thankfully, Henry was fine although he refused to return to the stage after that incident."

Everyone, except Henry, erupted into laughter. In my mind, I imagined Henry as a child, hanging upside down, a swinging green bob at the end of a pendulum. Henry stood there with his arms folded. Eventually, his stern, disapproving mouth slackened into a faint smile. He soon joined our laughter.

"Okay, fine," Henry admitted, "it was funny! You're lucky I can laugh at myself, or I might never forgive any of you!"

Elizabeth walked over to Henry and hugged him. "Oh, you worked so hard preparing for that play. I'm sorry it ended that way."

Henry wrapped his arms around his mother, standing above her with his eyes closed. "It's okay, Mom." In that embrace, he reverted to that little boy in a Peter Pan costume.

Mama watched them, a mother and son, and then glanced at me. "I'm sorry, Henry, if I embarrassed you. I'm the one who asked your mother for these childhood stories of you."

"No worries, Margaret. I will return the favor when your parents visit. When are they coming this summer? We should have a party! More of an audience for your walk of shame down memory lane."

Mama laughed. "I suppose I deserve that! They are coming next week."

"I didn't know they were coming that early!" I said. "We really should have a huge party for everyone! Henry, you must see my telescope! By the way, who is Charlie?"

"Charlie is my little brother. He lives in London. My parents usually spend the entire summer with him. And, I would love to see your telescope, Michael!"

"At Henry's insistence, we're delaying our trip to London for part of the summer, Michael," Elizabeth said, "so we'll definitely see more of you."

"I would like that." I smiled.

"Me too!" Mama agreed. "And more stories of Peter Pan!"

Henry growled at her. "Unfortunately, I must abandon you all and return to my store. I've already been gone too long."

I wondered if he was escaping before more stories of him resurfaced.

Mama said, "Oh, we must be going too. We'll walk down with you, Henry. Lizzie and John, it has been a pleasure to meet you. Thank you for the tea and the laugh. We can't wait to see you again."

We shook John's rugged hand and hugged Lizzie, who smelled of roses, goodbye with a promise to see them soon. Before we left the bookshop, I ran to the back for a closer look at the mural. I scanned it carefully, still clutching the book in my hand. Just on the edge of the enchanted forest, I spotted a tall oak tree with a large knothole in the middle of the trunk. Several items protruded from the cavity, too minuscule to identify by sight, but I already knew what they were—chewing gum, a ball of twine, two carved dolls, Indian head pennies, a pocket watch, and a spelling medal.

CHAPTER 14

POPCORN CRAVINGS

Rather than reading *To Kill a Mockingbird* again, I decided to loan it to Lucy, who had a sadness about her that persisted beyond the night she had frightened me as I looked into my telescope. I did not know the cause but surmised it was due to something more serious than a haircut. In my experience, however, I found girls to be strange, complex creatures who were perfectly capable of getting upset by trivial matters such as hair. No matter the cause, I decided a good book would cheer her up.

Lucy and Aunt Louise came over to our house the evening after we met Henry's parents. Mama and Aunt Louise sat outside on the back patio while Lucy and I loitered around the front yard, near the cliff, where I had set up my telescope again. I ran inside and returned with the book.

"I have a book for you to borrow." I hid the book behind me with a Cheshire grin upon my face.

Lucy, balancing on the cobblestone fence, immediately looked up from her path to me, searching for a glimpse of the book with zealous eyes.

I pulled it out from behind my back. "It's titled *To Kill a Mockingbird*, and you won't be able to put it down."

She jumped from the fence and ran over to me with bare feet. I handed her the book and watched as she scanned the front cover, just as I had.

Lucy smiled as she asked, "What's it about?"

I grinned broadly again, a devilish tinge in the corners this time. "I'm afraid I can't tell you. Just trust me and read it."

"Okay," she replied, "but since you won't tell me anything about it, I'll start right now and completely ignore you."

I laughed at her earnestness as she walked back to the fence and sat with crossed legs upon the stones. She indeed opened the book and began reading it with the aid of her flashlight, periodically tucking her short curls behind her ears. I thought of the thrill I had felt when hearing the first sentence, the curiosity that propelled me to read more and more, and how Lucy would be changed after she had read the last page.

After watching her for a minute, I resumed my study of the night sky and my attempt at tracking the moon's cycle in my notebook. I scanned the sky for the moon, first near the eastern horizon, gradually up towards the zenith, and then back down westward as far as I could see. The sky curved above my head, devoid of light apart from the faint twinkle of silvery stars, intermittent diamonds scattered about the immense black. I could not find even a sliver of the moon. I assumed this meant there was a new moon, positioned in front of the sun, unable to reflect the sunlight. From a book I had read at the library, I remembered that in a few days, the moon would appear in a crescent shape and grow larger and larger until reaching a full moon. Then, the full moon would grow smaller, the cycle in reverse, until it became a new moon once again.

Without lifting her eyes from the page, Lucy transitioned from the fence to sit upon the ground. I noted the date and new moon in my speckled black-and-white composition notebook. I returned to my telescope in order to hunt for stars instead when Aunt Louise suddenly came bursting through the front porch door as if there were some sort of emergency.

"My darlings! Darlings!"

Lucy and I climbed onto the cobblestone fence to discover the urgency.

"Oh, there you are! Would you like to go to the drive-in? I'm in the mood for popcorn, and Margaret has none."

"Yes!" I jumped into the air, the elation blasting my body from the fence.

Lucy agreed as well, though less enthusiastically than me. I always jumped at the chance to ride in Aunt Louise's new car—a 1960 Ford Thunderbird convertible. I remembered the first time I saw it the previous summer when Aunt Louise pulled it slowly, for added drama, into the driveway, parked, and blew the horn multiple times, laughing with her head back at our stunned faces. Birdie, as Aunt Louise called the car, was not one to blend in. Painted cherry red, Birdie was long, low, and shaped like a rectangle with bulges on the sides, brows above the headlights, pointed tail fins on the back, and six round taillights that looked like rocket boosters. Birdie looked as if she could fly. I had spent a long time inspecting every inch of Birdie and running my fingers over the paint, smooth and glossy, the wingspread emblems on the back and front, and the shiny cursive letters spelling "Thunderbird" on the bottom of the doors. It was the most glorious car I had ever seen in my life. I asked Lucy how Aunt Louise could afford such a car and if she were truly rich. Lucy told me she was filthy rich because her husband, who had died twenty years ago, was filthy rich, and they never had any children. She helped raise Lucy's father, the third son of her sister, and thought of him as her own.

"Are you able to drive, Great-aunt? Have you been drinking?"

Aunt Louise opened her mouth in disbelief. "Lucy Lou, how dare you! It's not your place to question me on this! I have not been drinking—er—since we left our house earlier. You should be careful, or Santa might forget you this Christmas!"

Santa? I thought to myself, surprised by this unusual threat.

I looked to Lucy for an explanation. She walked along the fence with a half smile upon her lips, trying to suppress her laughter by staring at the uneven stones. Mama walked outside and asked if we were indeed going to the drive-in. We all turned to look at Aunt Louise.

"Yes! Jump in Birdie!"

As we walked towards the car, I heard Lucy apologize to Aunt Louise before being pulled into her forgiving arms. Lucy had been acting differently, more rebellious and defiant, than previous summers. I wondered if it had anything to do with her being almost eleven years old, if perhaps the same would happen to me the following year, or if it had anything to do with her bouts of sadness. Perhaps all were connected in some way.

Birdie's top was still down, as it always was, from their drive to the beach house earlier. I had never once seen Birdie with her top up. I rubbed my hand along the three white buttons on the open door, upholstered in red and white, as I stepped past the front seat and climbed into the back, where two white buttons continued in a neat row on the sides. All of the seats were covered in red-and-white upholstery, red around the outside and white inside, with one white button in the center of the seats on the top and bottom. I peeked towards the driver's seat for a glimpse of the white steering wheel, large and thin, with the T-Bird in the center. Just above the back seat, midway, I spotted another T-Bird.

We backed out of the driveway and entered the tunnel of trees. I tilted my head back against the seat and watched as we passed beneath the reaching branches, gnarled hands stretching towards us in the darkness, softened by their green leaves. The shadows cast from the glow of headlights, short and long, shifted as we drove through the tunnel. The wind rushed against my face when we accelerated on the main road. I closed my eyes and savored the brisk air while the wind lifted my hair and then forced it down again, similar to when Nana tousled it. Mama's hair blew about wildly, blocking her from seeing anything. Aunt Louise had tied a scarf in her hair before we departed and laughed as Mama attempted to hold her hair back with her hands.

I whispered to Lucy, leaning towards her and trying to avoid her blowing curls, "What's with Santa Claus?"

"Aunt Louise dresses up as Santa every Christmas at her house with the suit, beard, jolly belly, everything."

Despite our efforts to stifle them, we snorted out our giggles at the image Lucy's words had shaped in our minds. To imagine Aunt Louise, in all her extravagance, dressed up as Santa Claus was almost too much, even for my imagination. Aunt Louise glared skeptically at us through the rearview mirror although I do not think she knew the reason for our laughter.

"All of the children sit on her lap for pictures, and she even hands out presents. When I was around two or three years old, I was terrified of her and refused to sit on her lap. We have a photograph of my dad holding me next to her with a look of sheer horror on my face. I guess if I don't stop asking questions, I'll be added to the naughty list and won't get a present this year."

Lucy and I continued whispering and giggling in the back seat as we drove outside of town to the drive-in, sitting in a large field on its own but not lonely in its surroundings. I had been to the theater several times but never in a car. I felt quite content that my first drive-in experience would occur in Birdie. As we approached, I spotted the lights of the oversized marquee ahead. Aunt Louise pulled Birdie in slowly, granting us time to read the film titles, the largest of which was the special feature—*The Wizard of Oz*. I had been wanting to see it for years, even more so after Lucy had told me about it that first summer. Lucy and I looked at one another, our eyes wide at the unexpected surprise.

Lucy leapt from her seat. "Wow! *The Wizard of Oz*! They never show that kind of movie at the drive-in. They're usually movies I've never heard of before!"

"I guess it's our lucky night!" Aunt Louise squealed before she paid for our admission, smacking Mama's hand for trying to give her money. She pulled into a parking space and glanced over at Mama. "Oh, Margaret, you must really borrow one of my scarves next time! Your hair is quite wild, darling!"

Mama leaned over to her right for a glimpse of her hair in the side mirror. She chuckled at her windblown hair, knotted into tangles. "I shall never get a brush through my hair again. Perhaps I'll just cut it off, like Lucy!"

Lucy hopped out of the car. "Michael and I will go buy the popcorn and drinks!"

I joined Lucy outside the car before Aunt Louise handed us money and we sprinted away. Lucy grabbed my hand and diverted our path to the children's playground. We each took a turn down the metal slide and then raced to the concession stand. When we returned with the popcorn and drinks, Lucy somehow convinced Aunt Louise to let us sit on the back of the car above the back seat. We both swore we would not wriggle too much or scratch her baby. Lucy and I nestled together, a popcorn bucket in our laps and Aunt Louise's shawl wrapped around our shoulders. It felt especially chilly when the wind blew.

At last, the screen lit up and sound began to play through the wired speaker, pulled from the stand next to us. The fluttering feeling in my stomach returned as I watched the opening credits, beginning with the MGM lion roaring over dramatic music. A black-and-white sky with drifting clouds appeared on screen, followed by large letters spelling "*The Wizard of Oz*" as slower, ethereal music played. Names filled the screen while the music flitted between fast, exciting bursts and dreamy lullabies. Already, the music had transported me to another world, long before

Dorothy landed in Oz. I was thunderstruck when Dorothy began to sing "Somewhere Over the Rainbow." I had never heard a voice like hers. I listened in wonder to the song as Lucy quietly sang along beside me.

Throughout the movie, Lucy leaned over and explained, in whispers, parts of the movie to me. I did not mind, however, for I knew she had been holding it inside for four whole years. Mama sat quietly, as entranced by the movie as me. Aunt Louise openly displayed her emotions. She gasped during the tornado scene, hummed along to "Follow the Yellow Brick Road," suddenly burst into laughter when the Tin Man whistled through his funnel, chanted along to "lions and tigers and bears, oh my!" and discontentedly growled when the wizard turned them away. Her favorite character of all was the Cowardly Lion. She laughed the most at his parts—when he trembled, fainted, jumped through the window, and donned his royal cloak.

Later that night, when I replayed the movie scenes in my mind, I attempted to pick my favorite one unsuccessfully. I loved every part of *The Wizard of Oz*, a movie I would watch many other times after that night. None would even come close to being as special as that first viewing—outside under the black sky, gusts of wind shaking the leaves in the surrounding trees and trying to carry our cover away, Lucy snuggling closer to me as our bodies shivered. I needed nothing that night, wanted nothing. The movie ended, returning us from the land of Oz to that open field. The stridulation of crickets, pouring from the woods, filled the newfound silence before we drove back home.

CHAPTER 15

MARTHA'S VINEYARD

The following Monday, Nana and Pops arrived earlier than usual, promising to stay longer than usual too. During their visits to the beach house, Mama gave them her larger bed while she bunked with me. Since they planned to stay two to three weeks and I had grown too big to fit comfortably in my bed with Mama, Pops suggested a solution—placing a bed for me on the screened front porch.

Nana jeered at Pops and his idea, smacking his upper arm. "*You* can sleep on the porch instead!"

Mama considered it a good idea. "I bet once you sleep outside, you'll never want to come inside again."

Nana rolled her eyes at Mama for agreeing with Pops and stomped to the kitchen in a tantrum.

"It's your decision, Michael. We can squeeze together and snuggle in your bed if you choose."

I replied, decidedly, "I like the idea of sleeping outside, sort of like camping!" To me, ten years old felt too old to sleep beside one's mother in a tiny bed. I kept this reason to myself.

"All right," Pops said, "let's go buy a bed for you. If we go this morning, perhaps they can deliver it today."

Pops refused to buy a frame or mattress unless they promised to deliver it the same day, unswayed by sales tactics such as upgrades or lower prices. His obstinacy, or prudence according to him, prevailed as the manager eventually yielded to his request. My bed was delivered later that day. We positioned it lengthwise against the house in case of rain; however, I did not worry about the weather too much because of the knee wall protecting the bottom third of the porch, with only the top screened portion permeable to rain. It never seemed to rain much at the beach in the summer anyway.

My first night of sleeping outside caused equal parts excitement and apprehension. Every little noise, from the trees, beach, and nearby creatures, caught my attention, preventing me from nodding off to sleep easily, instead fueling my overactive imagination. To calm myself, I thought about the phone conversation I had with Dad earlier that evening, replaying every tiny detail.

Dad remarked of my new sleeping arrangement, "There's nothing like sleeping outside, son. Your Uncle Junior and I used to sneak out at night during summer and sleep in their backyard when we were kids. One time, I remember your mama followed us. She was so small. She didn't say anything, just carried her blanket and pillow, placed it next to us, and went to sleep."

He laughed at the memory and the time of innocence to which it transported him. He had never spoken of these childhood memories with me before. I liked hearing him talk about growing up with Uncle Junior and Mama.

Dad said, "I miss practicing baseball with you. This apartment is so empty without you and your mama."

"I miss you too, Dad. Since you miss us so much, you'd better come visit us at the end of summer."

Dad laughed and replied, "I'm going to try my best if all continues to go well at work. I'm sleeping better, and everything seems to be going really well right now, Michael."

Dad sounded hopeful. I finally fell asleep that night imagining all three of them sneaking outside to sleep. The next morning, Mama came to my bed to see if I had survived my first night outside. I think she assumed she would wake up to me beside her in bed.

She sat down beside me, kissed my forehead, and whispered, "I'm thinking of throwing a garden party here for all of our friends and family. Do you think it's a good idea?"

I sat up immediately with a resounding answer. "I think it's a great idea!"

Mama smiled. "Okay, well, I'll need your help then if we are going to invite everyone."

After discussions with the intended guests, the date for the garden party was set for the following week since extra tables and chairs were needed to accommodate all the people. Aunt Louise, Lucy, Henry, his parents, and his aunt had all been invited. A few days after Nana and Pops arrived, we traveled to Martha's Vineyard for the day. I was thankful for the distraction as I could hardly wait for the garden party.

I awoke early that morning, unable to sleep any longer, and found Pops sipping his black coffee at the small table in the kitchen. Pops and I walked down the stone steps to the beach. There had always been something magical to me about waking up before anyone else, especially before sunrise, and having the quiet world to myself. Pops and I chatted about my telescope and baseball while the sun, burnt orange, peeked over the top of the ocean. We watched, in silent, stolen glances, as the sun rose slowly in the cloudless sky. For a brief moment, it looked as if the sun sat perfectly atop the water, a fiery ball balancing on the surface, until it continued its path upwards. The sunlight reflected off of the water as if from a mirror, forcing us to avert our eyes from the blinding light. We returned from our walk to the beach house for breakfast and soon after left to catch the ferry from Falmouth. I had never been to Martha's Vineyard, viewing only a distant glimpse of its land rising just above the ocean from the top of the lighthouse.

On our drive to the ferry, I thought of Lucy's remarks the night before. "Oh, be on the lookout for Martin Luther King, Jr. I hear he likes to vacation there. I've never seen him on any of our visits, but maybe you will be lucky!"

I wondered if Martin Luther King, Jr. and other activists met on the island to organize the sit-ins and freedom rides shown on the evening news. We parked our car, bought our ferry tickets, and waited until time to board. Our boat was already docked at the pier. To pass the time, I walked over to get a closer look at it. Medium-sized and white, the name *Vineyard Queen* was painted near the bow on a thin black stripe running across the entire length of the vessel. There were many other boats of various sizes nearby, pitching back and forth on the ripples of water, unable to move beyond their anchored point. I walked around and watched each teeter up and down on the waves as I inspected them, noting their differences and names, displayed on the back along with the cities from which they hailed. I spotted boats from all over the eastern coast, some with clever or quite silly names and some I did not quite comprehend. I pondered what I would name my own boat if I ever had one. Seagulls loitered around the pier, hovering in the air or sitting on top of the dock, squawking loudly while hunting food in people's hands or discarded on the ground.

They finally called for us to board, so I rejoined the others, already in line, before taking our seats near the center of the boat. After all the other passengers had boarded, the boat slowly lurched into motion as it pulled away from the pier and navigated down the narrow inlet. At this slower pace, it felt the same as riding in Aunt Louise's convertible with the top down. Once we exited the inlet and entered the open water, the boat accelerated, and the wind battered us from all sides instead of straight ahead. I could not see much beyond my seat.

Pops and I walked to the stern, at his suggestion, to watch the churning waves of the wake in an effort to quell his boredom. I loved the feeling of gliding up and down on the water, cutting through the waves, dappled with sunlight. It was a perfectly clear day. We were able to see far into the distance. The water on the ship's port side stretched to the back of forever. If we followed its waves, I wondered to which distant land it would take us.

Not long after we entered the Vineyard Sound, I turned to my left, starboard for the *Queen*, and saw a most extraordinary sight, one I thought I might be imagining at first. Initially, my gaze settled on the pallid gray rocks lining the edge, where the water met the land, creating an off-white border between the blue waves and verdure rising above. My eyes followed the green. Nestled on a grassy knoll, I spotted a two-story house with a red roof and white picket fence running alongside it. Beside the house, on the other side of the low fence, stood a white lighthouse with a black gallery and roof. It appeared before me as plainly as I had seen it four years earlier. I recognized it immediately, even at this distance. It was Nobska Light. I smiled and stared, unable to remove my gaze from its unexpected appearance before me like an old friend, still the same, constant beacon. I returned to the brick stairwell and the memory of climbing to the very top, being mesmerized by my first sight of the Fresnel lens, and looking out at the vast ocean, where we now sailed on the *Vineyard Queen*. *How much had occurred, how much time had passed since we were there*, I thought to myself.

I glanced at Pops, who also stared quietly at the lighthouse. "Remember when we visited?" I asked him.

"Of course! It was a perfect day! As far as I know, Hallett is still the lightkeeper there. It looks like a preserved memory, sitting there stuck in time."

I turned back to the lighthouse. "What a happy memory it is."

Pops wrapped his arm around me, and we watched as Nobska Light grew smaller and smaller as we sailed away, until it was no longer visible. Once the lighthouse had completely disappeared, Pops, reminded of another memory, spent the remainder of our trip to Martha's Vineyard recalling it to me.

"One time, my old buddy Clark and I went fishing on his little boat. We went way out to sea and sat there without any luck, roasting in the sun for hours. We were just about to reel in our lines and call it a day when Clark felt a sudden, powerful tug on his fishing pole. The line relaxed and then jerked again so forcefully that it pulled Clark violently out of the boat and right into the water with a splash. Clark released his pole and began swimming wildly back to the boat, afraid a shark was chasing him. I reached my arm over the side of the boat, ready to help him back inside, when I couldn't believe what I saw." He paused, keeping me in suspense for far too long.

"Pops! What happened next? What did you see?"

"Okay, okay, I'll tell you. Before Clark made it back to the boat, a massive creature burst from the ocean and swallowed him whole. The huge wave created by the monster pushed me and the little boat far away but thankfully didn't capsize it. All I could do was look in horror at the spot where the waves were still rippling on the surface, no sign of Clark anywhere."

"What happened to Clark, Pops?" I asked, curious but terrified of the answer.

"Oh, not long after that I went to his wedding."

"Wait! His *wedding*?"

"What? You didn't expect me to attend his funeral, did you?"

Unsatisfied, I stared at him in the same way Nana always did until he explained further.

"Oh, are you wondering how he escaped? You are a curious little thing! All right, I'll tell you. I just stared in disbelief, unable to move, for maybe a minute or so, perhaps longer, when I heard a loud noise below the surface and witnessed a jet stream of water shoot straight into the air. At the very top, I saw Clark flying up higher and higher until he fell back down into the water. Once his head resurfaced, I turned on the boat's engine and picked Clark up before he could be swallowed again."

"So, what swallowed him? What did he say afterwards?"

"Oh, we'll never know for sure. Ole Clark couldn't remember anything except thinking he was dead and then shooting into the air like he was a cowboy riding that geyser Old Faithful. I personally think it was a whale the size of Moby Dick that swallowed him and then sneezed him out. Perhaps the whale had hay fever or was just allergic to Clark or thought he tasted like old leather shoes."

"Oh, Pops!" I laughed, unsure if I believed any portion of his story.

We felt the ferry slow as we entered the harbor and then approached the dock at Oaks Bluff on the northeastern tip of Martha's Vineyard. Pops and I returned to our seats next to Mama and Nana. I spotted lots of smaller boats docked in the harbor ahead of us, heaving rhythmically like the ones in Falmouth. The ferry maneuvered slowly towards the unloading gate, located underneath an arching sign with the words "Oaks Bluff" written on it.

Once we had disembarked the ferry, Nana, looking relieved to be on land once again, asked, "How did you two go walking around that ship? I felt so seasick that I was afraid that if I moved from my seat, I might puke everywhere!"

"You haven't gained your sea legs, like us men!" Pops declared.

Nana simply stopped walking and glared at him with one of her frigid, unyielding stares, the very one that I had mimicked earlier, until Pops began sweating. He laughed nervously and then apologized. Content, Nana's face unfroze; her mouth curved into a broad smile. The first place Nana insisted on visiting was the Flying Horses Carousel. It was just a quick walk from where the *Vineyard Queen* had dropped us. We walked a few blocks to a building that resembled a barn with burgundy red slats on the exterior and its name painted in large white letters on the side. We walked around to the entrance, above which hung a sign that read "America's Oldest Carousel." As we walked up the steps and inside, I saw the carousel before me, looking small and unspectacular. It had a green floor with two rows of horses, larger ones on the outside and smaller ones on the inside, and a burgundy frame from which the horses were attached on black metal poles. I looked from the top of the frame all the way up to the exposed ceiling. The roof trusses, also painted burgundy, contrasted against the white rafters and beams.

"Shall we ride the carousel?" Nana asked with a childlike enthusiasm.

"I'm too old to ride, Nana. I'm ten years old now," I replied, looking around at the younger children sitting upon the horses.

Her face drooped. "Nonsense! You're still a child!"

Mama, overhearing our conversation and wanting to keep the peace, said, "Let's all ride together! After all, it's not every day you get to ride America's oldest carousel!"

I agreed, so Pops bought us all a ticket to ride. I picked a chestnut brown horse with a reddish tinge on the outside row and climbed onto it. I inspected the horses, hand-carved and painted with intricate saddles. They looked quite realistic with glass eyes and flowing manes and tails. I rubbed my horse's neck, shiny and smooth, and then touched the coarse hair of the mane carefully, wondering if it was real horsehair. Pops and Mama settled into a red carriage seat together. I giggled as Nana, at last, made a decision and attempted to climb the golden horse directly in front of mine. Pops eventually came over, against her wishes, to assist her after she had failed to make the climb after two attempts.

Nana looked back at me over her shoulder and smiled. "Let's see who grabs more rings!"

The carousel began to turn with Wurlitzer organ music playing in the background. There were two arms, one on the outside and one on the inside, stationed alongside the carousel that dispensed small rings. As the carousel rotated towards the arm, I reached over and pulled a ring from it. This was not too difficult since the horses were stationary and did not rise up and down like some newer carousels. Nana cackled as we circled around and grabbed the rings. I glanced behind me at Mama and Pops, who waved once they noticed me looking at them. Panels painted with water scenes and ships were hung from the radiating arms of each section and on the center of the platform. I looked at the paintings as we spun around until we approached the arm once more.

Once the carousel stopped, I looked down at the rings I had collected during the ride.

Before I could count them, Nana shouted, "The brass ring! I found the brass ring!"

Everyone stared at her exhibition of victory. For as long as I had known her, Nana was never one to be reserved in her emotions. I dismounted my horse, confounded by the stark difference between her and Mama.

As we exited the ride, I admitted to Mama, "That was pretty fun. I liked grabbing the rings."

Mama giggled quietly. "Not as much as your grandmother."

Together, we looked back at Nana, still crowing with a wide smile and flushed cheeks. Nana had won a free ride on the carousel for pulling the brass ring. Instead of riding again, Nana gave it to a little boy waiting with his family outside. He jumped up and down when Nana handed him the free ticket. We decided to eat lunch at a nearby restaurant before exploring the island further.

CHAPTER 16

OCEAN PARK

After lunch and consultation with our waitress, we decided to walk to Ocean Park since we had no car nor bicycles. Nana had never learned to ride a bicycle, and Pops remarked on how his old knees would need to be oiled before pedaling again. The waitress had also informed us of a beach directly across the street from the park in case we wanted to swim. She called it Inkwell Beach, which I thought was a peculiar name. It conjured a scene in my mind of people diving into thick black ink instead of water, which stained their skin once they reemerged from the sticky well.

Ocean Park consisted mostly of open green space. As soon as we arrived, I sprinted across the grass, bright green and inviting. The breeze, blowing in from the ocean, whipped my hair as I rushed into it. I darted past an elevated bandstand in the middle of the park and spied colorful rows of Victorian mansions lining the outside. After running the entire width, I rejoined Mama, Nana, and Pops, who were walking around the perimeter observing the beautiful houses. My favorites were the brightly colored ones. Next, we climbed up the steps to the top of the bandstand.

Pops said at the top, "That waitress said they have concerts here every night in the summer."

"Wow! I wish we could stay for one!" I replied. Mama and Nana agreed with me.

I looked towards the ocean, understanding perfectly why that particular name had been chosen for the park. Across the street, just as the waitress had said, I saw the beach, which appeared quite small beside the never-ending blue. I turned back to the park when I heard children's voices. Several children were riding bicycles along the paved paths that veined across the green space.

Below the bandstand, the ground sank into an artificial pond with a cement bottom. Inside the pond, several toy boats, mostly sailboats painted red or green, floated on top of the shallow water. Children stationed around the pond eagerly watched their boats as the wind blew against their minuscule sails. One motorboat painted white with a red stripe at the bottom raced past the others. I stared down at the water, peacefully watching the boats move in different directions—some fast, some slow, and some natant upon the stagnant water. One boy, around four or five years old, waded into the water after his sailboat capsized. A couple of younger children kicked the dirty water, up to their shins, along the edge of the pond.

I descended the bandstand and walked over to the boy with the motorboat for a closer look. The boy, younger than me, smiled proudly as he turned and asked if I wanted to see his boat. He removed it from the water and handed it to me. I turned it over in my hands, trying to discover how it worked. He watched my observations keenly.

The boy pointed to the top deck, painted brown, and explained, "It opens here, where the batteries go."

Part of the motor protruded from the deck's opening. I flipped the boat over to the red bottom, where the metal propeller shaft, attached to the motor on the top, extended from the hull. The propeller was connected at the end of the shaft. The batteries powered the motor, which caused the shaft and propeller to spin. As the propeller's blades spun in the water, the boat moved forward. Beside the propeller, I spotted a metal fin adhered to the stern.

I asked the boy while wiggling the fin, "Is this how it moves in different directions?"

He nodded before I handed the boat back to him. "Thanks! It's a cool boat."

I watched as the boy switched on the motor and then placed the boat back into the pond, speeding away as soon as he released it.

Nana sighed heavily as I approached. "I'm bored!"

"Well, how about we walk across the street to the beach?" Pops asked.

I shouted in agreement. Nana consented, only because of my excitement.

The beach was small, not much bigger than the beach at Nobska Light, but crowded with lots of families. I heard the screams of children playing together. As we walked down the wooden steps to the sand, I spotted lots of colorful umbrellas and a jetty of rocks, stacked on top of one another, running from the shoreline into the water. All four of us stood there for a moment, glancing around at all of the people, searching for a nice spot to sit. Pops led the way, snaking between the crowd, to an open area near the jetty.

Before we removed our shoes, Pops suggested an excursion on the rocks.

"Dad!" Mama protested. "That's just what we need—for you and Michael to fall into the water!"

"Oh, come on! Don't act like you wouldn't have been the first one out there when you were a child, Maggie. You were even crazier than your brother!"

I smiled, hearing Pops call Mama that nickname, which he rarely did. Nana's eyes cut sharply to them. Mama and Pops stared at each other. I watched, wondering who would crack first. Pops' mouth turned slightly up at the corner. Mama noticed and pointed at his face. They both began laughing. Nana rolled her eyes at them.

"Okay," Mama relented, "but please be careful."

"Michael will be careful. Your father will end up falling in." Nana turned to Pops. "If you do, just start swimming to the mainland, and we'll meet you there!"

Pops said nothing in reply. He merely grunted as we headed to the rocks. We held hands as we precariously stepped from rock to rock, steadying ourselves before adding our full weight. Trying to find a good stepping place reminded me of a puzzle. We weaved our way to the end of the jetty, where it lowered into the water and disappeared. We stared out at the high seas for a few minutes.

I tossed a small rock that I had discovered along the way into the ocean. It landed with a modest splash. Pops found a rock settled between two larger ones. He stepped back on his right foot and threw it with his arm parallel to the water. The rock skipped along the surface in four dwindling hops, leaving little ripples behind each one. We turned around on the narrow tip to return when Pops lost his balance and began falling backwards, slowly, as he attempted to lean his body weight forward to counteract gravity. I grabbed his forearms and helped steady him.

Pops sighed in relief. "Thank you, Michael. I can't prove your Nana right by falling in."

We returned to Mama and Nana, who were sitting upon the beach towels. Mama was looking around, smiling at the joy before her. Nana bore a sour expression on her face as if she had just licked a lemon. I wondered how she could possibly be unhappy on such a glorious day. From Mama's carefree countenance, it did not appear to be caused by a fight between them.

As we approached them, Pops shouted at Nana, "Why so sour, pickle? I didn't fall in after all!"

Nana scrunched her nose and furrowed her brow. "No, it's not that." She paused, looked around, and then motioned with her hands. "Just look at all of the niggers on this beach."

All three of us wrenched our necks to look at Nana with our mouths open in shock. I looked again at our surroundings with eyes narrowed by her words and indeed noticed the many Black families enjoying themselves. I had never before seen that many Black families gathered on one beach, intermixed with the White families, all focused on their own pleasure on a beautiful day. I had also never heard Nana speak that way before. With one word, she had transformed into the Southerners that I had seen on TV with venom spewing from their bigoted mouths.

"Mom," Mama said sternly, "please don't use that word around me or Michael."

Nana huffed, looking at Pops to intervene and defend her as he usually did. Pops' face had hardened from shock to an indignant expression, one of disgust. His eyes shifted back to her at last as he spoke.

"Betty …" He hesitated, hunting for the appropriate words. It took him several minutes to find them.

"Betty, I know you grew up hearing that word in a world where Black people weren't really considered people at all but were, instead, reduced to a color."

He halted again, perhaps contemplating whether it was worth continuing, before he resumed. "Our life together has come to be defined by the War, which I don't like to talk about. But Black men volunteered to fight, even though they were segregated from the other men, always kept in their place even when going to their deaths. I've thought about that a lot over the years, about how they wanted to fight for a country that viewed them as second rate, as less than, simply due to their skin color, the same color of their mothers and fathers and their own children, a color precious to them. But, still, they went, just as scared as I had been, just as scared as our son, to fight for what is right and just. And they will forever have my respect. So, I would appreciate it, my love, if you never used that word in my presence again."

And then he walked away. Nana sat there with her mouth wide open, too stunned for rebuttal. Mama and I walked to the shoreline to feel the cool water wash over our feet. Nana's words had utterly shocked me. Despite my efforts to distract myself for the remainder of our time on the beach, they kept returning to the forefront of my thoughts. Nana had always displayed good manners and kindness to others in front of me. Upon further reflection, I had never witnessed her interact with any Black people, as if they did not exist in our world, in our everyday life. I stared intently at the families before me, laughing and swimming, children running and playing. Seeing them made me realize that I had never once seen any Black people visit the beach near our house.

When Pops returned from his long walk past the jetty, farther than I could follow with my eyes, we packed up everything in silence and walked back to catch the ferry. Nana sulked in her seat on the ride back to Falmouth. Mama joined Pops and me at the stern, watching Martha's Vineyard slip away behind the waves. I never heard Nana nor Pops mention the incident after that day. It took a few days, however, for them to act normal in one another's presence. My naive eyes had been opened by our trip to the island, without even catching a glimpse of Martin Luther King, Jr.

CHAPTER 17

GARDEN PARTY

Lucy and I walked to the library early one morning, part of our normal routine now, not long after we returned from Martha's Vineyard. There was a chill in the air as we set off towards downtown through the tunnel of trees, the morning sun shining behind us. Birds were warbling merry tunes, each in their own melody, and darting quickly from tree to tree. Their songs of trees were lifted with the wind, cold and salty, blowing from the sea as it rustled the forest green above our heads.

Lucy asked, "How was your trip to Martha's Vineyard?"

"It was fun," I replied, undecided if I should reveal what happened. I was not sure how to retell the events, afraid Lucy might judge Nana to be a terrible person. Instead, I avoided the particulars. "Lucy, have you ever seen any Black people or anybody that isn't White at our beach?"

Lucy stopped walking and looked skyward, blocked by thick leaves whispering to each other. "No, I guess I haven't. But it's a private beach, so I guess only White people own houses there."

I thought about the sign I had passed dozens of times, always ignoring, which gave notification of the beach being private and only open to residents, not the public.

"In the South, they don't even let Black people visit public beaches."

Lucy reminded me of Nana's disbelief at seeing Black people on Inkwell Beach. Nobody at Inkwell had told them to leave nor did they act like they did not belong there. Nana must have never seen Black people at a beach like that before. It did not excuse her behavior, though.

"Did you finish the book yet?" I asked Lucy, noticing the book within her hand.

"Almost! I'm torn between not being able to put it down and not wanting it to end."

"Well, you need to finish it so I can talk to you about it," I said, afraid I might spoil the book if I spoke further.

Lucy smiled, turned around to face me, and walked backwards. "I don't think it will take me too much longer. I've also been reading a lot about the sit-ins and Freedom Riders in the South lately. I wish I were older and could run away to join them." With her arms outstretched and head tilted back, her smiling face drenched in the sunbeams filtered through the trees, she said, "I want to be a Freedom Rider!"

"Maybe someday," I encouraged her. "We can join together."

"Deal!" Lucy agreed with a handshake.

I paused momentarily outside the library for a glimpse of the three stained-glass windows, which always captured my attention, no matter how many times I saw them. As we walked into the library through the arched doors, I searched for Ms. Prince. I heard her voice from behind her desk, her body blocked by a tall man to whom she was talking. Lucy and I approached and waited for her to finish with the gentleman. Ms. Prince peeked around his frame when she heard us and greeted us warmly.

"Well, hello, Michael!" the gentleman said.

It was then, when he turned to face us, that I realized it was Henry's father, John. I laughed to myself, thinking I should have known it was John since his hair also stuck up in the back like Henry's.

"Hello, Mr. Prince. I didn't realize that was you at first."

"I came to visit my sister this morning. Who is your friend?" He looked at Lucy.

"This is my friend Lucy. Lucy, this is Mr. John Prince, Henry's father."

Lucy held out her hand for a handshake, which amused Mr. Prince.

"Nice to meet you, Mr. Prince. We walk here several mornings a week. Henry looks almost exactly like you but different somehow. Maybe your noses or eyes are different, but I'd have to examine you side by side," Lucy expounded cheerfully.

"Yes, I love their visits," Ms. Prince remarked softly, perhaps to kindly remind Lucy to lower her voice.

"Wonderful. And, please, both of you call me John. I don't like all that formality."

Ms. Prince asked, "Can I help you find anything particular today, children?"

"Yes, I would like some books on the moon or space to help me learn how to use my new telescope," I answered.

"Let me take a look, dear. I will bring them to your usual table." Ms. Prince turned around to rummage through the filing cabinet.

Lucy retreated with her book to our table in the back.

John asked, "You have a telescope, Michael?"

"Yes, I just saved enough money to buy it for my tenth birthday in May. I'm still learning how to use it. I'm keeping a moon journal to track the phases."

"I'm a bit of an amateur myself, but I have a telescope and can give you a few pointers, if you'd like."

"That would be great! I don't really know what I'm doing," I admitted.

"Well, it helps to have someone who can show you. I have a group of friends that meet every now and then. One of them is quite serious about it, and he helped me a lot when I was just beginning."

"That's cool. It would be nice to have someone who knows what they're doing. Are you coming to our garden party this weekend?"

"Yes, I believe we are."

"I will set up my telescope. Maybe you could help me then if we have a clear night," I suggested.

"Sounds like a plan. I prefer to be up in the stars than talking at a party any day. Until Saturday." John bid me farewell with a wide smile and left the library.

After that, I found myself unable to concentrate on any of the books that Ms. Prince brought to me, which were not quite the subject material for which I had been searching. They were more children's books about space rather than guides to finding celestial objects. I had not the heart to tell Ms. Prince this, however, for fear of hurting her feelings. I contentedly spent the remainder of our time at the library daydreaming, first about the party and then, staring at the shifting brilliancy of the blue stained glass in the sunlight, about the moon and planets. When Lucy eventually suggested leaving the library, I was startled to discover my body still in the library when my mind had been above the clouds.

The day of the garden party finally arrived. I watched as two men unloaded a large table and chairs from a trailer pulled behind their truck. Pops was in charge of overseeing the delivery and set up of these, mostly because Nana and Mama were inside cooking and wanted him out of their way, achieved by cleverly assigning him a task. I dawdled outside with Pops for the entire afternoon and then set up my telescope, as there were no rain clouds in sight, before running inside to dress for the party. Lucy and Aunt Louise arrived earlier than the others. Lucy wore a cherry red dress, the same color as her bathing suit that first summer. Her short curls had been pulled back with only a few pieces falling around her face.

Aunt Louise had brought her liquor stash to our house the day before in her car, proclaiming herself the party's bartender, despite Nana's insistence of one being unnecessary. Aunt Louise scoffed at this notion and made a claim, irrefragable by her manner of speaking, that "all exceptional parties need stiff drinks to part the lips and loosen the tongue." I caught Nana rolling her eyes at this assertion. After Aunt Louise unloaded her haul and left, Nana declared her insane.

That evening, Aunt Louise walked into the beach house in an off-the-shoulder black cocktail dress, shouting to announce her arrival. I lingered in the front yard with Lucy and laughed as I heard Aunt Louise's screams from outside. I imagined Nana rolling her eyes again. Not long after, our final guests pulled into the driveway—John, Elizabeth, Henry, and Ms. Prince. When I spotted their car, I called for Pops to help me greet them, eager to introduce him to John, who seemed, to me, extraordinarily similar to Pops. Lucy went inside to tell the others. I ran to Henry's door first and jumped into him for a hug, careful not to damage the dark red roses he carried, followed by a quick wave to the rest after they exited the car.

I dragged Pops over to the group and said, "This is my grandfather George. Pops, this is John and Elizabeth, the parents of Henry, who you've met before. And this is Ms. Prince, Henry's aunt and my favorite librarian."

"Welcome, everyone!" Pops said, his deep voice booming.

"Thank you for inviting us," Elizabeth replied in her elegant accent. "Michael, would you please show us inside so we can take these dishes to your mother?"

"Sure! Follow me." I led the way up the stone path and into the house.

Pops and John waited outside while Elizabeth, Ms. Prince, and Henry trailed behind me to the kitchen. I was relieved when Henry took over the introductions so I could dash back outside to

Pops and John. I found them chatting by the edge of the cliff. Pops was pointing at the water, explaining something. I squeezed Pops from behind to subtly announce my return.

"Hey, buddy," Pops said before jumping right back into his story.

I waited until there was a break in their conversation. "Can I show you my telescope, John? It's right over here." I pointed to the left of where we stood.

"Absolutely!" John first observed the exterior of the telescope, walking all the way around it. Then, he moved closer and gently rubbed the scope. "May I?" he asked, holding out his hand with the palm up.

"Of course," I replied, liking him all the more for asking.

John peered through the finderscope, swiveling the main scope around at different angles. When he moved away from the eyepiece, he smiled broadly at me, the happiest I had seen him since we first met.

"Michael, you have a fine telescope. I can't wait to give her a try later tonight."

I felt happy to have John's approval. Pops then recounted the entire story of when we bought the telescope and my determination to purchase that particular one. He loved to tell that story. Once Pops had finished, they both chuckled in the same manner with a slight backwards tilt and their bellies pushed out.

"I don't think we can hide out here all night," Pops bemoaned.

We decided it was time to join the others and slowly marched inside the house.

"There you are," said Nana, carrying a casserole dish outside to the back patio. "Come on, everyone is out back."

We followed Nana outside, where the remaining introductions were made. Aunt Louise, eyeing the empty hands of Pops and John, ran inside and swiftly returned with two drinks.

She handed one to each. "Old-fashioned."

"Ugh, I am not!" Pops scoffed as Aunt Louise turned back and laughed briefly before sniffing out empty glasses.

Aunt Louise kept the drinks flowing as people waltzed from group to group of scattered conversations and eventually settled down for dinner. The table was beautifully set with a white tablecloth, rows of candles across the entire width, and Henry's roses, uprooted to an etched glass vase, in the center. The candlelight bent and bounced off the glassware and water, sending shimmering reflections dancing upon the tablecloth. My gaze lifted to the glowing faces around the table, cast in a golden hue by the afterglow of sunset and the flickering candles. Umbras fell on faces, shifting in the flame's glow throughout the evening as darkness slowly descended. I looked up in the twilight sky for a glimpse of the moon in the east but could not find it from where I sat. In a quiet pause, the susurrus of the sea and leaves overtook all else as Mama rose from her chair. She wore a simple blue dress that colored her gray eyes the same shade of light blue.

Mama shyly raised her glass, a faint rouge coloring her cheeks. "You all are very dear friends and family. I'd like to thank you for coming tonight. Cheers!" She took a sip of her drink, followed by everyone else. "I'm not one for clever toasts. If you desire one of those, I'll hand it over to Henry."

Henry smirked. "Thanks for putting me on the spot." He stood up, not appearing to mind the spotlight at all. "Hmm, all I have is—To empty heads, full hearts, and, depending on your proclivity, half-full or half-empty glasses. Cheers!"

Aunt Louise interjected, "If it's up to me, young man, it'll be full glasses all night! Cheers!"

Everyone laughed and replied, "Cheers!" before taking another drink.

I could not recall a happier evening or one with such ample laughter and cheer, perhaps due to Aunt Louise. Lucy and I were even able to sneak a drink of Nana's red wine as she seemed quite drunk and did not notice at all. We giggled as we looked at one another, the burning sensation lingering in our throats as we swallowed the contraband sips. Before dessert, Henry walked to our end and crouched down beside Nana, who sat at the head of the table.

Henry said charmingly, "I do hope you're enjoying yourself tonight."

"Oh, yes, I am quite enjoying myself." Nana giggled before taking another sip of her wine. She belched loudly but seemed too tipsy to care about such matters as polite manners, not excusing herself.

Henry smiled but dared not laugh at her. "I have a favor to ask of you. Do you remember any embarrassing stories of Margaret from childhood that you might share with me?"

I laughed and looked for Mama, who had just returned from inside and noticed their little chat; her eyes narrowed to thin, suspicious slits. I supposed Henry sought his revenge for the Peter Pan story, as he had promised Mama.

Nana replied sharply, "Oh, sure! The only problem is there are so many, it will be hard to choose just one."

"Excellent!" Henry fixed his eyes on Mama and smirked at her.

Mama's mouth opened as she surmised, based on Henry's pleased expression, the reason for his special attention to Nana. Mama shot up from her chair, walked over to the other side of Nana, and interrupted, determined to stop the storytelling. "I must know of what you are speaking."

Nana huffed, "Well, if you *must* know, we are discussing embarrassing stories about you, which I revealed were plentiful."

Mama's sharpened eyes stared daggers at Henry. Mortified by being the one revisiting old memories, she asked, "How could you? I thought you had forgotten about Peter Pan."

"Peter Pan never forgets," Henry whispered, quite amused with himself.

"The first one that comes to mind," Nana said, ignoring their Peter Pan business, "happened in elementary school at St. Mary's."

I listened more intently once I heard mention of my school. Lucy also appeared quite enthralled with the conversation. Mama's eyes shifted left and right as she tried to guess the chosen embarrassment.

"Margaret's father and I were called into the school to meet with the principal."

"Oh, God," Mama beseeched softly.

"Yes, God does have something to do with this one. We were called into the principal's office because of a love letter written by Margaret."

"Ah, young love," Henry commented.

"Not quite," Nana countered. "This love letter, which was quite long and detailed, was not addressed to a classmate."

Nana stared directly into Mama's eyes before continuing. "The passionate love letter, which even included a poem, was addressed to Father Mark, the priest."

We all erupted into laughter, except Mama, who covered her face, no doubt bright red, with her hands. Henry almost fell over from laughing so hard. He eventually, when he was able, stepped over next to Mama with tears in his eyes.

Henry said, "Well, at least you had heavenly high standards, even as a child."

Mama lurched at him, grabbing his arms held up defensively against her attack. She attempted to push him but was unable to budge his body at all with her small frame.

"'All children, except one, grow up,'" Mama said. (Barrie 7)

"Is that a statement or a threat? Now, now, what would Father Mark say to this violence, Margaret?"

Mama began laughing at his reproach, despite her anger, while they continued their pretend battle. They halted after their laughter overpowered them and won. Lucy and I could not help but join in as they cackled and snorted until they were both weeping. The only one immune to their frivolity was Nana, who simply sat observing their hysterics with critical eyes.

When they were quite finished and composed, which took some time, Henry said to Nana, "Oh, thank you for that. You really must come with George to my bookshop one morning for tea. I would love to hear more stories like this one." Before returning to his seat, he leaned in closer to Nana. "I would also pay for a copy of that love letter, if ever you come upon it."

Mama watched him walk back, about to return to her own seat at the other end, when Nana grabbed her arm and postponed her departure.

"Margaret, I need a word with you. I have seen the way you act around that man, the way you look at that man. Everyone who has eyes sees it! You are not a child but a married woman. Start acting like it!"

Everyone stared at them. Nana's mind had been pickled in the red wine for too long. She had lost all restraint. Her scolding of Mama had not been spoken privately but shouted for all to hear, including Henry.

Mama ran inside the house. Aunt Louise, the only one completely unfazed by the alcohol, stood up instantly, gazed directly into Nana's glazed eyes, huffed disapprovingly, and followed after Mama. Nobody else knew what to do, apart from Pops and John, who took advantage of the diversion and snuck around the house to the front yard, as if they had been waiting for such an opportunity to occur. Elizabeth leaned in to talk with Henry, who appeared upset. I abandoned my chair and chased after Pops and John, grabbing my composition notebook from my makeshift bedroom on the front porch before joining them.

CHAPTER 18

WAXING GIBBOUS

I had seen the moon during the afternoon, hanging low in the southeastern sky like a pale ghost, barely visible in the daytime light. Seeing the moon during the day always surprised me, even though I knew it never truly disappeared. The three of us were now able to see the moon from the front yard.

John remarked, "We will need to move your telescope for a better view or wait a bit until the moon has risen higher."

I had my suspicions that they wanted to escape all of the unfolding drama.

"Michael, what if we take your telescope down to the beach?" Pops suggested.

"That sounds like a good idea! Do you think we can carry it without falling down the steps?"

"I figure we've got a fifty-fifty shot."

"Don't worry. I can carry it down if you lead the way with a flashlight. We fought in a war, George. Can we not do this?" John said resolutely.

"Indeed. If only I hadn't drunk so much tonight," Pops lamented.

John laughed. "Ah, my friend, you must learn to sip slowly."

I ran back to the front porch and retrieved my flashlight before we began our descent. Pops insisted on going down first, for he did not trust himself and feared if he fell, he might take the rest of us tumbling down like dominoes. I went down second so I could hold the light for John, who trailed with the telescope in his hands awkwardly. We climbed down each step sluggishly, at a pace even slower than my very first trip down the cliff. It felt as if we would never make it to the bottom until, at last, we exhausted all the steps. John placed the telescope near the shoreline, at a distance where the angle allowed me to reach the eyepiece, in perfect view of the humped moon sitting high above our heads in the dark sky.

"I saw the moon earlier when it rose in the southeast. It's a waxing gibbous, just a few days after first quarter, according to my notebook."

"That's correct, Michael. I'm impressed by your knowledge. The moon is easy to find because it's so big, but it's good practice for you," John explained as I placed my eye on the finderscope's eyepiece.

I lifted the main scope up while I scanned the sky for the moon, which appeared quite suddenly in my field of vision as a bright, mottled object.

"I found it," I said to John and Pops, waiting patiently behind me.

John instructed, "Now that you're centered on your target, you can transition to the main scope for a magnified view. When you're searching for further objects like planets, you may need to also adjust the main scope after the finderscope."

"Planets? I can see planets with my telescope?"

"Sure! In August, Jupiter and Saturn become visible in the east, perfect for viewing in this very spot!"

"Can you see Saturn's rings?" asked Pops, smiling like a child.

"Yes, you can see the rings of Saturn along with the stripes and moons of Jupiter! One day, I promise to show you the planets, Michael. But first, you must practice on the moon and truly appreciate its splendor."

I walked to the side of the telescope and placed my right eye on the eyepiece with my left eye closed. I beheld the moon, filling the entire field of view with only a portion of its surface. For the first time, I saw the moon as if it had been pulled down in front of me. I was able to distinguish the speckled dark spots and craters, the depths and ridges around their edges. I paused, moved back a bit, and looked at Pops and John with the broadest smile upon my face.

"It's amazing, huh? This is probably the best time to observe the moon. When it's full, there's too much glare from the sun, which can damage your eyes if you look at it for too long." John approached the telescope and pointed up at the moon. "Look along the edge of light and dark. That's called the terminator. Along the terminator, you can see even more details in the shadows cast from the mountains."

I returned to the telescope and began scanning the terminator up and down the moon as John instructed.

"Look for a large crater, along or perhaps next to the terminator, in the center of dark spots. This crater is called Copernicus, named after the astronomer."

"I think I see it! So, the holes are craters, but what are the dark spots?" I asked John.

"Ancient astronomers once believed them to be oceans and seas, giving them names such as Mare Serenitatis, Sea of Serenity, and Sinus Iridum, Bay of Rainbows. They are still called these names today, but now we know they are actually plains of lava, not water."

"Sea of Serenity," I repeated, thinking of how Mama would love their poetic names. I attempted to guess the location of each. "Pops, it's your turn!" I relinquished the telescope reluctantly.

While Pops took his turn, interjected with plenty of "oh, golly" and chuckles, I stared at the moon, attempting to memorize its geography, hoping one day I might point up at any landmark and recite its name. From the direction of the stone steps, I heard Lucy calling my name over the perishing waves behind me. I ran to her.

"Oh, here you are! I looked everywhere for you! Henry and his mother are searching for John. I believe they wish to leave."

"All right, but before you deliver that news, you must come see the moon." I beckoned her towards the telescope.

"Hello, Lucy," said Pops. "Come have a look."

I felt as if, upon the beach, we had blast off to the moon, away from the party and all that had occurred. I did not wish to return to the ground yet. Lucy skipped on the sand in her bare feet, her shoes beside the bottom step, over to the telescope. I watched her as she approached the telescope cautiously and bent to the level of the eyepiece. She looked fixedly at the moon while she adjusted the scope in tiny increments, as if she were not a novice. Lucy, open-mouthed in astonishment, said nothing the entire time.

Alas, against my wishes, our trip to the moon ended when Lucy, finished with the telescope, walked over to us and said, "I think we should all return to the house now. Mrs. Betty is sobbing all alone on the back patio, and Mrs. Elizabeth and Henry are looking for you, John."

I turned and peered at the moon one last time that night before we trudged up the stone steps to what waited for us at the top.

CHAPTER 19

GHOSTS

I could not have imagined the glaring contrast between the quiet of moon gazing on the beach and the howling sobs of Nana behind the beach house, exacerbated by her continued drinking, alone, performing a one-woman opera. We heard her tragic aria at the top of the cliff. Pops turned around and seemingly considered fleeing back down the steps.

John walked over to Pops, staring at the beach below, and patted his shoulder. "Courage, soldier."

Pops knew he had nowhere to hide. He gulped, turned, and marched to a battle he could never win. After we returned, Henry and his family left. Aunt Louise stormed outside, expressed her disdain for how Nana had behaved, which had ruined the party, and then abandoned all hope of the party's revival.

Sleep did not appear to remedy the situation, for a lingering headache plagued Nana the following morning. She sat at the kitchen table in her sunglasses, refusing to speak to anyone during breakfast. Nana and Pops left shortly thereafter, a week or two before they planned to depart, without a word spoken between Mama and Nana. I felt sad as I watched them drive away from the beach house, stubborn pride preventing Nana from apologizing. All the happy times left to be shared vanished with the disappearing view of their car.

Mama and I spent that Sunday quietly with much on our minds, just the two of us. Mama did not mention what had occurred at the party, but I knew it replayed in her mind repeatedly, turning like a film reel. The following Monday, we resumed our normal routine and chose to omit from our recollection the tainted parts of the garden party and the trip to Martha's Vineyard, both caused by Nana, as when looking back at old photos selectively recalls only the happy moments associated with them. From the garden party, I chose to remember the glow of faces—the merry ones around the table and the moon's through my telescope for the first time.

After dinner on Wednesday evening, I walked down the stone steps to the beach with Mama, Aunt Louise, and Lucy. Gold flecked the western horizon. A few wispy clouds, thin like paper, hung high in the darkening sky with shades of deep purple and pink underneath. To the east, above the ocean, a hazy pink blended into the blue sky. We walked along the beach towards the south, in the opposite direction of the boardwalk, as the light dimmed slowly, as if a veil fell around us, draping us in shadows. Darkness had suddenly and completely consumed the light by the time we walked back. I looked to the water and spied a massive orange object peeking over the dark blue waves. For a brief moment, I was confused by what I saw, wondering if it was an illusion, until it grew bigger before my eyes.

"Look, Lucy. The full Strawberry Moon is rising."

We watched in wonder as the moon inched above the water, bewitched, as if it were instead an orb levitating by magic.

When it sat just above the horizon, Lucy said, "Oh, it looks so big and orange tonight!"

Indeed, I agreed with Lucy's observation. I had never seen the moon appear quite that large before, and I did not know the reason why. I dared not speak, only stare at the moon, revealing itself to us. I gazed upon the dark spots and tried to recall their names—Sea of Serenity, Sea of Tranquility. My eyes, even when squinting, were not powerful enough to see the craters nor the shadows of the mountains. Although I could not see them at that moment, I knew that I had discovered some of the moon's mysteries through my telescope, as if we now shared a secret unknown to most. We watched the moon rise out of the water and then far above it, seemingly growing smaller and paler the higher it rose. Lucy and I then pretended we were on the moon, walking on its surface all the way back to the stone steps, where we parted at the top.

As I lay in bed that night upon the porch, despite my bed inside being empty, my mind replayed the rising of the Strawberry Moon. Unable to quiet my mind, I tiptoed out of my bed to the front edge of the porch and looked up through the screen into the small slice of southeastern sky visible to me. Before me, surrounded by prodigious black, was the moon, perfectly round, shining a pallid yellow. I had sought the moon but was still overcome by its appearance and beauty, just as magnificent as the very first time I saw it. I smiled, content to catch one last glimpse to carry back to my bed and sustain me until I fell asleep.

I jumped into bed and heard the loud and constant trilling of crickets and katydids. A steady chirr thrummed in the background while chirps overlapped in short snippets of three, similar to a creaking door. From time to time, the wind whistled through the leaves. I closed my eyes, my wandering mind hypnotized by the soothing cadence, and surrendered to rest. At first, the sounds of night, typically muted by my bedroom walls, had kept me awake, but after becoming accustomed to the wind, rustling leaves, ebbing waves, and insects, I indeed preferred, as Mama had predicted, sleeping on the porch to anywhere else, including my bedroom at home.

Not an hour since I slept, I was startled awake by a noise beyond the porch. I wearily opened my eyes and allowed them to shut once more until I heard the noise again, more clearly the second time than the first. It sounded like my name. I sat up in bed for a better listen and discovered the voice of Lucy. I walked over to the screen door, scanning the front yard for her, and spotted a dark figure amongst the other shadows.

"Lucy?" I whispered, hoping it would be her that answered.

"Michael," Lucy replied quietly below the porch, "I'm sorry if I woke you, but I couldn't sleep and found myself walking here. Too sleepy for an adventure?"

I opened the porch door slowly, to diminish the sound of squeaky hinges, and joined Lucy.

"What kind of adventure?" I asked, suddenly not tired at all.

"A ghost hunt, if your curiosity must know."

I laughed quietly. "Where shall we hunt ghosts?"

"On the beach, of course. Grab your flashlight, unless you're too scared."

I crept back onto the porch and returned quickly with my flashlight. I paused for a second before closing the screen door and listened for any sound of Mama, hoping she would not wake to find my bed empty. Part of me felt exhilarated to be sneaking away without permission. Without saying a word, we walked over to the cliff and began descending the stone steps, the same steps six-year-old Lucy had longed to climb. The full moon hung high in the sky, lighting our adventure down to the beach. At the bottom, Lucy led the way south, the direction we had walked earlier that evening before watching the moonrise.

Lucy said, "Follow my example," as she began sweeping her flashlight from the water's edge up to the sand and back repeatedly.

The tide had risen much higher on the beach than earlier. I obeyed, equally intrigued and afraid of the hunt and what Lucy had in mind. Together, we shined our flashlights back and forth as a spotlight, searching for what I did not know. We continued anyway, for Lucy looked quite determined to find something. We walked in this manner for some time with the moon reflecting fully upon us, the wind blowing us to the reaching surf. I was beginning to think it was all just a jest until Lucy touched my arm, our steps and flashlights frozen in one spot.

"There! Look!" Lucy said in hushed exultation.

I concentrated, trying to identify anything unusual, when something tiny scuttled across the sand and disappeared.

"What's that?" I asked Lucy.

"Ghost crab. Come on! Let's find more."

We resumed the repetitive scanning of our lights, searching for the faintest movement among the little mounds of sand and debris washed ashore. It was tedious work but with a satisfying reward when two black eyes peered at us, petrified above their front claws and legs arched on each side. As we attempted to inch closer, for a better view of their translucent shells, the crabs scurried safely to a hole dug perfectly round in the sand. We shined our lights into the holes but could see nothing. This game carried on until we had walked further south than earlier in the evening.

I looked up once more, as our pace slowed, to find the full moon still shining high above our heads. I did not know why I always sought the moon, perhaps just to ensure it still hung there, to feel the comfort its constancy provided. I thought of Mama and prayed she slumbered peacefully, ignorant of my absence.

We stood upon the beach, our bare feet sinking into the sticky sand, wet from the rushing tide's advance. Lucy's gaze had been captured by something ahead of us, which utterly transfixed her. I looked from her to the object her eyes were set upon, expecting to find a horde of ghost crabs. Instead, a massive rock, with a dark and jagged silhouette, rose before us and blocked our path. I shined my flashlight from the bottom to the top and then left to right for an estimation of its size. It was the cliff itself, jutting into the water. The sand ended at its ascent from the earth.

"I think that's the sea cave my cousin David told me about," Lucy said as she shined her flashlight into a small rocky entrance in the cliff, surrounded by water.

Her words reminded me of the mistaken ruby cave that I had imagined on our drive that first summer.

"The cave he said was haunted?"

"Yes." Lucy turned to look at me.

For a moment, I considered this to be a part of her game, but her expression dismissed this thought. "I'm sure he was just trying to scare you, Lucy. Look, the entrance is underwater. The ghost or monster or witch would need to be a strong swimmer to come after us."

Lucy cracked a smile that faded quickly. "In that case," she said before she walked closer to the cliff.

She screamed as loudly as she could, releasing bottled sadness or rage, which echoed off of the rock and blew away with the wind. Afterwards, we both decided not to linger around the cave and focused on gaining some distance between us and it, just in case. We did not speak until the cave was out of sight.

"Do you need to talk about anything? I mean, it seems like something is bothering you, and I'm a good listener. You can tell me anything, Lucy."

Lucy sighed. "I've tried to bring it up many times this summer. I feel like I might explode if I don't talk about it with someone. My Aunt Louise doesn't want to discuss her. It's about my mom."

I had never heard Lucy talk much about her mother. She spoke of her father fondly and often but not her mother.

Lucy said, a weary heaviness to her voice, "When I was five years old, my mom came to pick me up early from school. She told me she wanted to see the Grand Canyon, which sounded like fun to me. First, we stopped at a department store and bought new dresses, shoes, makeup, and jewelry, bags and bags of new things. Mama put on one of her new dresses before we left. I remember her looking in the mirror, admiring herself, before she pulled out her new red lipstick and applied it skillfully to her lips, staining them a cherry color. She glanced at me in the mirror, watching her. She turned and applied the red lipstick to my lips also. I thought I looked a bit like a tiny clown, not beautiful like her, but I smiled, happy to match her in some way. We left the department store and began our drive out west. We ate in restaurants, slept in hotels, and did whatever we wanted. I had never felt happier until one morning a few days later. I didn't even know what city or state we were in. One morning, it was as if she had fallen from the highest mountain into the deepest pit. I couldn't get her out of bed. At first, I thought she was just really tired and needed to rest, so I didn't bother her, even though I was hungry. Mama stayed in bed, crying intermittently, unable to do anything. I picked up the telephone in our room but realized I didn't know our home number. I begged Mama to call my dad or drive us home. All she did was lie in bed and stare blankly at a wall. She eventually called my dad after I asked the man working the front desk of the hotel for some food. My dad had no idea where we went. She never told him anything."

Lucy paused and inhaled deeply. "So, you see, that is how my mom has always been—unpredictable. Either end of extremes.

Her days of bliss, which always ended in reckless despair, were never worth the misery. Would you like to fly like a bird for a few minutes if you knew you'd come crashing back down at the end? Right before we drove here, she left again. I don't know where she went or if she'll ever return."

With the last word, Lucy began wailing like the little girl wearing cherry red lipstick. She collapsed onto the sand, unable, in that moment, to bear the maturity beyond her years. I knelt down beside her and enveloped her jerking body in my arms. I squeezed her firmly as she cried, her salty tears mixing with the waves that rushed over us before being carried out to sea.

CHAPTER 20

SEA OF RAINS

June ended quietly, full of many memorable events. Warmer weather arrived with July. Mama and I spent our time alone or in the company of Lucy and Aunt Louise. The four of us walked downtown for the Fourth of July parade. Lucy and I sat on the sidewalk, watching the decorated cars and floats drive past, and rushed to grab candy tossed onto the street. That night, we spread a large blanket on the sand near the boardwalk. Lucy and I lay on our backs gazing at the sky, eagerly waiting for nightfall. A loud boom, sounding like a rocket, interrupted the chatter of people. The sound whizzed higher and higher above us until it exploded into colorful streaks against a black canvas. Mama and Aunt Louise joined us on the blanket, all four of us enthralled by the starbursts splattered across the night sky.

Later in July, we celebrated Lucy's birthday with a trip to the diner. I felt quite content with our predictable routine for the rest of summer. I had enjoyed the busy days of June and often found myself, in silent times, contemplating their events but reveled in the tranquility of lazy beach days and reading together on the back patio in the evenings, utilizing every last drop of sunlight. The remaining summer days swayed as gently and as slowly as Ella Fitzgerald's crooning on "Summertime."

The nights came alive when Lucy and I snuck down to the beach and walked to the cave, which became a little tradition for us. Although we dared not venture inside the cave, even when the tide was low enough to permit us, it transformed from a frightening place full of imaginary ghosts into our sanctuary, where we shouted our secrets and fears and pain and they remained, a final resting place for our mental hauntings. I had witnessed the relief in Lucy's face that night of hunting ghost crabs when she screamed at the rocks. Telling me the story of her mother and her issues did not solve them, but rather, their escape allowed Lucy to grieve and process them.

Following her example on a subsequent night, I screamed for as long and as loudly as I possibly could. I had always been a quiet, reserved person who disliked loud noises, but there was something absolutely liberating in the shouting. Once I finished screaming, I revealed to Lucy what Nana had said at Inkwell Beach and how confused her words and behavior towards Mama during the garden party had made me. Lucy listened thoughtfully and did not offer judgment, as I feared, but compassion and understanding. We talked extensively about both incidents and the sorrow they caused me.

We did not see Henry for more than three weeks after the garden party, longer than we had ever gone between visits. I believed Mama to be too embarrassed to face him or his family. I missed their company but did not speak of them for fear of upsetting Mama. We also avoided the library and Ms. Prince during this time. One morning, three and a half weeks after the garden party, Mama and I unexpectedly walked downtown to Henry's bookshop. Thick, menacing clouds filled the entire sky, blocking the sun and appearing as though they would release rain upon our heads at any moment. Mama carried an umbrella, just in case, as we trekked under the ominous gloom in quick steps to avoid the rain we somehow felt certain would come. The morning weather felt odd, more humid than usual, as if we walked through an invisible fog, trapping heat and making it feel warmer than it typically did at that hour. As we passed the park on our right, I looked at the tall trees along the far border of the open green space. They were stagnant, standing perfectly straight like soldiers protecting a fortress, instead of gently swaying. I noticed their leaves had been flipped over to reveal their pale green undersides. The trees looked peculiar without their summertime vibrancy, as they often do before a storm.

Upon our arrival at the bookshop, we both looked to Henry's desk, where he usually waited to help customers. Stacks of papers and books, large and small, covered his desk in a chaotic mess. Henry was not there, only his round eyeglasses, which he removed occasionally when he appeared tired, along with his favorite mug, the string of a tea bag overhanging one side. His voice could not be heard anywhere. Mama did not want to wait; the reason why I knew not, since we had no appointments nor plans of any kind the entire day. She removed a thick envelope from her purse, addressed to Henry, and placed it against his mug of tea. We were about to exit when we heard footfalls bounding down the stairs that led from Henry's apartment.

Henry's jolly voice called ahead of his body. "My apologies for keeping you waiting!"

We paused as Henry arrived at his desk, put on his spectacles, spotted the letter, and then glanced at us, lingering by the front door. A smile immediately spread upon his lips and then pervaded his entire face, as if nothing awkward had occurred and he wished to see no one else in the world more than us. Mama's eyes, which looked apprehensive upon seeing Henry before our escape, softened at his reaction and by the time she walked back towards him, sparkled with life once more. I ran ahead of Mama to greet Henry with a hug. I desperately wanted us to remain friends. It seemed unfair to lose a friendship over someone else's words, even if they were Nana's.

"Good morning, Henry," Mama said, light blue overtaking the gray in her eyes.

"Good morning!" Henry returned in song form with a devilish grin. "Have you been avoiding me, Margaret?"

His question surprised Mama. Scarlet red flushed her face and then cascaded down her neck and chest before vanishing slowly. She bent her head and smiled before looking up at him again.

"Perhaps," she said, not quite admitting to evasion. "I left a letter for you. I wanted to apologize to you, your parents, and your aunt. I admit that I write the words better than I speak them."

Henry stepped from behind the desk closer to Mama. "Oh, Margaret, apologize for what? You did nothing wrong. I shall read your letter and convey your apology to my family, if you wish.

Actually, I'm so glad you both are here. I will be traveling soon to see my little brother in England. My parents have gone on ahead of me and wanted me to tell you goodbye and they hope to see you next summer."

Henry then walked back to his desk and began rummaging through its contents, opening every drawer. He touched the top of his head and muttered to himself, "Now, where did I put it?" He looked up at us, staring at him in amusement, and explained, "You see, I hid something important, and now I can't remember where I hid it." He stood there a minute, his eyes shifting back and forth as he tried to remember, and then said, "Aha!" before opening the wide middle desk drawer.

I could not help but laugh at how his hair stuck up where he had rubbed it.

He removed something from the drawer and said to me, "Oh, yes, laugh at me, funny guy, but what I hid is something for *you!*" Henry laughed as he acknowledged, "I'm rubbish at organization!" He handed it to me. "It's from my father."

I inspected the item after I unfolded it. It was a map of a destination I had only visited in my imagination—the moon. The names of landmarks, printed on the blue-green surface, filled every inch. I recognized a few of the ones John had taught me. I looked to the left of the middle and found Copernicus, the large crater. Above Copernicus, I read the name Mare Imbrium, Sea of Rains, one I had not heard John mention that night on the beach.

I peered over the top of the map, beaming at Henry. "Please tell your father thank you! I wish I could tell him in person."

"I'll tell him, Michael. He told me to advise you to study the moon map for your next viewing together."

"I promise." I folded up the moon map once again.

"I think we should be going," Mama said with a hint of quivering sadness. "I suppose we must say our goodbyes now since we won't see you until next summer."

Henry sighed heavily. "Indeed, you are right." He grabbed my shoulders and pulled me into him for another hug. "I'll miss you, Michael."

I wrapped my arms around him, the map grasped in one hand, and squeezed him tightly with my eyes closed. I inhaled his scent—crisp, new books mixed with peppermint—and felt his warmth envelop me until I pulled away.

"I'll miss you too, Henry. It won't be the same here without you." I professed this sentiment easily, for Henry's absence would feel the same as waking one morning to find the ocean had evaporated overnight. He felt as integral to our summers as the beach itself.

Mama walked over for her goodbye with Henry. Instead of a full hug like mine, she only leaned in with the top half of her body for a sort of strange partial hug. Henry seemed uncertain about how to approach this farewell embrace and kissed her on the cheek softly, a surprise, it appeared, even to him.

"Goodbye, Margaret. I shall write to you of any new books I discover, if that's all right with you."

"Of course! Michael and I love your books and letters. We look forward to them. Oh, please be safe on your journey to visit your brother. And tell Elizabeth and John that we loved meeting them and hope to see them again soon."

"I will."

I thought I saw tears pooling in his eyes, glistening behind his glasses. We turned and left, pausing at the door for one more look and goodbye. As we stepped out, Mama dropped the umbrella into the bin beside the door. When we passed by the front window, I saw Henry opening Mama's letter. I looked up at Mama to see tears dripping slowly down her face.

She noticed me observing her and sniffled. "I hate goodbyes."

The wind blew wildly on our walk back to the beach house as the storm finally approached. I wondered why Mama had left the umbrella at Henry's bookshop when we might need it. Luckily, it was mostly our tears that fell on our walk back. We made it all the way to the tunnel of trees before the rain finally poured from the sky. We ran through the tunnel, the trees swaying violently around us, up the pathway, and safely onto the refuge of the porch. We watched the rain together, entranced by the pounding drops bouncing off the ground, blown sideways by the wind.

Before she retreated indoors, Mama recited:

Have you ever seen
A waltz between
The wind and drops of rain
Up and down the pavement
On a cloudy summer day?

I remained on the porch, alone, to watch the enchanting dance between the wind and rain. I loved how the summer rain painted the trees and grass a bright green right before my eyes, the hue swelling into a verdant glow with each drop. The rain continued for the rest of the day, leaving little seas of rain behind in the yard.

PART 3 – 1965

CHAPTER 21

CALM BEFORE THE STORM

I looked back on the end of summer in 1961, after Nana and Pops and then Henry had left, and overwhelmingly remembered its calm. Dad had been promoted at work and was unable to visit us at the beach as planned, so Mama and I surprised him and returned home a week early. We missed the end of summer dance in the little park, but I was ready to resume our typical lives at home. I spent the remainder of my summer playing baseball with my friends at the park. On the weekends, Mama, Dad, and I picnicked on lazy afternoons. Sometimes Pops joined us, without a sulking Nana, and we flew a kite together while Mama sat contentedly on a blanket under the shade of a tall oak tree, squinting one eye and laughing when the sun broke through the branches.

Just before I returned to school, Dad suggested I go to work with him one day. He was perhaps even more excited than I was that morning as we stepped in front of his building. I gasped as I followed each story of the towering buildings with my eyes, one at a time, all the way up to the top. As we made our way inside and up to his office, everyone we passed said good morning to us. They all seemed to know Dad. The men shook his hand and laughed as he cracked quick jokes that did not make sense to me. Dad must have spent many hours around his coworkers while we were at the beach. I no longer pondered how he passed the time on his own in the city. I watched as he interacted with them, dressed in his nice blue suit which perfectly fit his tall frame of 6 feet 4 inches, transforming into a charismatic actor with an easy smile and swift charm.

I spent most of the day alone in Dad's new office while he attended meetings. Thankfully, a large window in his office overlooked the street. I watched people walking on the sidewalk below, all in a hurry, and wondered where they were going and for what purpose. Never-ending traffic lined the road with cars, no more than an inch or two between them, honking repeatedly. I did not tell Dad, when we finally went home that evening, how relieved I was to leave after a boring day nor did I tell Mama, when she asked about the day's events, about all of the women who embarrassingly flirted and swooned around Dad, bringing him coffee or creating reasons to visit his office. On the elevator ride down upon our departure, Dad talked to a woman. She winked and smiled at me, revealing a smudge of red lipstick on her front tooth.

I overheard her asking, "Are you going for drinks with everyone on Friday, Jimmy?"

Dad replied, "Well, I'll have to ask the wife now." He leaned in closer and whispered something into her ear, which made her giggle.

"Nobody," as Dad referred to her when I asked her name, hugged Dad goodbye and tousled my hair, grown out and in need of a haircut, as she walked away. It felt strange to see Dad in another world, mingling with strangers in a mask, pretending to be the tall, handsome veteran, devoid of stress or demons. He seemed to play the part well.

At home that night, I found a letter from Lucy waiting for me on my pillow. It read:

Dear Michael,

I miss you already. It doesn't feel the same without you both here. Tonight, I found myself walking to your beach house. I sat outside the empty house, for I admit I was too afraid to walk to the cave without you.

Aunt Louise received a letter from her friend, the editor of the Vineyard Gazette, who told her Martin Luther King, Jr. was spending August in Martha's Vineyard! I had to write and tell you immediately and to remind you of your promise to join the Freedom Riders with me.

Love,
Lucy

P.S. I miss screaming with you.

I placed her letter under my pillow and read it again before falling asleep, adding it to the tin lunchbox, still hidden beneath my bed, after the second reading. In my dreams that night, I returned to walk on the beach with Lucy.

Summer break ended, and I began fifth grade. Time accelerated as if someone had spun a wheel, and events occurred faster than I could recall, with a few notable exceptions. Dad and I attended another Yankees baseball game, the last we would attend together, on October 1, 1961. We watched Roger Maris hit his 61st home run into right field during the fourth inning, breaking Babe Ruth's record, the only run of the entire game. Roger Maris reluctantly waved to the cheering crowd after he ran the bases. I clutched the game ticket tightly in my pocket on our way home that Sunday afternoon, and as soon as we entered our apartment, I hid it in the very bottom of the lunchbox, a paper slice of history.

In early December 1961, Henry mailed a package addressed to me, an auspicious arrival, for I was sick with influenza and stuck at home for a miserable week of fevers and body aches. Beneath the brown paper, I saw the cover of a new book—a gigantic peach growing from a tree upon a hillside it had overtaken in size. A little boy wearing red shorts and white nautical shirt stood below with his arms outstretched. I read the title *James and the Giant Peach* and opened to the first page instantly to discover how on earth a peach grew to be that big. I finished reading it over Christmas break, a gift for Mama, who patiently waited for her turn. That Christmas was the happiest one I remember from my childhood.

Mama and Nana had fully reconciled, at last, and we spent that Christmas all together.

The freezing temperatures outside frosted our windows white. Inside, the fireplace glowed orange. We all wore the paper crowns Mama and I had crafted out of different colored construction paper and sat on the ground huddled before the fire. We ate fire-roasted chestnuts and drank Nana's homemade eggnog, spiked with rum for the adults. After two cups of eggnog, Pops' cheeks were flushed with red. The color created by the fire and drink suited his merry disposition well. After the third cup, he began singing Christmas carols, and soon we all joined in, passing the rest of Christmas Eve in jolly tune.

We, all but Dad, walked to midnight mass that evening. As we entered the cathedral, the lights were dimmed, and all was quiet except the occasional cough or peep from younger children. It was my favorite mass all year. I always felt giddy from the anticipation of Christmas morning, only a few hours away. The plangent bells rang out as we took our seats, reverberating their deep hum around the hollow. At that dark hour, the call of the bells haunted those venerable grounds, casting a mysterious pall on the hushed prayers murmured within the shadows of the wooden pews. I became aware of my own maturity that night when, for the first time, I scanned the crowd to find Joe, who sat a few pews ahead of us, and discovered slumbering children with my own awakened eyes. It was the first midnight mass that I sat through in its entirety without nodding off once. The same could not be said for Pops, who fell asleep slumped over on Nana. The problem arose when he began snoring with his mouth wide open.

This produced a rather loud, guttural sound that echoed in the somber nave. I could not contain my giggles, which always had a habit of becoming uncontrollable in church. I leaned over to my right for another glimpse of Joe, who had heard my laughter, which he knew quite well as he was often the cause of it. I found him turned backwards, gazing in our direction. He laughed as I imitated Pops' snoring until his mother noticed and forced him to face forward again.

Nana elbowed Pops many times without success and eventually dug her elbow deep into his ribs until he woke up.

Snorting and disoriented, Pops shouted, "And also with you!"

Mama and I lost all control at this untimely response. We spat out the laughter from our pursed lips and then immediately attempted to reign it back in, resulting in snorts and other absurd noises. Nana looked mortified beside us and bowed her head in embarrassment as the congregation turned to stare at us. We were finally able to release it all outside the church at the conclusion of mass.

"Betty, it was your dang eggnog! Did you make it stronger than usual?"

"Perhaps I was a bit heavy-handed." Nana giggled mischievously. "But you are to blame for drinking three or four cups!"

It was past midnight when we walked back to our apartment, officially Christmas morning. A light flurry fell on us, dusting the path and our heads with white powder. I tilted my head back and watched the snowflakes floating down, delicate ice crystals with tiny facets dancing down on the cold air. They landed upon my pink face with soft, brumal kisses before disappearing on my warm skin. I attempted to catch some in my mouth which always proved to be more difficult. My breath escaped as a white fog when I exhaled.

Nana slept in my bed that night after I begged them to stay with us. Pops and I camped out in the living room; he took the couch while I bunked on the floor beneath him. Mama made me a little makeshift bed of pillows so I would be more comfortable. I did not mind the floor at all. Pops and I whispered in the darkness, the snow still softly falling outside the window, until we fell asleep.

CHAPTER 22

CONFESSIONS

I could recall, with perfect clarity, the first time I heard "Gnossienne No. 1." I was distracted, hardly noticing any music, when it began flowing from piano keys. From the first note, I was removed from reality to a haunting dream, obscured by mist, the melody spinning me around and around. Utterly ensnared, my soul lifted above my body to twirl in a dizzying bliss until it floated back down, forever altered by hearing it. I often wished to return to that revolving dream instead of the one I entered.

The winter of 1962, though not as harsh or unpredictable as the previous winter, trapped us in its chill, a repetitive, never-ending merry-go-round. Our life became a blur of extremities. First, an eerie silence fell over our home. Mama's favorite records no longer spun quietly in the background. The soulful voices of Billie Holiday, Ella Fitzgerald, and Louis Armstrong were suddenly hushed. Even as the frozen ground warmed and renewed with life, our apartment remained in the unbearable cold, round and round, unable to exit the perpetual blue. I wondered why life tended towards circles, recurring cycles spinning out of our control.

The only time cracks of light entered our realm, confined and desolate, occurred when Mama and I were separated from Dad. In his absence, we portrayed normality, constructing an illusionary house in which to temporarily reside. Mama and I almost forgot ourselves during our summers at the beach when, after a week, the routine, freedom, and familiarity of places and people lulled us into a void. Henry had painted a new picture on his mural, just as he always did. A giant flying peach had been added to the sky. Henry was unaware of how many times I had longed to sail away on a giant peach like James, picking up Lucy on the way to the cave so I could scream at the rocks with her and share the pain I could not bear to write about. In truth, I omitted the reality and did not tell Lucy nor anyone about our troubles, with the next two summers of 1962 and 1963 passing somewhat normally. Our days were spent in the same ways with the same people. Everything felt the same at the beach, but a beautiful mirage can only trick the mind for so long before the bleak reality returns.

I received a letter from Lucy, stuffed into a bulging envelope, in September 1963. She wrote pages and pages about the March on Washington and Martin Luther King, Jr.'s "I Have a Dream" speech, delivered before the reflecting pool of the Lincoln Memorial. She had begged Aunt Louise almost every day that summer to drive to DC for the march. She described the photographs of the crowd printed in newspapers, her thoughts on

the speech, her disappointment at missing history, and the blame
she placed on her aunt. I could not focus on her words when my
own world spun out of control. I did not finish reading her letter
or send a reply.

It was just two months later when President Kennedy was
assassinated in Texas. I first learned the President had been shot
at school when Father Paul unexpectedly entered our classroom
and delivered the somber news. I stared at the black speckled floor,
cold and hard against my knees, as he led our class in prayers.
Mama and I stopped at church to pray after I was released early
from school that day. There were many others in the church that
Friday, the week before Thanksgiving, hunting solace in the pews.
Mama sobbed quietly into her hands, clutching her white rosary,
as she knelt. The surreal tragedy unfolded on uninterrupted
television sets across the United States over the next four days,
ending with President Kennedy's funeral on Monday. We as a
nation spent the Thanksgiving holiday of 1963 in disbelief,
grieving our young president. On Thanksgiving Day, I watched
President Lyndon Johnson give a speech on television. He said,
"A great leader is dead. A great nation must move on. Yesterday is
not ours to recover, but tomorrow is ours to win or to lose. I am
resolved that we shall win the tomorrows before us."

We did not travel to the beach as anticipated in the summer
of 1964. Nana fell down her porch steps and broke her hip that
May, so we delayed our trip. Mama and I went to stay with Nana
and Pops to help her recover after her hip replacement. Pops was
relieved upon our arrival, for he felt overwhelmed playing the part
of caretaker to Nana, who had always taken care of him along with

everything else in the household. Dad, on the contrary, was furious when we left to stay with them, wanting us to stay home instead.

During her convalescence, Nana was visited unexpectedly by their new priest. He had just arrived from the Republic of the Congo to train at the small church near their house, where they worshiped on most Sunday mornings. Nana seemed quite surprised when Father Jean, a small man with a round, childlike face and large glasses, entered her bedroom in his black outfit and white collar. He smiled constantly and spoke with a French accent. Father Jean, pronounced like John in French, brought Nana and Pops the communion they missed at Sunday mass and prayed for her swift recovery.

When the priest left their house after his first visit, Nana remarked, "So, that's the new priest? I'm not so sure about him."

After lunch one day, when my afternoon boredom reached a peak, I walked down the street from my grandparents' house to the little stone church. I did not know why I found myself walking there and then opening the wooden doors, which were always unlocked. The heavy door stuck a bit when I pushed it and creaked loudly, echoing up to the high ceiling, when I forced it open. I felt like an intruder in the empty church as I entered and broke the silence. I walked to the left and took a seat in the back pew next to the stained-glass windows, the yellow and green diamonds softly glowing in the sunlight. I stared at the shadows cast on the stone ledge below the window. My gaze shifted to the carved wooden crucifix above the altar. When I was younger, I had become transfixed by it, my eyes wandering over its surface until I had studied every aspect of it—the corners of the cross, the stakes, the injuries, the crown of thorns, the banner on top of the cross, the expression on Jesus' face. I remembered reading the letters on the banner during mass and asking Nana what they meant afterwards. It was cool and dark inside the church. The only light streamed through the windows, and the only noise came from the creaking pew I sat upon. I returned to the winter of 1962. Everything went silent. The silence was followed by something worse.

"Michael?" I heard in a gentle voice behind me.

I turned around. "Hi, Father Jean."

His round face beamed like a child's. "Is your grandmother all right?" He had visited her the day before.

"She's fine. Thank you for asking. I just came here to be alone."

He shuffled over and sat next to me. "Do you have something on your mind?" he asked, pushing his glasses up on his nose.

I hesitated. "Well, I was wondering something about confession. Is it true that priests are bound by the confessional? I mean, do you have to keep what you hear a secret?"

"It's true. It's called the sacramental seal, a very important part of confession. You see, the act of confession requires absolute trust, and this ensures it."

I lifted my right hand and made the sign of the cross on my forehead, chest, left and then right shoulder. "Bless me, Father, for I have sinned. It has been a month since my last confession."

Father Jean looked into my eyes and waited for me to continue. Subtle crow's-feet, imprints from a lifetime of easy smiles, radiated out from his deep brown eyes. His dark brown skin glistened in the windows' glow, resembling fallen chestnuts in an autumn wood.

I sighed deeply. "My sin is breaking the fourth commandment. I do not honor my father. I *hate* him."

He sat contemplating my confession. Instead of moving forward by giving me my penance, he asked, "Why, my son, do you harbor this hatred for your father at such a young age?"

I did not know how to start my explanation nor how much I should divulge, so I returned to the beginning. "My father lost his job unexpectedly shortly after New Year's 1962, just when our life seemed to be going well. He began drinking again, more than I'd ever seen him before. My mama tried to help him, but he ignored her."

I began crying at the memory of what happened next—how life became a dance around Dad's alcoholism. It was not his falter that I condemned but his poisoned tongue, spatting malice at Mama every time he spoke to her. All of his rage focused on her. I would have happily shared his wrath to spare her the verbal abuse, jealousy, and subsequent isolation he inflicted on her, but I became, instead, invisible to him. Father Jean touched my shoulder, softly at first and then with more weight.

"He blames her for everything. Yells at her every time he's at home. The things he says to her." I stopped, my words unintelligible from my heaving sobs.

The truth continued in my head. At first, everything went silent, the kind of silence when you are afraid to speak. Then, everything was loud. Dad began screaming at Mama and throwing plates against walls. The blame, the control, the blaring screams, the words always sharper the next day, my mom smaller. He tightened his grip around Mama every day, forbidding her from seeing any of her friends or attending church without him. He even wanted to prevent us from staying with my grandparents. He wanted to control her very existence. Father Jean remained beside me until I composed myself once more.

My face felt numb. "I'm sorry for this and all of my sins."

Father Jean, after some time of quiet reflection, said, "Relieve the troubles of my heart and free me from my anguish. Look on my affliction and my distress and take away all my sins. Michael, pray ten Hail Marys and one Our Father. Forgive yourself. I also encourage you to talk to your father. Tell him all that you have told me. And then forgive him too."

I prayed the Act of Contrition aloud, and Father Jean absolved me of my sins.

Before he left, Father Jean turned to face me. "Michael, come talk to me anytime. I am always here for you."

I thanked him and mulled over his words long after he had gone. I wondered if it were possible to follow his advice. I doubted words could reach my father. Each day he seemed further away. I walked back to my grandparents' house and never told anyone where I had been.

Father Jean faithfully returned to visit Nana each week. He never mentioned my visits to the church, which continued every day until it was time for us to return home. Along with communion and prayers, Father Jean brought Nana baked goods that he prepared himself. He spoke of his mother's cooking and asked Nana for recipes and baking tips during their visits. In addition to baking, he also loved baseball and chatted with me and Pops about the game after his visits with Nana. I had never met a priest like him, one that seemed so normal, like us.

On Father Jean's last visit to their house, when Nana was able to ambulate on her own, I heard Nana sobbing from her bedroom following his departure.

I knocked gently on her door and asked, "Everything okay, Nana? What's the matter?"

She patted the bed, indicating for me to sit down beside her. She wiped tears from her eyes as I plopped down and rested my head on her shoulder.

"I'm going to miss my visits with Father Jean," Nana confessed to me.

Secretly, I would too. "Nana, you can still be friends with him, and you'll see him at church. I'm sure he'll come to your house for dinner too if you invite him."

Nana spluttered, "Oh, Michael, it's not just that. I'm so very ashamed of myself. I'm ashamed of the word I used at Martha's Vineyard and the hatred that has filled my old heart for many years. God saw that in me and sent Father Jean to show me how wrong I've been. I've asked for forgiveness from God and promised to never use such words ever again." She began weeping once more.

I hugged her, marveling at how her friendship with Father Jean, one person, had changed her. I felt proud of my grandmother, at her age, for altering her views on Black people, prejudice that had been planted in her mind long ago as a child.

Words she had heard in everyday conversation and, thus, accepted. Redemption, I learned that day, was never out of reach. It filled me with a slight optimism that Dad might redeem himself too.

I enjoyed the calm of being at Nana and Pops' house, but I longed for the beach and our friends. My hopes, aloft like a kite with invisible drafts, floated at the thought of traveling to the beach after the weeks we spent with Nana ended. The night we returned home, however, deflated all of my hope.

I was in my bed, reading under the covers past my bedtime, when I heard Dad return home, stumbling through the dark living room, cursing when he hit a side table and fell with a loud thud onto the hardwood floor. I laughed quietly as I heard him tumble and then mutter to himself the rest of the way to their bedroom. I returned to my book, expecting to read in solitude before drowsiness overtook my tired eyes, but instead, I was startled by Dad's voice screaming Mama's name. I listened intently but heard only silence followed by Dad's return to the corridor.

"Come here, Margaret!"

Mama sleepily whispered, "Quiet or you'll wake Michael. What's happening? Are you all right?" Her voice trailed off as she walked towards the living room.

I crept from my bed and tiptoed to my bedroom door, slightly ajar, to hear their conversation coming from the kitchen.

"What's *this*, Margaret?" Dad shouted, ignoring her recommendation about his volume.

I could not see what he had presented to her. I snuck down the creaking hallway, standing just at the end of it.

"It's a letter," Mama answered in a small voice.

Dad sneered, "Oh, it's *just* a letter. No! It's a letter from a man!"

My eyes shifted back and forth. *Henry*, I thought to myself.

He demanded in a screeching voice, "Read it out loud!"

Mama's voice quivered. "My dear Margaret, how are you and Michael? I must confess I feel your absence here this summer most keenly." She could not continue but began crying in soft whimpers.

"Don't worry! I've already read it!" he spat viciously.

I wanted to run to her. Before I found the courage to move my feet, I heard a loud smacking sound followed by a wretched cry similar to the wail of a baby animal in distress. Tears had streamed down and completely soaked my face by the time I made it to the kitchen. I arrived to witness Dad repeatedly hitting Mama. I felt ashamed of my cowardice, my hesitancy when I heard her cry for help.

I placed my body between theirs. "It's just a letter!"

Mama gasped, "Michael."

Dad pushed my body easily aside and grabbed Mama by her throat, his large hands wrapping around to the back. He squeezed her throat and said, "I forbid you to see this man or talk to him again." He turned to look directly into my eyes. "Both of you!" He released her and left the apartment without closing the front door.

I rushed to Mama and held her upon the floor while we both cried. The physical abuse continued after that night, when our illusionary house toppled, our hope eventually decaying over time into ineffectual delusion. Many nights, I was startled awake by Dad's drunken yelling and Mama's cries from behind their closed bedroom door. I lay in bed, tears drenching my pillow, listening to her suffer. I found myself harboring a deep hatred inside, festering more and more every day. Mama resolved to accept it, learning how to utilize makeup to conceal the bruises on her face and arms. I wondered why she did not ask for help or tell anybody, even her parents. I came close to telling Pops many times, when he noticed the sadness within my eyes, but I dared not utter the truth out of fear for Mama. I feared he would kill her if anyone discovered our family's secret. I dreamt of him strangling her often, and when I woke with a start, I wondered if I would find her dead. I eventually slept only a few hours at night due to the constant anxiety from the recurrent nightmares and the anticipation of abuse.

That year would be the darkest of my young life, when I lived half of a life, exhausted and terrified. It felt as if the sun would never return. When I finished eighth grade, I had fallen to the bottom of my class, barely passing the year. At least school offered me a brief release from home. Mama, however, was forced to stay home, always at his mercy. I watched, during this time, Mama withdraw into herself, slowly, until she was inside out. Everything about her dimmed. Her eyes turned a dull gray; the shimmer in them receded. She no longer laughed at the moments of magic unnoticed by others, the ones that occurred in the pauses of a conversation, the stillness of a winter morning, the crunch of fallen leaves, the flight of butterflies between bushes and trees. The extent of her depression went beyond the melancholy she typically cycled through and managed, as if the shackles had been weighed down by something, pulling her wasting body completely underwater. I was forced to watch it all happen, powerless to stop it.

When my teacher Sister Mary Catherine called Mama into school at the end of the year for a meeting to discuss my grades, I sat before her in the chair next to Mama, bruises beneath her clothes, and listened to her concern with rage bubbling in my body. I felt angry at Sister Mary Catherine for burdening Mama, angry at myself for my poor grades, angry at Dad for everything, and angry at God for abandoning us. As Mama and I walked home after the meeting, we were surrounded by the delights of late spring—vibrant flowers in full bloom and green trees with lush sheaths, open to the bright sun. The world was alive with buzzing sounds and warbling tunes. Fleeting butterflies floated near bushes, appearing as unexpectedly as the bubbles blown from a group of children past us. To me, however, everything was ashen and cold. Every day was the same. I no longer wanted to play baseball with Joe at the park or carry my telescope to the top of our building. I stopped responding to Lucy's letters, which arrived faithfully every few weeks despite the absence of reply. Dad forbade us from going to the beach that summer of 1965 during one of his inebriated rants, his verdict passed with pummeling fists. That very night, I devised my own plan to help us escape to the beach, determined not to be jailed with him for the entire summer.

CHAPTER 23

ESCAPE PLAN

The next Saturday, Nana and Pops visited our apartment to deliver a late birthday present. There had been no party for my fourteenth birthday. I did not care to celebrate the passing of such a horrible year. I hated my own reflection, which resembled my father's more and more each year. I had grown much taller, not quite as tall as Dad yet, but I had not gained an equivalent amount of weight, leaving me rather lanky and awkward in appearance. It made a difficult year even more so, for even my body felt foreign to me.

Dad was away from home when Nana and Pops arrived, so I took advantage of his absence to talk with them individually. I did not want Mama to know anything.

"Pops," I said when he came to my bedroom, "can I ask you for one more birthday present?"

"Sure," Pops answered, listening thoughtfully.

"Will you and Nana drive us to the beach?" I asked.

"Well, I'll have to talk with Betty. We did not plan on going until later this summer. I thought your mama told us you weren't going this summer."

"Pops," I pleaded in a squeaky voice as I sat beside him on the end of my bed, "we *need* to go. It's important, or I wouldn't ask you. Please promise you'll come and take us, no matter what my dad says."

I stared into his hazel eyes with golden flecks, tears in my own. "Please promise me."

"I promise."

We spoke no further on the topic, but I trusted his word. Nana required a softer, less direct approach. I waited to corner her later when Mama was distracted in a conversation with Pops. I followed her into the kitchen.

As she opened the door to inspect our bare refrigerator, I said, "Hi, Nana," which caused her to jump and squeal in surprise. I bent down to hug her, squeezing her short, plump frame with my lanky arms. "I've missed you and Pops."

She smelled of butter candy and floral perfume, the latter which reminded me of the matching floral curtains and bedspread in her bedroom, the same fragrance hanging in the air. I recalled sneaking into their bedroom as a child and being fascinated with her crystal perfume bottles, arranged on her dressing table, each with an oval pump and tassel at the end.

"Oh, we've missed you too, my sweet."

"Can I tell you my *secret* birthday wish?" I asked her.

Her curiosity piqued, she replied hastily, "Of course, my darling boy."

I smiled. "All I want is to ride in your car to the beach house next week. You, me, Pops, and Mama. Don't tell Mama, but I don't think she's planning on going this summer. If you come and drive us, though, she can't say no and ruin it. I want to go more than anything."

I knew Nana could not refuse me or the chance of playing hero, especially against Mama's wishes. I knew Mama would forgive my lie against her.

"Leave it to me," she said with a signature wink, her red lips drawn into a mischievous smirk.

I decided Dad must know nothing about our escape plan. I did not tell Mama either so she could maintain her innocence. I knew Dad would blame her. Mama had never learned the pretense of deception, maintaining that childlike predisposition towards honesty. Part of me felt uneasy with my trick of running away, fearing I may regret the consequences of it, but desperation often precipitates poor choices. The plan had been laid for the following Wednesday. I called Nana on the telephone to confirm before sneaking into Mama's bedroom and packing some clothes for her. I chose her favorite dresses from past summers, ones she had not worn since we last returned from the beach. I hoped wearing them would remind her of the unbroken version of herself. I hid both of our packed suitcases in my closet and waited.

I lay in bed on Tuesday night and prayed for Dad to be kept away from our apartment until after our departure. My mind, anxious with all the ways our plan may fail, kept me awake until the early morning hours. I awoke the following morning with a dream fresh on my thoughts—Dad choking Mama while I screamed, no sound escaping my mouth. I had a queasy feeling in my stomach that only worsened when I walked into the kitchen. Dad sat at the table eating his breakfast. Dread supplanted the joy that had lifted my spirit for a few days. I ate my breakfast quickly and then took up a post in front of the large window overlooking the front of our building, pacing back and forth, keeping watch for Nana and Pops. The warm morning sun streamed through the window.

With any luck, Dad would leave right after breakfast. He lingered at the table, reading the newspaper, crinkling annoyingly between his hands. I sent up another silent prayer to Mary as I marched, pleading for forgiveness of my deceit while beseeching her for help in our escape, the whole purpose of which was to rescue my very own mother. I bargained with God, frantically promising piousness and benevolence thereafter.

I watched through the window as Nana and Pops' car arrived earlier than expected. I felt unbridled panic as Pops parallel parked the car, soon on their way up. My mind became befuddled with ideas and possible dialogue swirling around, interrupted by a knock on our door.

"*Who* is that?" Dad grumbled as he stood up, his chair abruptly sliding on the kitchen floor with a grating sound. He flung open the door with indignation and asked in surprise as he saw Nana and Pops standing there, "What are *you* doing here so early?"

I stood by the window with horror in my widened eyes. Mama, who left the kitchen to see who stood at the door, noticed my expression, as did Nana and Pops.

"Margaret, you didn't tell me your parents were coming over this morning," Dad barked, without greeting Nana and Pops or inviting them inside.

Nana and Pops looked at one another and cautiously entered with uncomfortable steps.

Mama, also genuinely surprised to see them, said, "Oh, silly me, I must have forgotten."

"I invited them," I interjected confidently, veiled terror underneath, staring at Dad, "before we drive to the beach."

Nana and Pops wore a worried expression, Mama confused. Dad's face contorted into rabid fury. He turned his ire towards Mama.

He asked, without any attempt to conceal his animosity, "So, *are* you going to the beach then?"

Mama's eyes, which had fallen back down to the ground, lifted directly to mine and then to my lips.

I mouthed, "Please."

Mama had not been the only one reading the plea on my lips.

Pops stepped closer to Dad and spoke before any words escaped Mama's hesitant mouth. "Why, this is all our fault, I'm afraid. You see, we felt guilty that Michael and Margaret missed their beach trip last summer due to Betty's surgery, so we planned this little surprise. Margaret had no idea about the trip," Pops explained calmly. "I do hope you'll forgive our surprise. Is there any reason they can't come with us? Michael is so excited."

Dad's displeasure was obvious all the way from his face to his clenched fists. He shifted from one foot to the other in irritation, considering his excuse and trying to subdue his temper, which must have been challenging since he had become accustomed to exploding whenever he wanted over the past year. Mama dared not answer Pops' question but waited for Dad to speak for her. I observed the bloodshot madness stirring within his eyes as he pondered his reply, as we left the apartment, packed suitcases in our hands, and as he glared down at us from the apartment window, his burly arms folded about his chest. I imagined him shouting and hurling furniture in a violent tantrum after we drove away. At that moment, safe in the car, I did not care. Mama and I were out of his reach, unfettered birds released after a year of frigid captivity.

CHAPTER 24

THE EFFECTS OF GRAVITY

As we drove away from our apartment, Pops remarked, "Boy, James looks horrible! His skin and eyes are all yellow, and he seems to be drunk and angry all the time."

Nana, chiming in with her opinion, lectured, "Yes, he looks quite ill, George. But, Margaret, he is still your husband. You *must* support him during this trial. Remember divorce is *not* an option for Catholics."

Mama and I, sitting in the back seat, kept silent and looked at one another. My eyes implored her to tell them. Her eyes apologized. I grabbed her hand and held it in mine. Pops glanced in the rearview mirror at my face. He saw tears within my eyes but did not ask their cause.

On the long drive, I thought about the shifting tides, high tides raised upon the sand, demolishing sandcastles and erasing footprints in their reach, and low tides pulled back into the ocean, exposing the seabed underneath. From my pocket, I pulled the folded moon map, the one gifted to me by John. I had studied it for hours and hours, memorizing the geography and names printed upon it. I stared at the map, faded and creased from years of use. In one of the many books I had read about the moon in the library, I learned of how the tides were influenced by the moon. Spring tides, I had read, occur a day or two after new and full moons, when the gravitational pull of the moon combines with the pull of the sun. Their added effects result in a larger difference in low and high tides. Neap tides occur after first and third quarter moons, when the pull of the moon is counteracted by the pull of the sun, causing less difference in high and low tides.

My thoughts shifted to the effects people have on one another. By the time we traveled to the beach house that year, Mama was already submerged, her body sunk to the depths, her lungs full of water. She no longer fought it, did not attempt to swim, but had surrendered to her fate as her lifeless body floated at the bottom in stillness. The further we drove away from Dad, safe miles placed between us and him, the less I hoped his crushing gravity would weigh upon Mama. I could not watch her slowly slip away anymore. I planned our escape to save her life, hoping it would allow time for her to surface.

The first thing I did when we arrived at the beach house that evening was call Lucy. Not three minutes after I hung up the receiver, Birdie flew into the driveway, gravel slinging from her spinning tires. Mama and I darted outside when we heard the honking. Aunt Louise sprinted, for perhaps the first time in her life, to Mama, picked her up, and swung her around in circles like a child.

Lucy jumped from the front seat and walked towards me, wearing a rainbow-striped shirt dress, buttoned all the way down, the same one I had seen her wear two summers ago. It fit her like a new dress altogether. The hem had lifted on her legs as she grew taller, and the fabric hugged her figure where before it was loosely draped on her slender frame. She appeared more like a woman than a child, as if she had crossed an invisible line beyond childhood, never to return. Her hair, with soft brown curls, had grown long, past her shoulders. She smiled as she approached me, the tiniest gap between her front teeth, her large brown eyes staring unwaveringly into mine. I felt a rush in my stomach from seeing her again. It felt odd to see her this way. I knew I also looked strange in my transitioning body, a crab outgrowing my shell.

"Michael, you look different." Lucy's sweetness turned sour when she punched my arm. "You didn't respond to my letters. I thought you were dead."

I rubbed my tender arm, blood already pooling under the skin. "Forgive me?" I squeaked.

Lucy giggled at my changing voice. Her laugh remained steadfast through all the other changes. "Of course." She jumped into me for an overdue hug.

"I'll explain everything at the cave tonight," I whispered into her ear. Her hair smelled of lavender fields. For some reason, The Beatles song "I Want to Hold Your Hand" began pounding in my head. My heartbeat matched the fast rhythm.

When she pulled away, the music stopped. Lucy nodded in agreement. How I had longed to walk on the beach with her on so many of those cold, horrid nights. We looked over at Aunt

Louise, who held Mama as she wept in her arms. Mama appeared small inside her embrace, which persisted until Mama had exhausted both her tears and her jerking body.

I overheard Aunt Louise say, "You need a drink, my dear," at which Mama laughed feebly. A stiff drink cured all ailments, according to Aunt Louise.

Later that night, when I snuck from my bed on the porch and walked with Lucy on the beach, following the sand as far as we could, I made a promise to myself. I vowed to take full advantage of my freedom, to enjoy the summer because I knew, deep in my heart, it may be my last one. I screamed and screamed and screamed at the cave that night, releasing all the putrid bile inside of me, until my voice was left hoarse. Rather than face Lucy's anticipated questions, an idea came to my mind. I walked closer to the cliff and shined my flashlight at the cave's entrance.

"Look, Lucy! Look how low the tide is! The water has receded from the cave. Let's explore inside."

Lucy walked closer to me and shined her flashlight at the edge of the tide, pulled back beyond the cliff.

"Come on," I encouraged her. "We're too old to believe in ghosts anymore."

Lucy, never one to miss out on adventure, laughed. "Let's go!"

We stepped closer to the low and narrow entrance, eroded into an uneven archway of sorts. As we hunched down and entered, carefully, to avoid hitting our heads, I ran my hand along the jagged rocks, marveling at how the relentless water had carved the stone. The sand inside the cave felt damp and sticky as we walked on bare feet to the center, where it was high enough to allow us to stand upright. We examined the rocks on the sides and top of the cave in increments, aided by our flashlights, as we spun around. I did not spy a single ruby winking within the gray. We sat down together upon the sand and switched off our flashlights. After my eyes adjusted to the darkness, I was able to differentiate the night sky and water outside the entrance. The only sound I heard was the rushing tide, which sounded further away than it was. I felt safe inside the cave, as if no problem nor pain could reach us there.

"How is your mom?" I asked in a whisper.

"Better. She's been staying in an institution and receiving treatment for the past six months. I visit her on weekends when I'm home." Lucy added with a giggle that echoed, "I sneak chocolate to her during my visits."

"Can I tell you a secret?" I said in an impulse that surprised even me.

"Anything."

"But you must promise not to tell anyone, including your aunt."

"I promise."

"It's just," I began but hesitated. "It's not my secret. Nobody else in the world knows except one other. I thought telling you might help."

Lucy grabbed my hand. "You can tell me anything, everything, or nothing. Or we can just scream together."

I smiled, though invisible to her in the darkness. "My dad ..."

The words sliced my tongue while waiting to be spit out; the truth was painful to say aloud. Lucy waited patiently for my resolve.

"My dad," I began again slowly, "has been hitting Mama."

Lucy immediately turned, grabbed me, and pulled my body into hers for a hug. I wailed in her arms, my head against her chest. When able to speak coherently, I revealed more details, explaining how it began and then progressed to physical abuse.

"I'm afraid he'll kill her when we return home. Coming here this summer was my idea. My grandparents, who know none of this, helped us. It's all my fault."

"I swear to keep my promise to you, but don't you think you should tell someone? Tell your grandparents, perhaps?"

"Lucy, I don't know what to do," I said in despondence. "I'm afraid of silence as much as I'm afraid of the truth. What will cause the least amount of harm? How do I save her?"

I began crying once more. Lucy pulled my body into hers again.

"Adults are just fucked-up children with more responsibility than they deserve," Lucy declared bitterly.

We remained in that embrace for I know not how long nor how many tears we shed together. Before we left the cave and walked home, Lucy and I pierced the silence with cathartic shrieks, reverberating off the rugged walls.

CHAPTER 25

HELLO AGAIN

Two days after we arrived, Mama and I found ourselves breaking yet another of Dad's orders as we walked downtown to see Henry. I was unsure if Mama had written to him after Dad discovered his letter, but I suspected not since her flesh bore the penance for such a sin. My senses took in the pleasures encountered on our walk, ones I had experienced many times before but never as sweetly as when the future's uncertainty was at the forefront of my mind. Such worries were typically absent from my conscience, but I found myself matured by circumstances without my consent. I reveled in the tunnel of trees, the birds, the varied colors of flowers, the little green park, the view of Henry's bookshop and even its smell, when we entered.

We walked in the direction of his desk and, before he spotted us, saw him chatting with animated gestures to a young woman. Henry glanced up from the conversation with a quick smile and unsuspecting eyes. When he first noticed us, his eyes betrayed his absolute shock as they shifted away and returned quickly. He ran to us.

"Is it *really* you?" he asked, both of us altered in more than just appearance since our last meeting. Henry remained unchanged.

I affirmed in a deeper voice, "It's really us."

Henry beamed and hugged me, my growing body not much shorter than his.

"I hardly recognize you." Henry spoke his thoughts aloud as he studied me.

I laughed, imagining I must look quite different to that little boy he met all those years ago. Henry turned to Mama. She wore a pale yellow dress with tiny flowers all over it, one I had packed for her. It swallowed her wasting frame and enhanced the pallor of her skin. She looked like a haunted version of herself.

Mama said, "Hello, Henry. I'm sorry I never responded to your letter. I … I …" She broke down in tears, unable to provide an excuse.

Henry wrapped his arms around her. She buried her head in his chest and sobbed. Henry furrowed his brow and looked at me, his eyes troubled. Tears collected in my eyes, a few overflowing onto my face.

Henry attempted a joke. "Margaret, you don't have to say it. I know you missed me. I'm just so damn lovable, like a dog."

Mama feigned a small laugh tucked within his arms. She pulled her head up to look at him, her sunken cheeks and eyes glistening with tears. A smile, faint but true, curled the corner of her lips; her eyes were illuminated, ever so slightly, similar to the library's stained glass when the soft glow of sunlight peeked through a break in the clouds. Mama wiped her eyes and face dry with her fingers.

The young lady who Henry had been speaking with earlier had been watching our exchange curiously. She had short red hair with bangs. The top of her hair sat quite high above her head, granting a few inches of height to her petite frame. Henry noticed her staring and seemed to remember only then that she was still there where he had left her.

He gestured for us to follow him and said, "Margaret and Michael, I'd like to introduce you to Sandra."

In turn, Mama and I said hello to her.

Sandra shrieked with a wild look in her eyes and leapt to hug each of us. "Oh, I've heard Henry talk of you both. It's so nice to meet you! Call me Sandy. I know we'll all be best friends!"

Sandy appeared quite a bit younger than Henry and Mama. She skipped over to Henry, her heels clicking on the floor, and wrapped one arm around his waist.

"We must invite you over for dinner to become more acquainted. Henry and I love cooking together." Sandy gazed up at Henry with smitten eyes.

Mama smirked at Henry, hardly noticeable to untrained eyes, upon realizing the romantic nature of their relationship.

Sandy glanced at her watch. "Oh, I must dash, or I'll be late for work."

She grabbed Henry's face with both of her perfectly manicured hands and planted a kiss on his lips, lingering for a few seconds, as if she were stamping his face. She said goodbye and hurried off, the sound of her shoes receding as she departed. Henry's lips had indeed been stamped red by her lipstick. Mama and I giggled. Oh, how I had missed hearing her laugh.

"That's a nice color on you," Mama teased.

Henry swiftly scrubbed the color from his lips. "Blame my mother. She insisted I couldn't marry a book and must start dating a real woman." He laughed. "I thought Jane Eyre would suit me perfectly."

"Indeed." Mama laughed before continuing sincerely, "We are happy for you, Henry."

"Yes, but I do hope we'll see you this summer. Will she share you with us?" I had not foreseen Sandy's intrusion into my summer plans.

"Of course! We've got to make up the lost time this summer. I'm afraid Sandra follows me everywhere, though. She's quite attached for some unknown reason. She won't leave my side until she returns to university in the autumn."

Mama said, "Ah, she is a young one. She sees you as the older, more mature, handsome owner of a bookshop, I suppose. I can understand the appeal."

"Sure." Henry scratched his head, uncomfortable in the spotlight for the first time.

Mama noticed and assuaged his uneasiness. "In all seriousness, I really like her. She seems full of life. That will be good for you."

"Are you implying my soul is dead?" Henry quipped cheekily.

"Hmm, asleep, not dead."

Henry scoffed, "'Do you think because I am poor, obscure, plain and little that I am soulless and heartless?'" (Brontë 252)

I looked at Henry, initially confused by his question.

Mama did not laugh but smiled radiantly. "You read it."

Henry chuckled and begged, "Come up for tea. Now. Can you stay? Now that you're here before me, I don't want you to leave."

"Yes, we can stay," Mama answered. "Perhaps you can share your thoughts on *Jane Eyre*."

We followed Henry up the stairs to his apartment to recall all that had occurred while we were apart. Henry was unaware of the glaring omission in our memories.

CHAPTER 26

OATHS

Nana and Pops, our oblivious heroes, stayed at the beach for a few weeks before returning home. Mama and I were left without a car and any concrete plan for our mode of return home at the end of summer. Pops unknowingly suggested an obvious solution of my dad coming for a visit and then driving us home. I hugged each of them tightly before they departed and relayed my endless thanks for granting my birthday wish. I knew, of course, I would never truly be able to repay them for an act they did not fully comprehend at that time, but I also knew that as my grandparents, they would never ask for repayment. Mama and I happily spent our summer in the company of our dear friends. We did not speak to Dad during our stay at the beach house. He never called, and we were content to pretend he did not exist that summer.

Lucy and I spent most of our time together, always off on some adventure as we sought our independence. The whole town was ours, and we ventured everywhere from the beach to downtown and beyond, until we discovered every inch of land. We took daily trips to the library to visit Ms. Prince and to the boardwalk, playing arcade games, riding the Ferris wheel, or just walking amongst strangers. One evening, at the suggestion and generosity of Aunt Louise, we walked to the movie theater downtown to watch *The Sound of Music* while Mama and Aunt Louise sipped martinis with olives, Aunt Louise's drink of the summer, on the back patio.

Aunt Louise came within inches of my face and whispered, essence of gin and vermouth on her breath, "Take her to eat before the movie," before handing me money.

"Thank you. I know just where to take her."

I darted to my room and changed into a pair of khaki chinos and a short-sleeved button-down shirt with a blue checked pattern. As we walked through the tunnel of trees, bathed in the somber sunlight broken by branches and leaves, I silently said a Hail Mary and prayed for Mama to be granted the strength and encouragement to tell Aunt Louise about the abuse. I glanced at Lucy, who walked lightheartedly beside me, unaware of my prayers, in a pink gingham blouse and matching skirt. The beams of sunlight lit her brown eyes, changing them to shimmering amber.

The quiet of a weekday evening had overtaken downtown when we arrived. It appeared almost the same as it had the first time I saw it in 1957. We strolled over memories that reawakened in my mind. I saw myself and Lucy as children sitting on that very curb, the spot where we had watched the Fourth of July parade together. We were plugging our ears as the fire engines drove past us, their sirens blaring and lights flashing. We dared not remove our fingers, even to chase after the candy waiting upon the street, glistening in its shiny wrappers.

Returning to the present, I asked Lucy, "Care to eat before the movie? I'm hungry."

"Sure." Lucy shrugged.

I led the way past the pharmacy, stopped, and opened the door for Lucy. Upon entering, I stepped back to a familiar scene, immediately flooded with greasy scents and a view of the wide counter and red barstools above the checkered tile floor. "Wooly bully, wooly bully, wooly bully" flowed from the jukebox. Lucy joined in to sing the chorus and followed me to the same booth by the large window where Mama and I sat on our first visit. The seats looked the same, apart from the frayed and worn upholstery. I bounced from the edge of the booth to the center, a feat much easier with the stature of a six-year-old, and banged my knee on the table.

Lucy sat opposite to me, scanned the diner for a minute, and then stared directly into my eyes. "So, what are your thoughts on the war in Vietnam?"

"Uh …" I tugged at my collar as my skin began to burn, red creeping up my neck.

"We debated this very topic in school. I was rather thrilled to be on the team opposing the war. I find it is much easier to argue a position with which I already fundamentally agree. Imagine trying to argue in favor of the Vietnam War's principles," Lucy said in one breath with a huff at the conclusion.

"Imagine trying to argue in favor of any war's principles." At last, I articulated a thought outside of my head.

"True. But, at least others like World War Two, for instance, were fought for a worthy cause. I cannot, in all my rumination on the subject, find the reasons to justify the killing of civilians and sending our soldiers overseas in order to stop communism."

Thankfully, the waitress interrupted Lucy's fiery denunciation of the war when she approached and took my order. The strums of "My Girl" began to play.

Lucy sang along with The Temptations. "I went to my school prom this year. This was the prom song."

"Oh, you went to prom? Who did you go with?" I asked with a fraction of the ardor that smoldered inside me.

"A senior I met through student council asked me. He picked me up in his car and gave me a drag of his cigarette on the drive. The prom was a blast! I loved getting dressed up, dancing, and, of course, making my friends jealous. My date turned out to be a flake, though. He tried to kiss me in his car right outside my house!"

Envy struck me unexpectedly in a jolt. "What did you do?" I clenched my jaw briefly, hoping she walloped him.

"Well, he leaned over to my side with puckered lips and kept leaning, not getting the clue that I was pulling away from him." Lucy acted out his movements by slowly falling in her booth with her lips stuck out. She then tortured me with a pause, as I sat there with my mouth open, while she laughed. "So, he kept leaning in, but I refused to kiss him simply because he took me to prom. I reached my hand behind my back and opened the car door. I jumped out, said good night, and slammed the door in his face."

"He deserved worse for putting you in that position," I said, just as my food was placed before me.

Lucy reached over and snatched a fry from my plate. "Perhaps he's just been tackled too many times on the football field."

"Perhaps," I giggled as she grabbed my burger for a bite. "Were you president of the student council?"

"Vice president. Next year, I'll be president," she mumbled with a full mouth before sliding my milkshake towards her for a sip. "This is really good!" She took a prolonged drink.

"I thought you weren't hungry." I held up a french fry and challenged her. "I'll fight you for the shake!"

Lucy laughed and chose her weapon, the biggest fry on my plate. We battled with slashes of our salty daggers until she stabbed me in the chest.

Lucy entertained me with more stories from her school year and the dozens of clubs in which she was involved. There were no happy stories to share from my school year. I preferred to listen to her talk anyway. When my plate was empty and Lucy drank the last bit of milkshake, we set off for the movie theater.

I found myself glancing at Lucy repeatedly during the movie. I remembered the jealousy that arose in the diner, catching me by surprise, when she spoke of going to prom. I felt a swirling feeling in my stomach when our arms accidentally touched on the armrest. I longed to grab her hand and hold it within my own. I concealed these thoughts from her and pushed the unwanted feelings out of my own cognizance.

A week after the movie, Lucy and I snuck from our beds and met at the cave, a tradition we kept almost every night that summer. They were my favorite moments of the entire day, the time of secrets. Even when we had no secrets to tell, we debated politics, religion, music, and literature, never an awkward silence between us. Lucy spoke of her undying love for Elvis, her first crush. We talked about Bloody Sunday and the march from Selma to Montgomery and whether Congress would pass the Voting Rights Act. I felt I could ask her anything there, my courage uplifted by the cave's shadows.

That night, I asked Lucy, "Do you remember when I asked you last week why you didn't want to swim? Why did you yell at me that day?"

I had noticed that Lucy wore regular clothes to the beach on those days and seemed more distant than usual. When I asked her why, Lucy had screamed at me, "Because I'm a woman!" I had no idea what she meant. I kept thinking about her response until I finally asked her that night in the cave's darkness.

"Sorry I shouted at you. I was having my period last week, and I suppose I was mad about it. It's unfair that girls have to deal with bleeding every month and boys don't. I guess I directed my anger towards you, which was unkind."

My cheeks flushed red. I felt ignorant after asking her the question, but I knew nothing about the female menstrual cycle. Lucy did not embarrass me for my curiosity. We were able to broach forbidden topics like puberty, lust, and sex without judgment. Lucy seemed open and confident in discussing such things. She easily confessed to masturbating in front of a mirror.

"Otherwise," she said matter-of-factly, "how will I know what I like?"

I was relieved that she could not see my blushing face and the shame taught to me by the Catholic Church. At my school, the nuns preferred to pretend our genitals and hormones were shut in a black box, locked with a chastity belt welded with sin and guilt.

"Don't you think it's a sin to succumb to such urges?" I asked earnestly, repeating what I had heard on the matter.

Lucy looked at me with a baffled expression. "Sin? Why would it be a sin? It's a natural feeling. What do they teach in your church? Perhaps this is why my aunt has no time for religion. We hardly ever go to church. All I know is my aunt taught me that these feelings are normal during puberty. It's normal to explore your body."

"The Church prefers us to be asexual beings with pure thoughts. They teach us that such urges are sinful and should be repressed," I explained.

Lucy derided the notion. "Oh, well, I don't believe that at all! Are we all to be saints then?"

I laughed. "I believe the Church would be fine with that."

"Then whose soul would need saving?" Lucy quipped cleverly. "Churches would become obsolete if we were all saints."

"Ah, then the Church holds us to a standard that can never be met. They will always be relevant if we poor sinners keep failing."

"Exactly!" Lucy giggled. "Don't you have anyone at school that you like? Someone that makes your stomach flutter?"

"Sort of. There is a girl I've known since kindergarten. We held hands one time." I dared not speak truthfully of the person who caused such feelings for me.

Lucy looked at me and admitted, "I'm not sure if I deserve you sometimes. You're too good, too pure. I'm a bad influence on you."

She moved from sitting beside me to directly in front of me, her face close to mine, and took both of my hands in her own. Her almond eyes, visible in the glow of the flashlight upon the sand, peered into mine. "I swear to you, Michael McCarthy, I will always protect our friendship and make time for you, even if I'm busy changing the world. Now it's your turn to pledge the oath of friendship."

"I swear to you, Lucy Monsoor, I will always protect our friendship and make time for you, no matter what."

Lucy smiled at my alternate ending. Unlike her, I did not know what I desired my future to be. After the past year, I could not see beyond the next day. She seemed to know everything. I looked at her and felt an urge, one that I had been battling internally all summer, every time I was in her presence. Without thinking, I acted. I leaned in, eliminating the remaining distance between us, and kissed her on the lips. I realized, after I pulled my lips away, that I should not have sealed a friendship oath in that manner, but the impulse quite overtook me in the moment. I did not speak but waited for her reaction. I wondered if she might think of me in the same way as her prom date. Lucy seemed surprised, at first, sitting there looking at me, not knowing what to do or say.

"I-I'm sorry," I stammered to break the silence. "I know we're friends, but I …"

I debated with myself whether she would laugh or slap me while I fought the compulsion to run away. Instead, she unexpectedly chose another option. Lucy leaned in and kissed me, not a mere peck on the lips like mine. Her tongue parted my lips and entered my mouth. I felt quite lost in the logistics of kissing, as a novice, but I followed Lucy's lead and mimicked her movements. I enjoyed the feeling of our lips together. I could not explain exactly why, but the soft touch of her lips flooded my body with a peculiar feeling.

We walked back home in silence that night, each contemplating what had occurred. I could not recall walking home at all but found myself in bed somehow. I hoped, as I lay in bed upon our return, that my secret love for her did not have to remain hidden in the cave like all the other secrets. Most importantly, I prayed that the kiss would not alter our friendship in any way.

CHAPTER 27

RETURN OF PETER PAN

I awakened before sunrise the following morning with the kiss replaying in my mind. Rather than lying in bed and dwelling on whether Lucy regretted the kiss or hated me for it, I walked to the edge of the cliff to listen to the waves, rolling in and out. I recalled the memory of our walk back from the theater after watching *The Sound of Music*. We had walked leisurely on the sidewalk, discussing our first impressions of the movie. Our path was lit by lampposts and a section of string lights hung from tree branches. We stopped by the trees to admire the lights.

Lucy had begun singing the opening line of "The Sound of Music" as she twirled around, her hair and pink skirt chasing after her body. She tilted her head back and closed her eyes, spinning in the golden light. I stood there staring at the way she danced and how her wild eyes, ebony pools, looked at me after she had finished, her lips parted in a wide grin. She was the most perfect creature my eyes had ever beheld. I had feared my unwavering gaze that night might expose my newest secret, reluctantly flourishing in my heart from that night onwards. I did not want the feelings, but they persisted despite my objections. I had no choice as her "amber hands" pulled me against my will (Dickinson 104). As the sun rose, I sat and watched the water, listening to the world awaken slowly around me, until time for breakfast.

Thankfully, I did not see Lucy that day. Henry and Sandy were coming over to the beach house for dinner that night. Aunt Louise had helped Mama complete her shopping the day before in her car, Birdie, and even insisted on teaching Mama how to make the perfect martini for her guests. Mama and I hung around the house the whole day preparing for the dinner party. Even at Mama's suggestion, I did not want to walk down to the beach for fear of seeing Lucy. I was unsure how to act around her after the kiss. In truth, I wished I only thought of her as a friend. I did not want romantic feelings for her. I had witnessed the demise of childhood friendships at school when hormones, attachment, and jealousy became involved. Instead of risking an awkward encounter with Lucy, I hovered around Mama as if I were a toddler again.

Since we had arrived at the beach, I slowly watched Mama transform into her old self once more. Aunt Louise personally ensured she ate and drank well. The nourishment as well as sunlight from our morning walks colored her pale skin. Her spirit, shining through her sparkling eyes, now more blue than gray, had been revived through freedom. The old bruises, hidden under her clothes, faded, no new ones to take their place. I pondered how we would return to that tiny cage, waiting with its narrow bars at home.

Sandy and Henry arrived promptly at seven o'clock. Mama and I both had become fond of Sandy in the time we spent with her. In some ways, she seemed closer in age to me than Mama and Henry. She had a childlike quality about her. I watched her as she stared at Henry during their discussions of literature. Usually, it was Henry and Mama talking with Sandy observing and giggling intermittently at something Henry said. I wondered why she did not comment more, especially since she studied literature at university. I suspected her area of study had been inspired by Henry. Perhaps Sandy felt intimidated by Henry's vast knowledge as I sometimes did. Any semblance of shyness disappeared when music played, however, as she spontaneously jumped up and began dancing and singing, sometimes dragging me or Henry along begrudgingly. She smoked and laughed too loud when she drank, but she made even the mundane activities seem fun.

Sandy looked rather beautiful as she exited Henry's car, wearing a light pink cocktail dress with a trim of sequins at the bottom. I blushed slightly when I noticed how it snugly fit her curvy figure before looking away. Her hair rose higher than ever, a feat of hairspray engineering, and the potent scent of her perfume lingered long after she walked away. Henry wore a light gray suit, the same style he owned in a few colors. He always looked the same, apart from the thin pink necktie with wide stripes he now wore. Sandy adjusted Henry's tie, almost the exact color of her dress, before we went inside the house. Henry looked uncomfortable, repeatedly looking down at the tie, quite eccentric for his particular taste.

I led Henry and Sandy out to the back patio while Mama, a proficient student of Aunt Louise's, prepared three martini glasses, loaned by the master herself. The dinner proved to be a welcome distraction from Lucy and the kiss, which invaded my thoughts that evening. I worried about meeting her later that night for our walk to the cave. There was ample laughter and interesting conversation to engage my wandering mind. After dinner, the drinking continued, and a game of Henry's invention began. In the game, each player must tell either a secret about themselves or an amusing story.

Mama began the game by telling a rather scandalous story about Nana and Pops. "My parents are very conservative Catholics," Mama prefaced her story for Sandy, who did not know them. "My parents met another couple at a church fundraising event, and they all became very close friends. They even went on vacation together. When they returned from the vacation, my parents did not speak to them nor see them again. I thought this was odd, so I asked my dad if anything had happened to cause a fight." Mama started laughing uncontrollably at the cause of their rift before she revealed it to us. "My dad quietly informed me that they are no longer friends with them because they discovered that they are swingers. And they asked my parents to swing with them!"

It would take several years before I fully understood the joke. After the laughter had subsided from Mama's tale, it was Sandy's turn.

Sandy said, "I can't think of a good story, so I'll tell a secret. I'd rather get married and be a housewife than study at university," staring at Henry the entire time.

I wondered if her revelation was less a secret and more a hint. Whatever it was, it prompted Mama to lecture her on the importance of independence before considering marriage. Sandy promised, during a serious interlude in the game, to heed Mama's advice and finish college before getting married.

Henry, under the influence of too many martinis, stood up and delivered an impassioned portion of Hamlet's most famous soliloquy. I was rather impressed that he remembered more than the infamous opening line, even though he had forgotten the rules of his own game. Henry recited:

> To be, or not to be, that is the question:
> Whether 'tis nobler in the mind to suffer
> The slings and arrows of outrageous fortune,
> Or to take arms against a sea of troubles
> And by opposing end them. To die—to sleep,
> No more; and by a sleep to say we end
> The heart-ache and the thousand natural shocks
> That flesh is heir to: 'tis a consummation
> Devoutly to be wish'd. To die, to sleep;
> To sleep, perchance to dream—ay, there's the rub:
> For in that sleep of death what dreams may come,
> When we have shuffled off this mortal coil,
> Must give us pause—there's the respect
> That makes calamity of so long life (Shakespeare 3.1.56–69).

Mama stood up and clapped enthusiastically, along with Sandy and me.

Mama shouted, "Bravo! Bravo! Ladies and gentlemen, Peter Pan has, at last, returned to the stage!"

Henry fell to the ground in the middle of his bow. Sandy appeared confused by the reference to Peter Pan. Nevertheless, she cackled boisterously and pretended she understood its meaning. Henry and Mama began to cry from the laughter. The return of cheerful tears, or cheers, as Mama used to call them, stopped me in my own laughter. It had been more than a year of only sad ones. I stood there observing Mama, forming a memory of how beautiful she looked to carry me through the turbulent times ahead. Henry rose from the ground and excused himself to go inside the house. Soon after, Mama followed him into the house to refill the martini glasses and bring out dessert.

Sandy asked for music, so I ran to the kitchen to fetch the radio. Henry was in the kitchen with Mama, helping her assemble the dessert plates and silverware on a tray. They were both still giggling, presumably about the return of Peter Pan, when I arrived.

"I'm bringing the radio outside," I said as I entered.

"Good idea!" Henry remarked.

The telephone rang as I turned to leave the kitchen.

"Oh, I'll get it." Henry picked up the receiver and shouted merrily, "Hello! Margaret and Michael's residence. Peter Pan speaking!"

I turned back again, afraid it might be Lucy calling to inform me that I kiss like a slobbering donkey and she never wanted to see me again. I quickly surmised it was someone other than Lucy by the expression on Henry's face. His broad smile narrowed to a disturbed gape as he listened to the words spoken to him. He pulled the receiver away from his ear and offered it to Mama.

Henry said quietly, "I think it's your husband."

Mama dropped one of the martini glasses onto the ground. It shattered into a hundred sharp pieces. Dad's screams were heard from the phone in angry mumbles. Terror overcame Mama. She began to cry as she took the phone from Henry and listened. Mama became more and more hysterical the more she heard.

Henry snatched the phone from her trembling hand. "Stop it, sir! You are upsetting Margaret and Michael!"

Dad yelled something at Henry that caused him to slam the phone down.

Henry said, "He says he's driving here tonight to take care of you both. Margaret, what does that mean?"

Mama looked at me and then collapsed. When her weight fell upon them, the fragments of glass clinked together and then scratched the floor. She wailed on top of the broken shards as the tiny pieces cut her skin. Henry lifted her safely onto a chair and then approached me in a frenzied panic.

"Michael, what's going on? What does your father mean? Tell me so I can help you."

I glanced from Mama to Henry several times, stuck in the middle of betrayal or help, and began crying.

"He's been hurting her, hitting her for a while." I jumped into Henry's body after the secret left my lips and buried my face in his chest. "I didn't know what to do. I didn't know what to do. Oh, God, he's really going to kill her this time!"

Henry hugged me and placed a hand on my head. "I won't let him harm either of you."

Once Mama and I had stopped crying, the glass had been swept, and Henry had sufficiently sobered up after two cups of coffee, he drove Sandy home and returned with a shotgun. Henry locked the doors, and we three stayed together all night in the living room. Every noise caused my heart to race. Mama made a bed for me on the couch while she and Henry sipped coffee. I resisted sleep for as long as I could but found my eyes closing as a result of my early morning awakening and the gentle caress of Mama's hand on my head. Before I fully succumbed to sleep, I heard Mama and Henry talking.

"Why didn't you tell me, Margaret? Don't you trust me?" Henry questioned her years of silence.

"Of course I trust you. There's no one I trust more." Mama breathed out wearily before continuing with a tremulous voice. "I suppose I thought if I kept silent, things would at least remain the same. I could endure the pain if Michael was safe."

"Oh, it's unbearable," Henry cried, "to think of you and Michael living like that."

I floated to sleep before hearing any more of their conversation and before Dad's imminent arrival, our summer at the beach ending when I shut my heavy lids. I dreamt Mama, Henry, and I were standing on a teetering rowboat in the middle of the ocean. We appeared so small between the black and stormy sky and waves. Henry held his shotgun up in anticipation as hungry sharks circled around us in the unsettled water.

PART 4 – 1969

CHAPTER 28

PHANTOMS

I jolted awake suddenly on the couch, remembering Dad's threat, afraid of what I might discover upon opening my eyes. The morning sun beamed through the three small panes at the bottom of the east-facing windows. I had counted the twelve square panes of each window during our first summer at the beach house. With one eye squinted, I spotted Henry's gun propped up in the corner beside the front door, still closed and locked. I saw no obvious signs of a struggle in the living room nor any other car parked in the driveway when I ran to the window to look outside. I heard voices in the kitchen and followed them to find Mama and Henry eating breakfast. They both appeared tired, and I assumed they did not sleep at all.

The terror all began the night before with a telephone call from Dad and ended the morning after with one from Pops, who relayed news of a car accident. The drive home in the back of Henry's car felt disorienting, as when I spun around in circles too many times as a child; images outside the car all converged together in my vision, intermixing with disorganized thoughts during the silent miles. We did not know the details of the crash; however, a pervasive question returned again and again to my mind—what would have happened if Dad had made it to the beach house? This question preoccupied my mind for the rest of the trip like an unwelcome intruder.

When we arrived at Nana and Pops' house, a whirlwind swept Mama and me up and carried us unwillingly into a distorted reality tinged with bewilderment, denial, and anger. Two police officers visited us the following afternoon. We sat on Nana's floral couch beside each other, holding hands, as we waited for information.

The older officer, who removed the cap from his greased silver hair, said, "Ma'am, I'm sorry. Your husband is dead," in a composed, experienced tone.

After that, the sound coming from his mouth was muffled into incoherent words. My ears no longer heard, nor my mind comprehended their meaning, as if he spoke a foreign language. All of my senses narrowed to a singular object. I stared, unable to shift my gaze from Nana's pink Fostoria candy dish, placed in the center of the coffee table. My eyes fixated upon the smooth pattern etched into the glass, raised facets that rose and fell like tiny pyramids lined up beside one another. I glanced at the zigzag halfway down, where the two halves of the bowl and lid met. I used to carefully trace my finger along the glass years ago, when I was too afraid to grab the tiny knob on top of the lid and open it, terrified I would drop and break it if I tried. I spied the stacks of bright colors and shapes through the dish—white-and-blue striped rectangles; circular peppermints; ribbons of yellow, red, and green; purple candies shaped like miniature pillows; and round white ones with cherries in the center. The sight of them conjured a phantom taste of their cloying sweetness in my mouth, the clicking sound of them hitting my teeth.

I learned the details later that night from Mama as we lay in bed, neither of us able to sleep. I turned over on my side towards her, lying on her back with her hands clasped across her chest, and asked her to repeat the officer's words.

"Your father crashed the car down an embankment and into a tree. He was driving drunk. They even found a half-empty bottle in the passenger seat. They don't think he suffered."

A few minutes passed between us in silence.

"So, he *was* on his way to the beach house?" I flipped onto my back and stared at the ceiling. "Mama, what would have happened if he made it to us?" I whispered, releasing the disturbing question which had haunted my thoughts the entire car ride back home.

No answer was attempted by either of us that night. We cried in the darkness; the reason why we knew not.

Did Dad deserve our pity? Our tears? Or did we cry for ourselves? For relief?

Pops drove us to our apartment the following day so we could pack some more clothes. We were not quite ready to return home yet. Pops dropped us off, promising to return in two hours. He drove to pick up Henry from his hotel and take him out for lunch as a thanks for driving us home. Henry refused to leave us, offering his assistance and support, if needed. We did not see him until the funeral, but I felt better with him nearby.

As we entered the apartment, part of me feared Dad might be waiting for us and not dead, after all. Quiet, abandoned rooms were all that greeted us. An empty bottle of liquor sat on a table. I walked to my room and began gathering clothes, a few books, and my baseball glove from the top of the closet in case Pops wanted to play catch. I finished in no time, quickly stuffing them into my backpack, and went to my parents' room in search of Mama. I found her sitting upon the floor, surrounded by a mess of crumpled papers. I sat down beside her and picked up one of the pages. It was a handwritten letter. I did not read it but looked at Mama for an explanation as to why they were scattered on the floor.

"Your father discovered my box of letters. That must have been why he called that night."

After some time, Mama said, "Michael, your father wasn't perfect, but there was a time when I loved him very much, as did your Uncle Junior. He always seemed to be a part of our family, for as long as I can remember. But, sometimes when you're very young and inexperienced, you think you want something that you may not want when you get older. People mature and change as they encounter life, and their childhood fantasies are overtaken by the harsh realities of adulthood."

I attempted to connect her words to the letters. I glanced down at the pile of scribbled words and spotted a recurring name—Harry.

Mama noticed my curious observations. "When I was about your age, during the war, Nana and I spent our summers at the beach house. The same one we still visit. Pops and my brother were both away fighting in the war, and we found ourselves wanting to escape from our home and the daily reminders of them and their absence. During the summers, I met a friend at the beach whose father was also away fighting. We spent the entire summer together, outside exploring the beach and town all day. I never wanted to return to the beach house, full of just as much grief, anguish that Nana could not leave behind. It was nice to have a friend who understood how I felt and with whom I could talk about anything. Much like you and Lucy. We became very close and exchanged letters for a few years until we lost touch. The war ended, your father returned, and I married him. I never knew what happened to my friend."

"Harry?" I asked, looking down at the letters again.

Mama smiled. "Yes, little bird."

It had been a long time since she had called me that.

"So, did you ever find out what happened to Harry?" I asked, quite interested to know his fate.

"Not for many years until I returned to the beach with you."

I considered who Harry could be.

"Harry had traveled abroad to attend university before eventually returning to open a bookshop. We became friends again."

The truth struck me like a jolt of lightning. "Henry."

"Yes, he was called Harry as a child."

I spent some time sitting there with her, allowing her words to seep into my understanding, to alter past events with their revelation. I helped Mama gather all of the letters, smooth the wrinkles out, and return them safely to their box.

Before I left the bedroom, I stopped and turned back to face Mama. "I know Dad just died, but you should not feel guilty if you love Henry."

CHAPTER 29

RESURRECTION

Mama spent the next few days arranging Dad's funeral. Though Dad had long ago lost his faith, his service was held in our church since he was baptized and raised as a Catholic. His burial was a small affair, only attended by me, Mama, Nana, Pops, his uncle, whom I had never met, and Henry, apart from the military honor guard. I stared at the striped American flag, draped over his casket and later folded precisely before being presented to Mama. I counted as the soldiers folded the flag, in the same manner I used to fold notes for my friends at school, exactly thirteen times until only a triangle of blue with white stars remained. The final salute reminded me of a photograph I had seen of John F. Kennedy's funeral procession, when the president's son raised his tiny hand to his head and saluted his father.

I did not shed a single tear at Dad's funeral. Nana was the only one who did cry, quite uncontrollably, as the casket was lowered into the ground. Perhaps she thought of her own son and the military funeral he never received, still labeled as missing in action all these years later. Mama accepted the folded flag stoically, mourning the boy she loved as a child, best friend to her older brother, who never truly returned from the war. I admired her ability to differentiate the two and forgive the monster he became.

After Dad's funeral, Mama cut her hair short, liberating herself and beginning anew. She began working in a restaurant the next week and signed up for college classes in the fall, the latter at the behest of Pops, who insisted on paying Mama's tuition as well as helping us with our household expenses, his own atonement for the abuse he learned about after Dad died. I began my first year of high school just before Mama began her college classes. Happiness, at last, returned to our home, melting the cold that had trapped us inside. Music and laughter abounded within the walls of our tiny apartment as Mama and I both studied and completed homework in the evenings. We were happy.

During the school years, I spent the weekends on my own, riding skateboards, hanging at parties or dance halls, and eventually cruising in friends' cars while Mama worked. The days of high school were savored on the weekends, my time of freedom from nuns and exams. I experienced my first taste of intoxication, the oblivious state with muted emotions and blunted senses, and partially understood why my dad preferred to spend his days in such a state. Something I could never understand nor forgive was the abuse, the thought of which gave the alcohol a bitter aftertaste.

When Dad died, I felt no sadness, only relief along with a burning hatred towards him, growing more and more wild each day. I hated that I grew tall like him and saw his face when I looked in the mirror, when I only wanted to become the opposite of him.

My unresolved rage resulted in a period of fist fights and violent outbursts. In the year after his sudden death, I struggled in school as a result of the fighting. I often skipped classes to avoid causing trouble for Mama, walking around the city, lost in my brooding. I wished I could visit Father Jean and talk to him. Instead, I wrote him long letters about the feelings I wanted to express in person but could not. For some reason I did not understand, writing my anger onto paper, scribbling each seething word without inhibition, helped. Father Jean replied not with letters of advice but with envelopes of baseball cards, his favorite recipes, and a small picture of Saint Jude. Slowly, day by day, with the passage of time, strokes of my pencil, and Mama's support, my anger subsided, and I was able to release enough of the past in order to live. It would take many more years, though, before I matured enough to face his ghost, always in the background haunting my thoughts.

On a cold winter day after Dad's death, a letter, addressed to Mama, arrived. I curiously observed her as she unfolded the letter with a smile and then read the lines carefully, her eyes focused on each word before eventually filling with tears. After she had finished, she released a small laugh, clutched the letter to her chest, and then read it again. Her eyes lifted to meet mine.

"It's from Harry," Mama said, wiping her face. "It's a letter worthy of Captain Wentworth."

I never read the letter nor grasped Mama's meaning about Captain Wentworth, but I knew his letter restarted their regular correspondence by mail and preceded a visit from Henry himself. Thereafter, Henry's letters arrived weekly, and he began visiting us regularly throughout the year, treating us to plays, concerts, and trips to museums. Sometimes we met him for a weekend away from the city.

Because Mama worked full time in the summers to make up for lost income during the school year, we only visited the beach house for a few weeks the next several summers until she received her degree. I spent my limited time at the beach with Lucy. She mostly talked of fights with her boyfriend and asked my advice from a male perspective as I discreetly rolled my eyes. I never knew what to tell her since I had no experience with relationships. I still found it difficult to approach new people. I also preferred casual dating in order to avoid the exact drama Lucy described to me. I wanted to be free of giggling, silly girls. In truth, I despised her boyfriend and all of the time he spent with Lucy throughout the year. I also blamed him for taking up so much of our precious time at the beach together, always occupying our conversations. We never discussed the kiss, and I pretended it never occurred.

During the summer of 1968, we traveled to the beach a few weeks after the assassination of Robert Kennedy following his win of the presidential primary in California. Still reeling from the assassination of Martin Luther King, Jr. and news that President Johnson would not seek reelection, so many Americans had placed their hopes on another President Kennedy to unite the country. It was a summer of uncertainty. Everything in my life was changing rapidly and felt out of my control. Lucy would soon celebrate her eighteenth birthday and begin her undergraduate degree in political science at a women's college in the autumn. My happiness for Lucy was tinged with the fear that she was leaving me behind.

Lucy and I escaped to the cave on our very first night at the beach to catch up on the events of our lives over the past year. On our walk, she confessed to me that she had broken up with her longtime boyfriend, the one I had been forced to hear about the last few summers. She and her boyfriend had broken up and gotten back together many times, so I doubted it would last. I quickly changed the subject from her breakup. She did not seem upset about it, and I did not want to discuss it.

"What did you think of 'Strange Fruit'?" I asked, curious to hear her reaction to it ever since Mama had played it for me all the way back in April.

Earlier that evening at our beach house, I had played a song for Lucy on our record player, one I had wanted to share with her on the night of Martin Luther King, Jr.'s death. Lucy had called me on the phone that night in early April. We cried together, sharing our sorrow over the line and remembering our pact to join the Freedom Riders when we were younger. After our phone conversation ended, Mama played her Billie Holiday record *Lady Sings the Blues*, moving the needle forward until she found a particular song. I had heard the song before, but it was the first time I listened to the lyrics as she enunciated every shocking line with her raspy voice:

Southern trees bear a strange fruit
Blood on the leaves and blood at the root
Black body swinging in the Southern breeze
Strange fruit hanging from the poplar trees

Pastoral scene of the gallant South
The bulging eyes and the twisted mouth
Scent of magnolia, sweet and fresh
Then the sudden smell of burning flesh
Here is a fruit for the crows to pluck
For the rain to gather, for the wind to suck
For the sun to rot, for the tree to drop
Here is a strange and bitter crop (Allan).

"It's a powerful song," Lucy said on our walk to the cave. "It made me furious and wretched at the same time." Lucy had cried earlier as she listened to the words, once again releasing the anguish of Reverend King's murder. "It's genius to compare lynched bodies to unusual fruit on Southern trees. The descriptions are so vivid and raw that you can visualize the sight and even the smell of bodies hanging on trees."

"Yeah," I agreed. "It might not be a comforting song, but it's one that every American should hear."

We began discussing recent events, and soon Lucy huffed and paced around as she ranted. "We, as White people, need to do more to help change the system of racial injustice, even if the current system benefits us. We are too afraid to lose our comforts, so we speak of our outrage behind closed doors. We must go outside and protest and fight for change. I hope our next president fights for such justice and also ends the Vietnam War. I can't believe at eighteen years old you can go fight a war but can't even vote. I want to vote in the next presidential election."

Lucy appeared ready to march all the way to DC, a protest sign in hand, at that very moment. She would prove to be quite a passionate student. I imagined her as one of those pupils with their hands constantly raised, always ready with an opinion to express, whereas I blended in with the class and only spoke when absolutely necessary. Observing her speak in such a manner, I was reminded of our past discussions of *To Kill a Mockingbird* and could not suppress my laughter.

Lucy noticed my amusement, became offended by my affront, and chased me out of the cave until I tripped and fell on the sand, face down. Lucy sat upon my back as the tide washed over me, drenching my T-shirt and jeans.

"That will teach you to laugh at me," Lucy taunted.

I resigned with a sigh. "I'm sorry. You just looked so serious, like you were running for political office or something."

The tide returned and soaked my face. The salty water rushed up my nose and left a nasty taste in my mouth. Without any warning, I suddenly jerked my body up with my arms, throwing Lucy off of my back and onto the ground with a shriek. Lucy still thought of us as little children, when she was bigger than me. We both lay there on our backs, our wet clothes sticking to our skin. We looked at each other and giggled.

"Lucy," I informed her, "I'm much stronger than you now."

She smirked. "I guess I always thought I would be able to beat you up."

I laughed, remembering when she tackled me on the cliff years ago as I looked through my telescope. "Will you forget me when you go to college?" I asked, afraid of the truth.

Lucy smiled, her eyes piercing mine with their intensity. I dared not look away.

"Oh, Michael, don't be silly. I will never forget you. You are my very best friend. Do you remember the oath we made in the cave to one another? We will always be bound together."

Her words comforted me, but returning to the night of the oath summoned the memory of our kiss. Though I had kissed other girls since then, I felt happy knowing Lucy would always be my first. It seemed fitting since we had grown up in so many ways together. We were better as friends so that nothing could tear us away from each other. Before Mama and I left the beach a short two weeks later, I bid farewell to Lucy and wished her good luck in school.

I hugged her tightly, not wanting to let go, and pleaded through tears, "Promise me I'll see you next summer."

"I promise." Lucy wiped away my tears and then handed me a ripped half of our photographs from the boardwalk.

I believed she would keep her promise. On the car ride home, I cried softly while reliving our last evening together. We had walked to the boardwalk under shifting skies, a kaleidoscope of pastel colors, as the sun set on our left. The night, in many ways, resembled our walk to the boardwalk when we first met in 1957. Much was the same, and much had changed since then. The footprints we cast in the sand were larger and deeper, our shadows elongated. We were no longer children with round cheeks and skinny limbs. Music drifted from the boardwalk as we approached. The pier jutted over the water, supported on wooden stilts. The Ferris wheel turned round and round.

We shared a root beer float, our straws dueling for the last sip. Lucy laughed as our heads butted over the glass. We watched people coming and going, wondering where they called home. We observed one woman retreating from the beach with a bright red sunburn on her face, neck, and chest. I imagined it felt like a hot knife sliced her skin every time she talked or conveyed any emotion. I, myself, had felt the sting of such sunburns. She looked even more ridiculous when she removed her sunglasses, and a white outline remained on her face, as if she were wearing a white domino mask. Once the lady had walked out of our sight, Lucy and I giggled uncontrollably, like we were five years old again.

We walked on the boardwalk between the shops and stopped along the way to take our traditional picture in a photo booth. Mae's, the old arcade we had visited during our first trip to the boardwalk, was no longer there. By the time we walked to the end of the boardwalk and back again, a band had set up and begun playing. A few groups of teenagers were scattered around the periphery. As we neared the music, Lucy squealed, grabbed my hand, and pulled me to the makeshift dance floor in front of the band. She spun around and jumped wildly, her hair flying about her face. Her navy blue plaid skirt, knee-length with a white blouse tucked in the top, lifted up her legs as she danced. She looked exquisitely happy and beautiful. I attempted to follow her moves, laughing as we danced the Twist, the Mashed Potato, the Frug, and the Freddie as fast as our bodies would allow. I tried to remember the dances I had seen on *American Bandstand*. A few years prior, when I secretly cared more about girls' opinions and knew less about them, I meticulously watched the show, trying to learn the latest dance moves in order to impress them.

More and more couples joined us on the dance floor, but I hardly noticed them, faded objects in the background. To me, Lucy and I were the only beings in the universe, our eyes locked onto one another as our bodies, untamed, moved to the music's beat.

Back in the car, I glanced at Mama, softly humming along with the radio.

She noticed and asked, "Do you want to drive?"

"Sure, when we stop for gas. Mama, do you think you and Henry will ever get married? One more year and I'll be heading to college, like Lucy."

Mama smiled as she contemplated her response. "Henry and I have discussed our future. Henry wants to get married, but …"

"Are you afraid to get married because of what happened with Dad?"

"That's one of the reasons. I love Henry very much and don't want to lose him. But part of me is tired of being defined by my husband, only existing through the man in my life. Women seem to always stand in the shadow of their husbands. I've never been happier taking classes, meeting new people, debating ideas, and, most of all, being free. I suppose I'm afraid to lose that independence." It was the same advice she had shared with Sandy.

"Oh, Mama, do you really believe Henry will take that away from you? Will lock you in a cage?"

"I don't think so. But I also believed my marriage to your father would be different. I believed he would let me return to college one day when you were old enough."

"Then Dad still has power over you, even from the grave. You deserve to be happy, Mama. I'm growing up and won't be around forever."

She reached over and rubbed my head softly. "I know, little bird. Don't fly away and leave me just yet."

CHAPTER 30

KALEIDOSCOPE EYES

Once we made it back home, Mama returned to work, and I landed my very own job at a record store. I was trained by a college student named Jane, who I would replace when she returned to school at the end of summer. Jane had a face full of freckles and straight red hair, the same color as Henry's former girlfriend Sandy. She had a cool, mellow attitude and never seemed bothered by silence. I found it easy to talk with her. One Saturday night, the last time we worked together, Jane asked me if I wanted to smoke with her. I agreed in order to pass the last hour before closing. The store was empty, all customers out enjoying their weekends instead.

Jane put *Sgt. Pepper's Lonely Hearts Club Band* on the record player and lit up her hand-rolled cigarette. She took a slow drag and handed it to me. I had smoked once or twice at parties, so I hoped I would not cough in front of Jane, who coolly inhaled each puff, savoring it before exhaling the smoke through her pursed lips slowly. It did not take long for me to realize that we were smoking something other than tobacco. My head felt as if it were being inflated with helium as The Beatles aptly hummed about getting high with their friends in the background.

I was transported to a psychedelic world when "Lucy in the Sky with Diamonds" began playing next. I closed my heavy lids and attempted to steady my wobbly legs and oversized, inflated head. For a brief moment, Lucy and I were floating in the black sky amongst the stars. Jane grabbed my hand and pulled me back to Earth. We began swaying to the music with our bodies close together. I caressed her soft hair that cascaded all the way down her back. Through her shirt, her bare breasts pressed into my chest as we danced. With my reticence temporarily dispelled, I kissed her without thinking, tasting the marijuana flavor on her lips, redolent of a smoldering campfire in the woods. As we kissed, she took my hand and placed it on one of her breasts. I was thankful that we were both high at that moment, else I might have fled in embarrassment. We continued that stoned intimacy, our bodies entangled in a trance of dancing, touching, and kissing, for the remainder of our shift. We walked to a nearby restaurant together after closing the record store. Over a plate of shared fries, Jane laughed at the way my face blushed when she mentioned sex. It was not a sardonic laugh meant to ridicule but one of playful maturity.

"You still have lots of growing up to do, Michael," Jane said before we parted that night. "Good luck your senior year. I hope to see you next summer."

I walked home alone in a hypnotic fog, taking my time meandering the streets until my mind cleared. As I walked the lonely sidewalks, I recalled a night earlier that summer I had spent with Lucy at the cave. I had asked her to sneak a bottle from Aunt Louise's liquor stash. We drank to Lucy's cousin David, the one who had warned her about the haunted cave. She told me he had just been drafted to the Vietnam War. We toasted all of the casualties of America's wars—past, present, and future. I thought of Uncle Junior.

Lucy raised the bottle of sloshing amber liquid. "To our peaceful president and his broken promise to 'seek no wider war.'"

After several large gulps, I staggered out of the cave, followed by a giggling Lucy, and lay down on the sand with my arms spread out on both sides of my body. I stared at the sky, which I perceived to be spinning faster than it did, and spied a few twinkling diamonds set in the vault of heaven.

I began singing "Lucy in the Sky with Diamonds." Lucy slumped to the ground beside me, and together, we sang the remaining two lines of the chorus and the extended "ah" at the end. We laughed after we had finished.

I twisted my gaze to her. "Which girl are you in the song?"

Lucy smiled. "Aren't they all the same?" She shrugged. "I'm *just* Lucy."

I repeated, "Just Lucy."

When I eventually made it home, I avoided eye contact with Mama and hurried to my bedroom. My head still felt dizzy when I collapsed onto my bed, my room revolving around me before settling in its correct orientation. Waiting for my head to deflate in bed, I felt shame for touching Jane's breast. My friends, who bragged whenever they kissed a girl, would have laughed if they discovered my thoughts. I had no adult with whom to discuss such matters comfortably. The Church disseminated plenty of guilt and talk of abstinence but offered no discussion on the normalcy of such desires. I could not even bear to admit the acts or feelings during weekly confession after Friday mass. I tried my best to resist such urges, but sometimes they overtook me as they had earlier that night with Jane. Thinking about our kiss and the soft feeling of her breast in my hand sent a sensation of electricity shooting down my body. I touched myself that night, thinking of someone other than Jane.

In early August 1968, Mama and I met Henry and his parents in the mountains of upstate New York for a short getaway before the school year began. I rather liked being surrounded by trees in a fortress of green. John brought his telescope along, and on a clear night, he and I hiked to find a clear spot for stargazing. He set up his telescope on a hill and waited for the sky to darken sufficiently. First, he scanned the eastern sky with his eyes until he found a bright spot, as he explained, that did not twinkle like a star but remained constant.

"Ah, there it is," John said, as if he had spotted a familiar face in a crowd.

He pointed the telescope in that general direction and sought the object in the finderscope. Once he had discovered it in the finderscope, he switched to the main scope, adjusting its position in small increments until he found it again. This methodical work took quite a long time. He then twisted the dial to focus the image. He smiled proudly and offered me a look. I approached the telescope, careful not to move it as I bent down and peered through the eyepiece. My eyesight adjusted quickly to the view through the lens, and inside, I saw a small round object with distinct stripes of tan, almost a shade of orange, and off-white. Out to the sides, I saw tiny yellow dots.

Bewildered by what I observed, I pulled my head away from the telescope and looked at John with my mouth open wide in astonishment.

"Jupiter," John said, verifying the planet was indeed what I gazed upon.

"Are those some of its moons on the perimeter?" I asked.

"Yes, a few of its many, many moons."

I walked back for another glimpse of the gas giant, orbiting the sun millions of miles away from where we stood. I stared at Jupiter until my neck and back ached from bending over.

"Ready for another surprise?" John asked, quite enjoying the suspense.

He repeated the same steps as before, first adjusting the telescope up and to the right the second time. I peered into the distance where the telescope pointed, searching for the speck he sought to magnify. It took John even longer to find the second celestial object, but I knew it would be worth the wait. John stepped back and allowed me to look once more when he had finished. In the left corner, I beheld a sphere with tilted rings encircling it.

"Saturn," I said aloud, certain of its identification.

After I had spent as long as I could marveling at the sight of Saturn and its rings, I expressed my gratitude to John for showing me the moon and the planets.

"You're welcome, Michael. I promised you all those years ago I'd show you the planets. To be honest, it's nice to have someone who enjoys it as much as me. Someone to share it with," John said, acknowledging his own gratification in our mutual love of space.

On our hike back to the cabins, John recalled a story he thought I would find interesting. "In September 1950, before you were even born, I remember when the sky turned dark during the day, without warning. It was as if a black haze suddenly filled the sky. The sun disappeared and then reappeared through the passing haze but looked blue instead of yellow. Some claimed it looked purple. People feared it was caused by a nuclear bomb. The same phenomenon occurred that night with the moon. Indeed, we saw a true blue moon!"

"Unbelievable! A true blue moon. Did you ever learn what caused it?"

"Yes. Believe it or not, it was all caused by a large forest fire in Canada. Some didn't truly believe that explanation because it didn't smell of smoke or appear red as it usually does."

"I wish I could have seen it. I'll have to ask my mother if she remembers it."

During the remainder of our hike, we discussed blue moons; supermoons, when the moon's orbit is closest to Earth; and blood moons, occurring during a total lunar eclipse when red light is scattered from Earth's atmosphere onto the moon. On that night, John and I did not know that the crew of Apollo 8 would become the first to successfully orbit the moon a few months later on Christmas Eve.

It was quite late when we arrived back at the campsite. Mama, Henry, and Elizabeth sat around the campfire, waiting for us. Upon our return, we roasted marshmallows on long, thin sticks. As I had always done, I stuck my marshmallow directly into the center of the flames. I loved setting it ablaze, the white disappearing within dancing orange, until I blew it out to reveal a black crust around a melted, gooey center. Mama preferred a slow, even method to achieve the perfect brown color. The fire crackled and bounced on the firewood; the smoke billowed out, leaving a burnt scent on everything it touched. Henry taught us songs he sang as a Boy Scout. My favorite one was about an Austrian being repeatedly interrupted while yodeling on a mountaintop.

Henry stood up after we finished singing and asked for everyone's attention. He beckoned for Mama with his hand, and she joined him.

"Years ago, I met a lonely girl with a blonde braid down her back, wandering the beach by herself. We bonded over our shared experience of the war and the absence of our loved ones. We spent every minute together those summers. Before we parted one summer, I plucked up the courage to kiss her on the lips, for I feared I'd never see her again." Henry paused before continuing. "And believe it or not, that sweet girl smacked me." Henry laughed and looked at Mama, who slyly grinned. "Years and years passed until she walked into my bookshop one day with her little boy. She took my heart with her all those years ago, and it shall be hers until she leaves this world. I'm happy to announce that Margaret and I are getting married!"

Congratulations and cheers erupted around the fire. I pretended to be surprised but already knew the happy news. Mama and Henry had discussed it with me earlier that day, wanting me to be the first to know. Elizabeth ran to the cabin and returned with a bottle of wine.

"This will have to suffice in place of champagne," Elizabeth proclaimed, holding the bottle up in the air.

We each took turns, first Mama and Henry, passing the red wine around and drinking straight from the bottle until it emptied. I sat there staring at Mama, her face glowing in the firelight. The flames moved within her blue eyes, illuminated from within. At last, she was happy.

CHAPTER 31

CELEBRATIONS

M y senior year of high school rushed by with college applications, tours of campuses, and work at the record store after school and on weekends. I also joined my school's track team after discovering how running cleared my mind and provided an outlet for all of my pent-up anger towards Dad. On weekend mornings before work, I trained at the nearby park, the same one where I played baseball as a child. I ran on the sidewalk that snaked around the outside, staring at the baseball diamond in the center, and reminisced about the little boy I used to be. I sometimes missed those days of innocence and simplicity as I stood on the precipice of adulthood.

Mama graduated in May of 1969 with her teaching degree, just before I turned eighteen years old. I graduated high school the following month. After the conclusion of my ceremony, when I walked across the stage and received my diploma, I hunted for Mama and Henry among the sea of dispersed people, standing packed together. Thankfully, I had grown as tall as my father, which gave me an advantage above the others. I first spotted Henry's head, distinguishable by the hair sticking up in the back, and made my way over, pushing past the blockade to reach them. I heard a familiar laugh as I neared, which took me by surprise. When they came into view, I saw a young woman from behind wearing a jumper dress over a long-sleeved shirt. Her straight brown hair swept all the way down her back and ended at the bottom of her rather short hem. I did not recognize who it was until she turned around and looked at me. Deep mocha eyes stared into mine, releasing that flitting winged creature in my stomach. I saw the slightest gap between her front teeth when she smiled, so small that normal people would never know of its existence. She ran towards me and jumped up into my arms.

"Congrats, Michael! And happy belated birthday!" Lucy squealed and kissed my cheek.

Still holding her in my arms, I squeezed her tightly and then spun her around. The tassel from my graduation cap smacked her in the face.

"Sorry," I apologized as I set her back down and removed my cap. "I can't believe you came! What a surprise!"

A group of giggling girls walked past us and said, "Hi, Michael," in unison before giggling away again. I rolled my eyes. Lucy tousled my hair, causing it to fall onto my face. I had let it grow out long on the top. I swept it to the side again.

"I remember advising you one time to grow out your hair like this. I wanted you to look like Elvis," Lucy teased. "And now look, you've got your very own fan club!"

"Very funny! I see you've not lost your sense of humor at college. Come on, I want to see your aunt."

I was relieved to return home and remove my sweltering gown, a final torment inflicted on students. Everyone gathered in our apartment, a merry group packed into our small living room along with boxes piled in corners, before we went out for a celebratory dinner in honor of mine and Mama's graduations. We had much for which to be thankful.

I slept in my bedroom, which seemed to grow tinier each year, for the last night in two days' time, glancing around my room in the dark with a bittersweet sentiment. Its walls had witnessed the happiest as well as the darkest days of my life. The last box I carried out came from under my bed—a lunchbox with a broken handle. I was not sad to leave our apartment, along with the bitterest memories, closed behind the door as we left forever.

I rode with Mama to the beach, driving on the same path that we had taken every summer escape since 1957, even though the subsequent construction of interstates had shortened the trip. My wandering mind took me back to my last day of high school. I thought of my friends, many of whom I had known since kindergarten. We had spent so much time together, growing up, learning how to be people, and I had parted with most of them for good on graduation night. That thought had not occurred to me before then. The truth hit me in the car as I drove further away from them and our old life. I was standing at a crossroads, about to pass an arbitrary line separating childhood from adulthood. With high school over, my mind was, at last, free and clear to dive beyond the shallow waters of necessity, beyond exams and deadlines, and become lost exploring the depths of our previous summers at the beach as well as the boundless future spread out before me.

My thoughts soon roamed to a subject which my mind always gravitated towards, no matter how far away it seemed. I returned to the night of my graduation, to the moment I witnessed Lucy turn around to face me, when I finally realized it was her and she ran and jumped into my arms. When we walked back to our apartment after dinner that night, Lucy and I sat on my childhood bed and talked. She chatted nonstop about her college courses, new friends, and the coffee shop where she studied. I listened as she waved her hands and spoke without allowing me to ask questions or comment. She was still that little girl with the pigtails and large gap between her front teeth, but she was also now a woman who seemed much more mature and confident.

A woman, I thought to myself. In my head, Lucy screamed at me again, "Because I'm a woman!" as she had during the summer of 1965. I laughed at my younger self in the car when I thought back on how much I did not know at that time and how stupid I felt when Lucy later clarified the situation.

Mama heard my chuckle and turned her attention to me. I felt her staring at me as I wandered in my thoughts, just as I had stared at her on our very first trip. I glanced at her quickly and smirked. I noticed tears within her eyes.

"What's wrong, Mama?"

"Nothing, really. I just realized that this is the last time we'll drive on these roads to the beach together. Do you remember our first trip?"

"Yes, I remember how excited I was during the drive." I thought of the pie we had eaten on our first trip, the one she had drawn on the map, and the look of disappointment on Mama's face when we had returned a subsequent year to find the diner closed.

"I just wanted to run away that summer from your dad. I didn't want to fight with him anymore. That wasn't the first time you went to the beach house, though. I took you when you were a baby. As a young mother, I felt like I was suffocating in that apartment and had to escape. I always seemed to run away to the beach house. It's been our sanctuary."

Mama turned her head to look out the window before returning her gaze. "And now, you're a man driving me to the beach. Oh, time is a fickle measurement. It never alters except in our minds, disobeying our wishes. It passes slowly when we want it to fly and quickly when we want it to stop. How I wish to rewind its hands for one more hour of your childhood." A stream of tears trickled down her face.

I returned my focus to the road, considering her lament on the passage of time. The car moved steadily over the asphalt, each section quickly disappearing below the tires. They were the miles I had tried to memorize at six years old and, now at eighteen, the ones I could never forget, the ones my life had passed over. As I steered our car along those roads, forever embedded into my mind, I was reminded of the little boy who attempted to commit every turn to memory, every exit, clutching an Esso map with a pie drawn upon it and inhaling the smell of the ocean. For the rest of our drive, I pondered the passage of time in my own way, from when I was that little boy, filled with the excitement of a summer trip, all the way up to the man I had become, ready to leave for university at the end of summer.

When we arrived at the beach house, my rumination on past events and the elapse of time was forsaken. We unpacked a few of the moving boxes, but the final preparations for Mama and Henry's wedding took precedence above all else. Aunt Louise took her duty as matron of honor quite seriously, and without being asked, she also took on the role of wedding planner, with a particular interest in the reception afterwards. Lucy and I laughed and laughed at the madness that possessed her, barking orders and demanding perfection for the big day. She set up office in our beach house, making telephone calls and meeting with vendors and caterers. It was all out of character for her, but I knew she wanted the day to be special for Mama's sake. We all helped in any way we could, mostly by staying out of Aunt Louise's way until the wedding day arrived.

CHAPTER 32

THE WEDDING

On the morning of the wedding, Mama and I took a stroll on the beach after waking early to a blue dawn. We wanted some quiet time alone before the hectic activities commenced. It marked the end of our time together as a family of two.

"Today's the day," Mama remarked, looking up at me, studying my face for a long time in the rising sun.

"Do you see Dad when you look at me?" I asked, recalling what I saw in my own reflection.

My question surprised her. We walked in silence before she replied. "Yes, you bear a striking resemblance to your father. You're the same height, and your jawline, eyes, and nose are a perfect copy. Your hair and eye color remind me of your Uncle Junior, though. When I look into your eyes, it's like looking into his again."

She sighed heavily. Her mind transported her somewhere else. "When your uncle and I were children, we spent a month of every summer vacation in Tennessee with Nana's parents. We lived outside, wandering in the tall grass of the meadow with the wildflowers and butterflies and attempting to scale the round hay bales after the grass had been cut and bound. We roamed the woods and climbed trees, pretending we escaped from a gang of bandits who had kidnapped us. At night, we chased lightning bugs and caught them in our hands. Looking at you reminds me of these cherished memories I shared with my brother. I filled my little red notebook with poems about them, but I could never speak them aloud until now. That is why you've never heard these stories before. After all this time, the memories finally overshadow the loss of him. You remind me of him and your father during happy times."

"Mama," I said with a quaver in my voice, "how do I look in the mirror and see him after what he did?"

"You look in the mirror and see yourself, a person who did nothing wrong, you see a reminder of the man who went to war before he was able to live and returned home imperfect because of that. You see the man I loved, the man who loved baseball and you. You decide not to make the same mistakes he did because you are not him or his choices. You look in the mirror and see my blue eyes staring back at you, full of pride and the deepest love."

She paused before continuing. "Michael, you may resemble your father, but you are *not* him. In you, I see the better parts of us all. I hope you remember that. There's a box of your father's belongings in my bedroom closet. I think you should look through it when you're ready."

Mama then changed the subject back to the wedding. "I'm afraid I'm not ready for the craziness of today. I wonder if we should have eloped."

I laughed. "You would break Aunt Louise's heart. Don't worry. I think it will be a great day. I'm glad all of us can celebrate together."

"Are you *really* okay with me marrying Henry?"

I wrapped my arm around her shoulder, my shadow towering above hers, my right eye squinted in the sun. "Mama, it's a bit late for that question. I love you and Henry. I'm happy for you. I also feel quite lucky to have Henry as a stepfather. Plus, now I won't worry about you as much when I leave for college. Be happy, please."

When we climbed to the top of the cliff after our walk, we spotted Birdie, red and gleaming, parked in the driveway. Lucy and Aunt Louise frantically burst through the screen door and returned to the car for more supplies—dresses, bags, and boxes of mysterious objects. We ran to help them. Aunt Louise looked frazzled with her windblown hair, a panicked expression marring her face. I had never once seen her appear as unpolished as she did in that moment.

Pops whispered, "And so it begins," to me, dread in his eyes, as the women gathered in the beach house and immediately began debating hairstyles and nail polish.

Just as Aunt Louise began handing out mimosas, Pops and I quickly retreated to Henry's apartment to hang out with him and his brother, Charlie. We left Mama, Nana, Aunt Louise, and Lucy the entire house to prepare for the wedding. I wondered what would take them so long to get ready but did not want to stay in order to satisfy my curiosity. It took the men less than five minutes to get dressed and comb their hair.

When I returned that evening with the men of the wedding party, I first saw the beach from above while standing on the cliff. The wind blew with faint whiffs of June blooms, and the churning waves perished onto the sand in the same manner they always had. An unfamiliar feeling hung in the air as I looked down on the scene below me. Wooden folding chairs were arranged in two sections, lined up forming straight rows across, with blue ribbons tied into tidy bows on the chairs that formed the aisle. Before the chairs stood an arbor decorated with the same blue ribbon, woven around the top and legs, and simple bouquets of white flowers, one hung on each side. A string quartet played softly as the guests arrived in irregular intervals and filled the empty seats.

Pops returned to the beach house to wait with Mama and the others while Henry, Charlie, and I descended the steps in our suits and dress shoes. After we were out of sight, to prevent the bride and groom from seeing one another, Pops and Aunt Louise drove their cars to the public parking lot on the way to the boardwalk so the women would not have to climb down the stone steps in their gowns. Nevertheless, the thought of them tiptoeing down the cliff in their formal dresses conjured a diverting prospect in my mind while I waited for them to arrive.

The families were the last to be seated before the ceremony began. Charlie escorted his aunt, Ms. Prince, to her chair in the front row on Henry's side. John and Elizabeth followed, walking down the aisle together and sitting beside Ms. Prince. Elizabeth wore a beautiful yellow dress and matching brimmed hat. John looked like an older version of Henry in a light gray suit so similar to one I had seen Henry wear previously that I thought it might belong to him.

Nana stubbornly refused to remove her shoes and go barefoot "like a barbarian," so she walked cautiously from the parking lot on quivering ankles as her heels disappeared into the unsteady sand. I enjoyed her amusing walk in her pink dress and matching pillbox hat, her strawberry blonde curls billowing out around her face, with her arms outstretched on either side of her body and blue eyes focused on the ground, as if she were walking on a tightrope. When she finally completed her arduous journey, I escorted Nana down the aisle to her seat in the front row on Mama's side. Nana lost her balance several times as her ankles overturned, almost toppling us into the chairs. The mother of the bride continued smiling, however, as she paraded past the wedding guests. I dropped off Nana, the last to be seated, and returned to take my place in the procession line at the back. Henry entered from the side and stood under the arbor, joining his friend who had agreed to officiate the ceremony.

Nana had begged Father Jean to marry them. It was an impossible request, in any event, outside the confines of a Catholic Church. Much to Nana's disappointment, Mama and Henry preferred a simple wedding on the beach where they first met rather than a formal wedding inside a church. Her best efforts, a combination of nagging and prayer, could not persuade them otherwise.

On my return trip down the aisle after leaving Nana, I caught my first proper glimpse of Lucy. The sun shone around her from the west, encompassing her figure in a halo of light. She stood beside Charlie in her sleeveless two-tone dress, laughing. I took my place in line behind Lucy and Charlie, shifting my weight from foot to foot as I waited, and observed her more closely. The top of her dress, covered in white lace flowers, conformed to her body, held with thin straps that scooped down her chest in the middle. Underneath, an aqua blue sash encircled the high waist, tied with a bow in the back. The bottom, aqua blue satin, flowed out from her waist to her thighs, ending above the knee. Her long hair had been pulled up and pinned in the back with matching flowers, daisies I surmised, a haphazard garden atop her chestnut brown hair. A few hairs dangled in the front, blown back and forth by the wind across her chest, brushing against her collarbones. When she turned around to face me, I noticed the scar on her chest, a jagged white dash upon her tanned skin. I had heard the story many times. As a child, she had slipped while climbing a tree, a branch ripping her flesh on the way down. My eyes followed the contours of her collarbone and bare neck up to her face, colored with makeup. Her lips were stained a sharp red, her cheeks dappled with pink. I peered into her eyes, citrine in the sunlight, somehow appearing larger and more magnetic, outlined in a ring of black eyeliner and shaded on the lid and brow bone with eyeshadow.

At last, signaled by the change in sheet music, Charlie and Lucy began the wedding procession, arm in arm, down the sand pathway. My eyes followed Lucy the entire length of the aisle. I felt a twinge of unfounded jealousy watching her walk with Charlie, their bodies colliding when the sand collapsed below their feet. I felt it should be me beside her, but as best man, it was my duty to escort Aunt Louise and take my place beside Henry. Lucy and Charlie diverged to the left and right, respectively, once they reached the arbor. Charlie looked small standing next to Henry, who was several inches taller with broader shoulders.

I turned to find Aunt Louise, who was not waiting with me but shuffling quickly in my direction wearing a long satin dress with a sheer overlay. Aunt Louise had forgone her longstanding tradition of black and instead wore aqua blue to match the rest of the wedding party. As she rushed towards me, Aunt Louise appeared to have composed herself from earlier, looking like a completely different person with her hair pulled back, every strand in its perfect place, and her typical serene expression washed over her face. I suspected the mimosas had helped her achieve this stark transformation.

Before we began our trip down the aisle, Aunt Louise turned to me and asked, "Are you ready for this, Michael?"

I answered quickly, without hesitation, "I'm ready."

Aunt Louise grabbed my face with both of her hands. Her bouquet of tulips pressed against my cheek. "You are a remarkable human being."

She released my face, hooked her arm in mine, and we marched past the rows of chairs to the front. I shook Henry's hand before taking my place beside him. While waiting for Mama and Pops, I scanned the smiling faces in the crowd, focusing on those of Elizabeth, John, Ms. Prince, and Nana. Mama and Pops approached the aisle and waited with locked arms for the music to begin. Pops looked handsome in the simple navy blue suit and matching tie all the men wore. I glanced at Henry. His eyes were fixated unwaveringly upon Mama. Mama wore a sleeveless white dress with a lace tulip overlay, high neck, and empire waist, tied with a sash. It was a simple dress, without frill or volume, that suited her perfectly. She wore no veil nor hat. Her hair, cut short after Dad had died, was curled and styled back away from her beautiful face and bright blue eyes. Her face radiated pure happiness. Aunt Louise began blubbering quite uncontrollably when she saw Mama. The wedding march lifted from the instruments, and everyone stood and turned to look at Mama and Pops. As they walked, Mama smiled at the guests on both sides and then looked directly into my eyes until Pops offered her hand to Henry.

When they recited their vows, Mama began crying steady tears, which did not stop until long after they kissed and were declared husband and wife. Mama hugged me, tears still streaming down her face.

"Cheers, Mama. I love you." I bent down and kissed her wet cheek.

After the service, the guests trudged across the sand to the public parking lot. The family and wedding party remained behind to take pictures while the others headed to the reception, which was held at the downtown park under a large white tent, perhaps the same one used for the annual summer dance. I first spotted the white tent as Pops' car climbed the small hill, and it rose in my view slowly. Even at eighteen years old, I gasped when

I saw it unexpectedly pitched on the green space. Underneath the tent, round tables covered with white tablecloths dotted the lush summer grass. The tables were set with plates, glasses, silverware, and cloth napkins. Crystal vases stuffed with white hydrangeas, their blooms forming circles, tufts of baby's breath, and a few dark red roses formed the centerpieces, enclosed by a ring of candles. String lights hung above the dance floor in the center and stretched to the ends of the tent. In the corner, a four-tier wedding cake, frosted with white icing and topped with a bride and groom figurine, posed majestically upon a rectangular table with white tablecloth. A similar table beside it held champagne flutes, ready to be filled after dinner.

Guests staggered in and took their seats. Loud chatter and laughter overwhelmed the tent until Mama and Henry arrived to a standing ovation. Mama cupped her hands over her mouth as she looked around the tent, awestruck by the decorations. I watched Mama as she scanned faces in the crowd, stopped when she found Aunt Louise, and smiled at her. As Mama and Henry greeted their guests, I walked over to Aunt Louise and hugged her.

"What's this for, young man?" she chuckled after I bent down and kissed the top of her perpetually brown head.

"You made Mama happy. The wedding is beautiful, thanks to you."

"Well, I'm filthy rich with no children, so who else should I spend it on but the ones I love?" Aunt Louise sighed heavily and then left me to hunt for a drink.

After we were sufficiently stuffed with dinner and cake, Mama and Henry walked onto the dance floor for their first dance as the band began playing a slow song. That night, unlike the first summer, when Mama and Henry danced together, the ring she wore on her finger belonged to him. Observing them twirl around the dance floor, I wondered when and how Mama had discovered Henry's identity. *Did she know when she danced with him that first summer? Is that what she whispered into his ear?*

"Busy?" a voice interrupted my thoughts and startled me.

I looked at Lucy, who held out her hand to me. "Shall we dance?"

I grinned, took her hand, and joined Mama and Henry on the dance floor. We danced with our bodies close together.

Lucy said softly into my ear, "You look quite nice in a suit, Mr. McCarthy."

"Oh, don't call me that. This suit is choking me. I can't wait to take it off."

Lucy giggled as I spun her around and dipped her to the floor. We bounced over to where Mama and Henry danced and finished the song beside them. I took Mama's hand for the next dance.

Mama looked into my eyes. "Oh, Michael, I am so very happy. Can you believe how much life has changed? I never thought I'd be this happy again."

Like Mama, I had never been happier than I was that marvelous night. With champagne flowing and inhibitions loosened, we danced the night away. I danced with Nana, Aunt Louise, and Elizabeth before being approached by an unlikely partner. I thought, at first, my eyes deceived me until I saw her sky-high red hair. I accepted her offer to dance, confused as to why she attended her ex-boyfriend's wedding.

As we swayed on the dance floor, she asked, "Do you remember me?"

"Of course. You're Sandy. Are you here to ruin the wedding? You're a bit late for that."

Sandy tilted her head back and cackled as loudly as I remembered at my cheeky reply. "No, I am not here for that, although I am surprised to be here myself. It's true I was left quite heartbroken by Henry, but all that's in the past now. Even after I had cried my tears and looked back on it, I knew Henry was always in love with your mother. I am thankful for her advice to finish school. I listened and just completed my first year of a master's program."

"That's great, Sandy. I'm really happy for you. I'm sure Henry and Mama never meant to hurt you. I will begin university myself this fall."

"You can't be that old already," Sandy scoffed. "You were all awkward and gawky the last time I saw you, you poor thing. And did I catch you peeking down my dress a few times that summer?"

My cheeks blushed, burning hot, but I found that I did not mind after the champagne's effects. "Oh, I would never do that," I dismissed her accusation.

She giggled uncontrollably. "Never mind. You were just a boy. I didn't mean to embarrass you. You're a sweet kid who's grown up."

Sandy lifted my arm and twirled under it, her dress flaring out. "And you've got the ladies after you." She motioned with a tilt of her head. "Over there."

I looked in that direction and saw Lucy staring at us before swiftly averting her eyes. I had noticed Lucy's gaze, transfixed on me since the wedding ceremony, even as she danced with other partners. I tried my best not to let my eyes linger on Lucy.

"Oh, that's just Lucy," I corrected her. "She's my best friend." My mouth curled slightly in one corner. *Just Lucy*, I repeated silently in my head.

Sandy grinned slyly, giving me a devilish look. "Oh, my mistake."

I felt rather hot when my dance with Sandy ended, not having a chance to rest yet. Sweat pooled in beads on my forehead.

I walked over to where Lucy stood drinking champagne and asked, "Fancy a walk outside?"

She gulped the last of her flute in a move reminiscent of her dear great-aunt, scrunching her nose as the bubbles fizzled inside. "Ah," she gasped, "bubble brain." She shook her head, grabbed my arm, and said, "Let's go!"

As soon as we exited, the cool air hit me with an instant respite from the heat. I removed my jacket as we walked into the woods, where we had chased children's voices years before. The dirt path, bounded by trees on both sides, remained the same, an unspoiled memory that transported us back in time to 1957.

"Do you remember when we caught fireflies at the summer dance?" Lucy asked as we ventured deeper into the forest, overtaken by shadows.

"Of course I do. And I remember the tree swing and the dancing."

A large gust of wind blew, surprising us and the trees, their limbs violently waving and leaves shivering. The sound of crickets or frogs hummed in the distance. We followed the path between the trees until we discovered the swing gently rocking on its own. Lucy ran in her high heels like a child and jumped onto the wooden seat. She pushed herself backwards but did not swing very high.

"Need a push?" I offered, once I had caught up with her.

"Oh, yes please! I want to swing all the way to the treetops!"

I pulled the swing back as far as I could and whispered, "Hold on," before pushing her forward with all of my strength.

Lucy squealed and began laughing as she rushed ahead. I pushed her repeatedly until the long twisted ropes climbed higher and higher into the sky before falling backwards again. At the top, the hair around Lucy's face bounced as she reversed direction, the innocent joy of a child on her face when she tilted her head back. I pushed Lucy for a while, for she begged me to continue, hoping time would stop passing. It evidently did not obey her because soon we were surrounded by darkness and with it, a certain stillness. We set off on the path to return when we were halted in our steps by the appearance of neon yellow lights, tiny lanterns hovering in the dim light. We froze, petrified by the thought of them vanishing, carrying their twinkling lights away with them. They floated, rising and falling, in almost indiscernible increments. We stood there, simply enjoying the magic before we left it behind us in the woods.

We eventually wandered back to the tent and spent the remainder of the evening dancing. Aunt Louise challenged Henry to a dance-off. Everyone else formed a circle on the dance floor, and each took turns, back and forth, showcasing their finest dance moves. The crowd clapped and cheered until Aunt Louise attempted the splits, nearly ripped her evening gown as her legs locked halfway down, refusing to spread any further, and tipped over onto the floor. Lucy and I rushed to help her and once we had confirmed she was not injured, fell to the floor beside her, overtaken by a fit of giggles. For her effort, Henry declared Aunt Louise the undisputed winner, and the spectators erupted into applause for her. Slowly, the guests departed the tent until only our closest family and friends remained.

It was well past midnight when Charlie approached me with Elizabeth and John to say goodbye. "It was a pleasure to finally meet you, Michael. I fly back to London in the morning. You have an open invitation to visit me anytime you want. I really hope you come."

Elizabeth added, "Yes, we can all go together. I would love to show you around England."

"Sounds like a great destination for my first airplane ride! Safe travels, Charlie. I hope to see you again soon," I replied, shaking his hand.

I hugged Elizabeth and John, who I had considered family long before the wedding. The three of them then left together. Upon first introduction, I liked Charlie. He was one of those people everyone liked. He was clever but in a more subtle, less ostentatious way than his older brother. In many ways, he was more like his mother with the same delicate, feminine features. I felt disappointed he could not stay longer but looked forward to visiting him in the future.

Eventually, the tent emptied, and the celebration ended. Aunt Louise was the most disappointed of all when the night was truly over. I walked back to the beach house alone that night, wanting to enjoy the quietness of the early hours by myself. The last guest to leave, I hesitated on the sidewalk and turned back for one final glimpse of the tent before I continued ahead. Mama and Henry were still swaying on the dance floor, stars just above their heads.

CHAPTER 33

GHOSTS IN CLOSETS

The next morning, everyone, except me, abandoned the beach house. Mama and Henry traveled to Nantucket for their honeymoon while Nana and Pops returned home. That night, when I found myself alone in the beach house, the overwhelming silence disquieted me. In my restlessness, I walked around the house and eventually to Mama's bedroom. I sat on the bed, peering around her room, when I suddenly remembered Mama's words on the morning of the wedding. I entered her closet and stood there for a moment, recalling how I had once searched for Narnia beyond the back.

Upon a shelf, I discovered the box of Dad's belongings, "Jimmy" written on the top in Mama's handwriting. I sat upon the floor in the closet and began rifling through its contents. On top, I spotted his leather wallet, discolored over time, folded in half with worn edges and a few threads sticking out. I placed it to the side, unable to face it yet. I pulled out a chain of metal dog tags, clanking against one another, and inspected their inscription. The name "James P McCarthy" was stamped on the top line, followed by a series of numbers and letters, his mother's name, and home address. Loose photographs in black and white were stacked underneath the dog tags. In one of the photographs, I saw two boys standing beside each other in baseball uniforms. A young girl stood next to the shorter boy, resting his elbow on her head. The taller boy looked like me. Next, I found a bundle of letters, bound with a pink ribbon. I removed the first one from its weathered envelope and opened it. Water stains had blotched the paper with pale brown spots of discoloration, smudging some of the cursive words.

Dear Margaret,

How are you? How are your parents? It's hot and rains here all the time. But the rain only makes the air thicker and hotter somehow. I try to make friends with the other soldiers, but it makes their deaths even harder. Most nights I can't sleep but when I do, I always dream of being at your house with Junior again. We're playing baseball in your yard. I think of him all the time wondering where he is and how he's doing.

Thanks for your letters. They're the only mail I get. It makes me smile to read about home. Have you had any news of Junior? I wish we could have stayed together so I could look after him. Write back, little sister, and tell me what you're up to.

Jimmy

I returned to the wallet, which had been with him when he died, and unfolded it slowly. Inside, his driver's license was tucked inside a pocket on the left. I opened the center to find a few dollar bills, faded to pale green and ripped at the top. I searched the remaining areas, containing nothing of consequence to me—a receipt and a scrap of paper with a phone number scribbled on it. Behind the front row of pockets on the right side, I felt a bulge without an apparent cause. I lifted the side of a hidden pocket with my fingers and found a stack of items wedged in the back. I pulled them out and examined the creased red paper on top: a ticket with a large "81" printed in red ink. I recognized it immediately because I owned a matching ticket, hidden in the bottom of my old lunchbox. It was the ticket stub from the Yankees game when Roger Maris broke the home run record. I shuffled to the next item and saw myself as a kid, wearing my old baseball uniform and holding a bat up, ready to swing. The last item was another photograph, one of Mama and Dad, smiling proudly, with a chubby baby sitting on their laps. I did not realize I was crying until my vision became blurred by the tears welling inside my eyes, breaking through the dam of anger and resentment I had built up over many years against my father. I sat on the ground and wept with the photographs in my hands and wallet on my lap.

The loneliness of night disappeared with the rising sun. Lucy knew I was on my own and came over every day to keep me company. I was perfectly happy to have her to myself. We spent the afternoons on the beach, lounging on the sand and occasionally cooling ourselves with a swim. She wore a red bikini and her long hair braided into two pigtails. Her hair, which she now straightened, still curled when it got wet. I preferred her curly hair, the locks of the little girl who poked my burning pink flesh and offered me a drink. The evenings passed on the back patio, listening to records and talking. Lucy read to me from her Emily Dickinson poetry book, the one from her seventh birthday, dog-eared pages marking her favorite poems.

Lucy said, "'There's a certain slant of light,'" and began reciting it aloud:

> There's a certain slant of light,
> On winter afternoons,
> That oppresses, like the weight
> Of cathedral tunes.
>
> Heavenly hurt it gives us;
> We can find no scar,
> But internal difference
> Where the meanings are.
>
> None may teach it anything,
> 'T is the seal, despair, —
> An imperial affliction
> Sent us of the air.
>
> When it comes, the landscape listens,
> Shadows hold their breath;
> When it goes, 't is like the distance
> On the look of death. (Dickinson 106)

The poem reminded me of the oppressive winter that had trapped me and Mama in 1962 and all that had occurred during the subsequent years of secrets. Lucy and I no longer walked to the cave at night. I supposed we were too old for such traditions. Perhaps, we had run out of secrets or, in our maturity, wanted to hang onto them. She regaled me with stories from college on morning walks to the library, where she introduced me to books she had read in her classes. I paused before we entered the library, looking along the edge of the stones up to the stained-glass windows, which still captured my gaze, no matter how many times they appeared before me.

I found Lucy quite changed in her hippie clothing and libertarian speech after only one year away at college. She spoke of the protests on campus, open ideas, and the many students who were just like her, wanting to absorb everything and impact the world in a meaningful way. Compared to her, I was dormant, forever the little boy glancing up at the library's façade.

"It's so different from high school, Michael," she explained one night. "Students are there because they chose to be, not because they were forced. It makes a difference. Oh, Michael, all of us are happy now. Do you think it will last? Even my mom is doing well. She began a new medication recently. I think she might be released soon. She promised to visit me when I return to school."

Lucy spoke of the future and traveling abroad after college, perhaps joining the Peace Corps. It seemed fitting for her since she was always trying to join some cause. Her words filled me with encouragement. Lucy was right. For the first time, all the people dearest to me were happy. I dared to hope it would last.

CHAPTER 34

BUCK MOON

On the morning of July 16, I watched the launch of Apollo 11 from the living room television. My stomach churned, and my heart raced during the last ten seconds of the countdown. After the countdown ended, I saw fire and then a plume of smoke when the boosters ignited. I heard a voice from mission control say, "Liftoff! We have a liftoff, ..." as the spacecraft shot straight up into the air, headed for the moon.

Four days later on July 20, the Lunar Module *Eagle* landed on the moon in the Sea of Tranquility. I spent most of that day watching the continuous television coverage, afraid to miss any of it. I listened to the astronauts rattle off their steps calmly as they descended to the moon's surface. I held my breath in the final moments until Neil Armstrong confirmed, "The *Eagle* has landed."

Later that night, we held a party for Lucy's nineteenth birthday at the beach house. Mama, Henry, John, Elizabeth, Aunt Louise, Lucy, and I gathered around the television when Neil

Armstrong prepared to walk on the moon. The whole room went quiet as we glued our eyes to the screen. We watched the black-and-white footage of Neil Armstrong jumping from the ladder onto the moon's surface, which he described as "fine and powdery," and immortalizing his infamous line over static, "That's one small step for man, one giant leap for mankind."

The moon landing reignited my fascination with the moon. I found myself staring up at the moon every night, much the same as when I was a little boy, watching it wax bigger and bigger until the night of the full moon, called the Buck Moon in July, and thereafter as it waned smaller and smaller in the subsequent days. One night, a few days after the Buck Moon, I observed it hanging in the sky from the front porch, the breeze blowing through the screen, before going to bed. I attempted to recall the names of the craters and seas printed upon my old moon map.

I heard a noise in the distance, to the right of the beach house, and spotted Lucy exiting the tunnel of trees, heading towards me with something in her hand. I smiled, remembering the many nights we snuck down to the beach and the thrill I felt of getting caught. I had never told anyone of our nightly meetings, even Mama. Lucy saw me watching her as she approached. She stopped below the porch and looked up at me, her curls falling on her face. Wearing her white nightgown, she appeared before me like an apparition in the moonlight.

Lucy grinned. "Fancy a walk?"

"Sure." I snuck down to join her.

I knew our time together whittled down, in the same way the days beyond summer solstice grew shorter, until we parted ways for our respective universities. We descended those familiar stone steps and traversed the path of our childhood to the cave, still waiting there for more secrets. Lucy and I sat outside together on the sand, taking swigs from the bottle she carried with her. It was an unusually hot night. Sweat began to drench the back of my shirt. There was a sadness about Lucy that deepened as she drank. From her nightgown pocket, she pulled a joint and a lighter.

"I was saving this for our last night together, but tonight will do," she murmured as she lit the cigarette perched between her lips.

We savored each puff while finishing off the bottle of liquor, and before the weed carried us away, Lucy stood, without saying a word, and removed her nightgown and then her underwear, tossing each onto the sand without a care. She ran into the ocean, skipping over the waves.

She swam a little distance past the shallow water and shouted, "Aren't you coming?"

Without thinking, I undressed and waded into the water. Minuscule shards leapt from the waves and bit my flesh, the chill creeping up my body until the water swallowed me completely with weightlessness. Lucy laughed as I swam to the spot where she treaded water.

"There's nothing like swimming naked. It's freeing!" she declared to the sky before splashing me directly in the face, the briny flavor filling my nose and mouth.

I splashed her back and swam away quickly while she plotted her revenge. She chased after me, eventually grabbing my leg when she realized she would never catch up to me. She pulled my leg backwards towards her. I spun around, unable to swim against the resistance, to face her punishment. Her damp face glowed in the moonlight, shimmering softly on the restless water. She took my hand and pulled her own body closer to mine, our faces inches apart. She kissed me as our naked bodies embraced, holding each other up in the rocking waves that attempted to pull us apart. Hot blood, boiling in my vessels, pumped through my body as I felt her, all of her, press into me.

Lucy pulled away from the kiss. "Come on. Follow me."

We swam to the shore and walked with dripping bodies over the specks of sand, clinging to our feet. Lucy turned to face me, and I saw her naked body in the moonlight. The water glistened upon her wet skin. Her breasts curved on top of her chest, her nipples protruding from the center, their peaks casting shadows onto the valley that sloped between her breasts and then opened up to her abdomen, belly button, and the wide shape of her hips. I dared to look down at her pubic hair for a brief moment before returning my gaze to her eyes. She was observing my body too.

She took my hand and led me to the cave, her back slanting from her neck over the bony glimpse of her shoulder blades and spine, climbing onto her round bottom. We knelt down in the darkness of the cave and found each other's lips again. The familiar spark returned to my stomach, the same one that appeared the first time we kissed. My heart began thumping more wildly, and I felt blood pounding underneath my skin everywhere simultaneously.

I admitted, at a loss, my head spinning, "I've never done this."

Lucy did not reply but took my hand and placed it on her breast, cold and peppered with goosebumps. Water from her hair dripped onto my forearms. I focused on the rhythmic drips as she guided my movements. For a moment, I wanted to laugh at how she took control, an action so typical of her character.

I brushed her hair behind her back and slowly traced my fingers over her collarbone and then down to the scar on her chest. I touched the remnant of torn flesh, replaced by a cleft of rough tissue. I kissed the scar and inhaled her scent, her skin smelling of salt and something else, something familiar. She gently pushed me to the wet sand on my back and climbed on top of me. I felt her heart beating against my chest as she placed her weight on me. Our bodies melded into one, moving back and forth as the tide rushed in and out, in and out.

Lucy collapsed onto my chest as we caught our breath, our heaving chests rising and falling together. It did not feel sinful to be with her. I lay there in a blissful daze, feeling outside of my own body.

"Lucy, I have a confession. I've been wanting to do that for a long time. The cave has kept my secret since we first kissed all those summers ago."

"Why didn't you tell me?"

"Because you're not just a kiss or a fling or a girlfriend. You're my best friend."

"Well, you certainly concealed your feelings from me rather well over all those years. Or maybe I should have paid more attention." After a long pause, Lucy said, "My dad called me tonight, and I came to you straight after. I needed you, only you."

We held each other in the darkness for a long time until our heartbeats and breathing normalized. The sensation of her skin upon mine felt unlike anything I had ever experienced. I never wanted to move, to part from her.

Lucy sighed heavily. "Michael, we're leaving tomorrow."

"Why? What happened?" I selfishly wanted more time with her.

"It's my mom. My dad called earlier to tell me she's not doing well." She began weeping on my chest, her body jerking with sobs.

"I don't understand it, Michael. She was doing really well. She had just started a new antidepressant. I visited her before we drove here. For the first time in years, she seemed better. We made plans. Sometimes I wonder if she'll ever get better."

I wrapped her body in my arms, desperate to shield her from the type of agony I had felt in my own life. "Lucy, please don't cry. I'll do anything to help you."

"I know," she said, sniffling. "I love you, Michael. I have loved you since I first spotted you on the beach burning under the sun. Do you remember?"

"You poked my pink skin, and suddenly, that moment marked a before and an after. Before Lucy and after Lucy. Of course I remember. I remember *everything*. I love you, Lucy."

Exhausted, we hugged in the cave, as we did so many times through the pain, happiness, and uncertainties in our lives. Those were the last secrets we whispered to the cave. Each in turn, an "I love you" spoken aloud, aloft in the air, and gone the next second as we fell asleep in each other's arms.

EPILOGUE

A recurring dream tortured my sleep from that night onwards: rushing water, relentless waves, violent pushing and pulling, thrashing rocks, surrender, gasping, gurgling, rancid taste in my mouth, imperfect moon, twisted sounds, slipping fingertips, the call of my name, muttered then sinking, bubbly froth, scraping sand, consuming black. Some nights I awakened in a dry sweat, drenched as if I had just returned from the surf.

When summer ended, I announced to my family that I had withdrawn from university and enlisted in the army. Before I left for basic training, I borrowed Mama's car and drove to Nobska Point. I grinned as I pulled into a parking space, remembering when Nana had bashed Pops with her purse over that very parking lot. I stopped before the wooden steps that led up to the lighthouse, lit by the setting sun. I looked up at the black-and-white tower as my six-year-old self did years before, inspecting its simplicity. There were no frills nor adornments on its exterior. It had been constructed for an essential purpose: warn vessels of the coastline. I pondered then, as I had many times over the years, about the endearing allure of lighthouses and why so many seek them out on land. I supposed it was not because of their pragmatic purpose but their symbolism. They represent eternal hope. They are a pulsing light in an unpredictable sea, literal or figurative. Perhaps that was why I found myself driving there that evening, following the old steps of my childhood, searching for a comforting beacon to follow.

I attempted with each step to retrace the path I took in 1957 to stand beside the lighthouse on the knoll. No matter how perfectly I placed my feet, I could not find that feeling of wonder. I found no hope on my visit there. I only saw an old lighthouse, small and unremarkable, absent of luster. The magic had evaporated. Its sight recalled a memory to which I could not return in the same way. After I drove home that night, unable to catch the ghost of innocence I chased there, I reflected on the visit in scribbled words written in my red journal, gifted to me by Mama on the day of my graduation.

I sense
Distorted memories
Scents of childhood
Just beyond my grasp

Is this how
Life plays out
Trading hope
For maturity?

Were those
Innocent eyes
Required to see
Magic in obscurity?

Or is looking back
Like frosted glass
Only the best parts
Shine through?

Our minds
Distort the memories
Until we're not sure
What is true.

Mama held me for a long time before I boarded the bus with other young men, some who were drafted and some who volunteered, like me. She still smelled of laundry detergent and flowers. I thought of all the times she had asked me to reconsider my enlistment.

Mama begged, "Please take care of yourself. Please come home."

Henry hugged me and said, "We love you, and we'll see you when you return," as if the latter were guaranteed.

Father Jean came with Pops to wish me luck. He carried the stack of letters I had written to him. He held them up and simply said, "Write to me."

Pops stood there looking at me, without saying a word, tears streaming down his face, the second and last time I saw him cry. I already knew the words he did not speak. Nana could not bring herself to say goodbye. Instead, she took to bed for several days. Father Jean faithfully visited Nana every afternoon and prayed the rosary with her after I left.

In a few weeks, I was shipped to Vietnam to fight for a cause in which I did not believe. But it has never been the duty of a soldier to weigh the reasons for war, merely pawns to win or lose the battles. I wondered in the sleepless hours of the flight, as others before and after me have, if life was predetermined for us, if our actions or choices truly bear any consequence or if we merely play out our parts, already written for us. Are we able to escape our parents, or do we just become them in the end? The answer, and whether my father's or my uncle's fate waited for me ahead, each destructive in different ways, did not matter. Life continued, despite our musings or our objections, despite chasing ghosts at old lighthouses. After all, what is life but simply a series of events strung together—happy, tragic, miraculous—an existence that must eventually come to an end.

I never saw Lucy again, only her image in the photographs from the boardwalk, still moments of our childhood, tucked inside a worn book of poetry that I carried with me. Her voice reciting her favorite poems echoed in my head. As I flew over the Pacific Ocean, bits of clouds and sky blurred together outside the window in the morning sun. I was trapped in my thoughts again. My mind was occupied with both nothing and the obscure everything. Flashes of scenes over the years played in my mind—

a vibrant sunset, stone steps, blue glass, the boardwalk, a Ferris wheel with a star in the center, a black-and-white lighthouse, a carousel of horses, a Deluxe Skyscope, the moon's surface, and a secret cave.

I thought of Henry's mural and my last glimpse of it. I had carried the final box of Henry's belongings down from his apartment and walked to the back of his bookshop for one last look before I left. I smiled as I stepped down into the children's area, familiar but smaller, and scanned the magical scenes and characters on the wall. On the beach, I noticed two figures from behind, walking on the sand. Above them, a full moon, painted blue, sat in the sky, hot air balloons and a giant peach floating just beyond. I had indeed lived in the time of blue moons, when real men walked on the moon, and I was granted the chance to grow up with a girl whom I loved and who loved me too.

We have arrived at one ending, which is much like the beginning. I question whether time is a straight line, for it is not within my infinite mind. This is my truth. Until the absolute end, I shall be deep within, wandering in my mind, lost in the time of blue moons.

REFERENCES

1. Gibran, Khalil. "On Clothes." *The Prophet*. Alfred A. Knopf. 1923, p. 42.

2. Wordsworth, William. "I wandered lonely." *Poems by William Wordsworth: Including Lyrical Ballads and the Miscellaneous Pieces of the Author*, Longman, et al. 1815. p. 328–329.

3. Friends of Nobska Light. 2023. www.friendsofnobska.org. Accessed July 17, 2020.

4. Dickinson, Emily. "Tell all the truth but tell it slant." Amherst Manuscript #372. Amherst College Digital Collections. https://acdc.amherst.edu/view/EmilyDickinson/ed0372. Accessed July 17, 2020.

5. Dickinson, Emily. "The moon was but a chin of gold." *Poems by Emily Dickinson Third Series*, edited by Mabel Loomis Todd, Little, Brown, and Co., 1896, p. 125.

6. Barrie, James Matthew. *Peter and Wendy*. Germany, Grosset & Dunlap, 1911, p. 7.

7. Brontë, Charlotte. *Jane Eyre*. United Kingdom, J. M. Dent & sons Limited, 1922, p. 252.

8. Dickinson, Emily. "The moon is distant from the Sea." *Poems by Emily Dickinson Second Series*, edited by T.W. Higginson and Mabel Loomis Todd, Roberts Brothers, 1892, p. 104.

9. Shakespeare, William. *Hamlet*. Ireland, Bloomsbury Publishing Plc, 1902, 3.1.56–69.

10. **Strange Fruit**
    Words and Music by Lewis Allan
    Copyright ©1939 (Renewed) by Music Sales Corporation
    All Rights outside the United States Controlled by Edward B. Marks Music Company
    International Copyright Secured All Rights Reserved
    Used by Permission
    Reprinted by Permission of Hal Leonard LLC

11. Dickinson, Emily. "There's a certain slant of light." *Poems by Emily Dickinson*, edited by Mabel Loomis Todd and T.W. Higginson, Roberts Brothers, 1890, p. 106.

drhmnour@gmail.com